In the Queen's Service

The Queen's beloved voice. "Remove your gloves, Mr. Obeck."

He did so.

"Put your right hand inside your dispatch case—the Queen commands."

Obeck complied.

The Queen spoke slowly. "Now, with your left hand, press the Destruct button. Again, my direct command."

Obeck looked at the red shield over the button. He twisted it off, stared at the brass DESTRUCT stud, thinking that now he knew how like her mother she was.

He knelt. He waited; Rachel II Valeria, Queen of the Human Realm, said nothing. Obeck's left index finger moved toward the little brass stud. . . .

He pulled his hand from the case. *TpatTpatTpatTpat* went the pulser. . . .

Books by John M. Ford

The Princes of the Air
Web of Angels

Published by TIMESCAPE BOOKS

JOHN M. FORD

THE PRINCES OF THE AIR

A TIMESCAPE BOOK
PUBLISHED BY POCKET BOOKS NEW YORK

Another *Original* publication of TIMESCAPE BOOKS

A Timescape Book published by
POCKET BOOKS, a Simon & Schuster division of
GULF & WESTERN CORPORATION
1230 Avenue of the Americas, New York, N.Y. 10020

ISBN: 0-671-44482-4

First Timescape Books printing November, 1982

10 9 8 7 6 5 4 3 2 1

POCKET and colophon are trademarks of Simon & Schuster.

Use of the trademark TIMESCAPE is by exclusive license
from Gregory Benford, the trademark owner.

Printed in the U.S.A.

Part One: The Players and the Game

Part Two: Deeper Shades of Blue

Part Three: The Knight on the Cross

Epilogue: In the Age of Gold

He that pursues his safety from the school
Of state must learn to be madman or fool.

—from *The Lover's Melancholy*

Knights in ladies' service have no free will.

—from *Honour Triumphant*

PART ONE

The Players and the Game

Many speak of Robin Hood
That never bent his bow;
Many talk of Little John
That never did him know.

—Traditional

Chapter 1
Authentic Simulations

Orden Obeck tugged at his blue Student's gown, trying to let in some breeze; the air was not cool but it was quite dry, pleasant on sweat-wet skin. As Obeck adjusted, a fold of cloth covered his brass indenture pin. He exposed it again instantly. There were probably no physical proctors near, but Obeck had earned his freedom of the streets by being scrupulous of the pin and the Clock that watched it, and this was no time to risk any of that freedom.

No rattling the chain now, Obeck thought, when in ten days more we can break it.

He did not allow himself that thought for long. He looked at his plain steel wristec, issued by the same government that had hung the brass pin on his collar. Obeck wondered occasionally if the timepiece also had a circuit to track the wearer.

Riyah Zain had a day of twenty-one hours Standard: the wristec read two minutes to eleven. Obeck was on time. Good. Timing was everything in street games. He turned a corner, and the sun struck him like a sack of sand.

Just past the meridian, Riyah Primary was a ladle of molten metal in a white quenching sky. One of the two moons was up, faint in the haze.

Sharp-tasting dust floated in the streets, dulling the alabaster of the buildings. Not far overhead a windbeater went *whop . . . whop* in the idle breeze. Powerload boxes on steel brackets droned and clicked, and the black cables between them seemed soft in the heat.

It was not a day to be out of shade—certainly not one to stand still in the sun—yet a small crowd was gathered around a young man with a tray of red jewels, watching as stones leaped between his fingers and shone on his velvet. Obeck moved closer, drifting unnoticed into the fringe of the crowd.

The stoneseller wore a lizard-leather vest over an open green shirt, tan trousers loose around the ankles, well-broken sand boots. He squinted a bit in the light, accentuating his smile; there was sweat on his smooth, very dark skin.

"Sangrads, sirs and dames, yes, true sangrads, square cuts, ovals, tears of the desert—any shape, any weight, one hundred marks."

"Real sangrads for a hundred?"

"Where'd they come from?"

The young man with the tray grinned whitely. "I'm not saying I dug them." A few onlookers drifted away. The stoneseller tilted his head, put out a finger to his cloth, and tipped a stone on end so that it flashed blood red in the daylight; the strays moved back. "It's said, you know, that stones once free of the earth that made them are free forever; you cannot enslave a diamond, a pi-crys, a sangrad—their lives are their own."

"If they're real—"

"Touch one. Please, one of you." He looked around, settled his look. "You, medame?" He extended two fingers toward a teardrop stone, turned his hand palm up.

A woman in a suncloak, its chiller rumbling on her shoulder, peeked over her dark glasses. Obeck could see the puffiness in her face, from the revi needle that kept her cells youthful. "Well . . ." she said, looking more at the seller than the wares. After only a moment she put out a finger, searched with it over the two dozen red jewels on the velvet. The one she finally touched was the teardrop the man in the vest had pointed out. Just like forcing an ace from the deck, Obeck thought. The woman said "Oh!" and pressed down more firmly. "Why, it's . . . quite pleasant."

"A mirror of mood, medame," the seller said, "cooled by the touch of your warm hand. Were your fingers chilled, the sangrad would warm to them." He shook back his coarse, wavy hair, looked directly into her half-shaded eyes, needle-young.

Orden Obeck took a step forward. "So it's a cool stone on a hot day," he said. "So is any pebble from the shade." Heads turned toward him, taking in his age, his gown, its Government College sash, and most especially the brass collar pin that said he belonged, service, soul, and soma, to a branch of the Royal Government.

"But . . ." said the woman, "it's getting damp. Moisture's condensing on it."

"Then he packed it in ice overnight," said Obeck wearily. "He'd keep it in an oven, if the day was to be cold—only being sure not to melt the plastic."

The stoneseller gave Obeck a look hotter than Riyah Primary. The woman, her finger still on the sangrad, said, "That's not . . . is that true?" Obeck read her voice; she was not Zaini, doubtless had never touched a sangrad.

The seller blinked, gave a dust-choked sigh. "True enough of some. But you're touching my stone." He looked around. "Any of you . . . all of you! Touch! If you would, medame . . . ?"

Not eagerly, the woman passed the sangrad around the crowd. There were hummings and humphings of surprise and delight at the stone's properties.

"Feel—you hold it warm, I'll hold cold—feel it tremble?" Only Orden Obeck refused, pointedly, to hold the red stone. Gradually the sangrad made its way back to the seller, who dusted it with a hand, put it back on his velvet.

"And now—"

There was a slight disturbance to one side, and the seller's eyes shifted. His jaw tightened. His fingers arched.

The crowd suddenly became aware of another person: a figure, not tall, wrapped in a wine-red robe. His face, mostly hidden by a hood, was very pale, as much whiter than the norm as the stoneseller's was darker. He wore slitted sun-visors, handmade. His arms were close to his sides.

In one slightly upraised hand were three red stones, two teardrops and a half-sphere—like the first seller's but larger than anything on the velvet.

"*Why,*" said the stoneseller, "are the streets so full today?"

A few people had already moved toward the red-robed man. He pushed back his hood a little, showing a high forehead, slightly flushed. The eyebrows above his visors were thick, prominent, his chin very sharp. One or two of the onlookers made startled noises. Obeck could easily tell why; though there were no signs of the revi needle, there seemed to be the pain of ages in that tight, pale face.

"What are you asking?" someone said.

"These are . . . my all." He pushed up his visors, exposing blue-black eyes, deeply sunken, enhancing the ancient effect. His knuckles whitened. "Matched . . . I should not like to separate them. But . . . as this fellow asks one hundred . . . two hundred marks each." His voice was quiet, but distinct.

Only the woman in the suncloak remained near the first stoneseller, and she did not look fully at him. *"Two—"* the dark youth said. "There is no reason among mortals in the midday sun." He carelessly bundled his stones into the velvet.

The woman turned toward him, her eyes concealed again. "Are you here . . . often?"

"Almost never, and I think never again." Then the corners of his mouth turned up. "But . . . under a high moon, when the air is cool and the stones are warm in response . . ." Eye to shaded eye with her, he put the bundle of sangrads on his shoulder, turned, and went away, whistling a song of the star Pilots.

I remember being where my vision told me true . . . .
I'll lay in a vector that will take me back to you.

Obeck was pushing between the crowd and the man in the robe, asking his pardons with a very clipped but very formal style. In a low but emphatic voice, he said, "Theo, you can't. What would they say if—"

"There is no one left to say but I," came the pale man's reply, also soft and potent, "and I carry my memories in my heart. Not my pocket."

"I know something about matched stones," said a man in a dazzling gilt vest. "I'll give you nine hundred for the set."

"It is more than—" said the pale man as the silver edges of hundred-mark cards fanned before him. "There are . . . eleven hundred marks here, sir."

"I count nine," the man in the vest said. "Call me wrong?"

"As you count them, then." The young man passed over the sangrads as if they weighed the world. He lowered his visors, pulled his hood forward. Orden Obeck took a last look at the crowd, put his arm across the broad, red-robed shoulders, and led the man away through the heat and haze and dust. Shortly they turned a corner and were gone.

Then, after a quick glance back, they slipped into a breezeway and moved rapidly, silently, parallel to the street they had just left, near enough to hear the buyer tell two companions: "Now there's one who sold his grief cheap. Feel this, will you? I never felt a passion-pebble cold as this. They've shown me warmer single stones over Cromarty's counter for a thousand a rock—and this a matched lobes-and-brow set!" Laughing, he gave the stones a toss in his hand and pocketed them, and with his friends moved off—passing the cloaked woman, who was tapping the street location into a personal secretary, checking the time on a gemstone wristec. She folded the persec and tucked it into her suncloak, then turned the cloak's chiller up a notch. Then she too departed, humming a romantic sort of song.

Obeck glanced at his own wristec. "Time for us to go as well, Theo. Allow David an hour to stow the jewelry and get back, and we'll—what's that?"

The man in the robe had begun to tuck his left hand into his sleeve. He turned it over. There were small white patches on the light skin. Obeck touched it, then realized he was only doing more damage and drew back. Theo had not flinched in the least. Obeck said, "You'll be lucky if you don't blister. That freeze-spray's for the stones, not you." He looked Theo in the face. "Next time . . . be more careful, will you?"

Theodor Cranach Valerian Norne turned his frostbitten hand over, put it away as one might tuck away a persec or wallet. His other hand came up with the stack of silver-edged cards. On his face was a look that was not a smile, or anything translatable into words.

"Well, when you put it that way," said Obeck, and the two of them walked on.

About an hour later Orden Obeck was seated in a caffe booth, head down over a book that lay flat on the table. Knuckles rapped the tabletop and Obeck looked up at David Koleman, who not long before had been selling red stones from a tray in the street. Offering them for sale, that is, because all but the teardrop sangrad had been the same polished cast plastic as Theo's set of three.

Koleman's vest had been turned leather side in, showing black silk. He had added mirrored glasses, a billed cap with the Starkadr Shipyards emblem, and a light-duty chiller collar to his clothing. He sat down in the booth opposite Obeck, pushed an empty coffeepot to one side, and said, "Theo still at it?"

"How otherwise? He said that when thou cam'st"—Obeck shook his head, grimaced—"when you got here, to wait for him."

Koleman knocked on the table again. "I can't wait. Besides, that weird ELI-Three language is starting to affect your mind."

Obeck sighed heavily, closed the Grammarion. "Thou'rt right," he said, and they both laughed. Koleman started to stand up; Obeck touched his wrist and brought him down again.

"The crowd was too big today, David."

Koleman grinned. "We were damn good on the hook today, weren't we?"

"Let's not hook that many again."

"Let them bid for Theo's heirlooms. Or—suppose I had to supply the overflow market? Imagine if we sold them all. Excepting the real one, of course." He reached into his pocket, produced the teardrop sangrad. He turned it over in his fingers, enjoying its feel. "I wonder if . . . tonight . . ."

"What about a blowup?"

". . . sort of like a battle favor. Have to leave the price up to her, of course. Not really profitable—wouldn't want to leave her a casting. That'd be cruel."

"David—"

"Receiving you clearly, Orden. You know exactly what about a blowup. I run the hook—I run like hell. Theo's got the hurrah—he runs like multicolored hell. You're the stall—you can act any way you want, call the city crackers if no honest citizen does. Blue hell, you're a Queen's Own shill! So what's the uncharted mass?"

"No mass. Just a flutter." Obeck put the Grammarion in his gown. "There's an examination in ten days. The top five . . ." Obeck looked at Koleman's face, but the glasses hid his eyes; Obeck saw only himself, twice, tiny. ". . . go to Novaya."

"Oh, *do* they now?" Koleman put a hand to his chin. "You never said Novaya. Not in ten days."

"I didn't want to say it. I don't want to think about it," Obeck said, knowing that there would be nothing else in his mind for the rest of the day. "It's not just going to the Queen's world. I'd be at the Royal Academy . . . I wouldn't be wearing the brass." Obeck touched his indenture pin, covered it with his hand, trying to imagine his clothes without it.

"Well, I'm glad you told me," Koleman said briskly. "We'll have to make some plans."

"David, I don't just have to pass the test. I have to make oh-oh-five in two hundred twelve."

"We'll make plans anyway. You always need plans—doesn't diplomat school teach you that? And remember, lad"—Koleman was a hundred eighty thousand hours old, Obeck fifteen thousand older—"there's no such thing as too big an audience." Koleman stood. "Let's go see if Theo's dead yet."

Obeck slipped a blue-edged ten-mark card into the table, which gave back eight red ones and a half-mark disk. As they left the caffe, a samech in apron and cap cleaned the booth.

The cardchanger at the Asterion Arcade, a samech, waved a white hand at Koleman and Obeck. Koleman said, "Afternoon, Goldie." Obeck went to the change booth, put his fingers in the samech's palm, and signed THEO STILL HERE?

Goldie nodded, held up both hands, showing six fingers. Obeck reached into his gown and handed the sapient mechanism a silver card. "Tens," he said. Goldie nodded again, put the hundred-mark card into a slot, and slid its white plastic index finger into a keysocket. A stack of blue-edged tens dropped into a chute before Obeck.

THANKS, Obeck wrote, and the samech waved again.

The Asterion Arcade had no lighting system as such. The game displays around the walls provided more than enough illumination. Near the door sat a guard, human, reading a book through nighteye goggles. Should something nasty happen, the power cutoff a few centimeters from his hand would make him master of the situation in seconds. His handstick and wired gauntlets would help. He sat quite still, and but for his tanned cheeks and his reading might well have been a samech.

The Arcade games were noisy as well as bright, though since the sounds were usually part of the play the speakers were directional. As they walked through the Arcade Koleman and Obeck heard music, then battle noises, bells, a voice cackling, "—but you *can't* escape now!" and the cheering of thousands.

In a deep corner, quieter and darker than the rest, were two rows of four cylinders each, running floor to indistinct ceiling, three meters across. All had curved, flush doors, some open with faint lights showing within, some closed. The doors bore the symbols of Sub-Sea, Armored, and Airspace Commands,

and numbers; Number Six, where they paused, had the tri-
angular emblem of Deepspace Command.

"Wonder how long he's been in?" Koleman said.

"Five's open," said Obeck. "We could—"

The door to Number Six opened and Theodor Cranach
Valerian Norne appeared; he stepped out and down. His red
robe was partly open in front, and there was a sheen of sweat
on his hard-muscled chest. His eyes were in deep shadow but
caught tiny sparks of light from game displays.

His knees buckled slightly, but he stood again before
Obeck's or Koleman's hands could reach him.

Koleman said, "What the hell did you set it on, Theo—
thirty?"

"Four-zero," Norne said, nearly whispering. Sweat dripped
from his narrow chin. "Fifty minutes. Duel."

Koleman was chuckling a little, but there was awe in it as
well. "The fluidics in real ships help you, Theo, they don't
fight you."

"A-B system shutdown, crossover shunt sticks and doesn't
pop the freedom failsafe."

"I guess that's supposed to explain it," Koleman said to
Obeck. "Want to get him dried off and revived a little, while
I—"

"I'll engineer for you," Norne said, his voice strong again,
though still not loud.

"Not at four-zero."

Norne shook his head.

Koleman turned to Obeck. "Feel like navigating?"

"Well, hell, yes."

They filed into the simulator. Norne and Obeck took pairs
of disposable goggles from a clip by the door; Koleman did not
change his glasses. Koleman slid into the center, forward-
facing couch, Obeck the left. Norne closed the door, said,
"Conroom secured," and got into the right-side couch,
gathering his robe closely about himself.

Koleman said, "Fifty minutes at . . , two-zero sound all
right?"

"All right," Obeck said.

"You have the con," said Norne.

A blue-edged card went into the pay slot. The credit counter
read 50. Koleman dialed in a control response of 2—correct
for normally functioning fluidics; 1 was too light, 3 equaled an
overloaded or damaged ship, 4 was unimaginable. Control
delay was dialed to 0, of course—real starships did not give

their crews extra seconds of decision time. Number of crew, three. Mission type, EVADER.

Koleman touched START MISSION. The cabin lights went out, the displays and indiks lit, white constellations on black poryl panels. With two exceptions, every bank and cluster of lamps and gauges was white on black, the screen displays monochrome, reading by position and pattern. Only the TALAN displays for airspace navigation, lifts, and landings, and the combat boards used color.

The half-circle wraparound "viewscreen" showed an apparently infinite pad under a cloudless near-black sky. The only features in the landscape were a control tower—a plain white obelisk with dark squares at its top—and the rocking wire cradle of a TALANtenna—though on closer look it was more suggested than detailed.

"What is the operational name of this vessel?" came a neutral voice from their headcushions.

Koleman adjusted his voiceboom. *"Condor,"* he said without hesitation. For Koleman it was always *Condor*. For Norne, *The Pale Horse*.

"QSC *Condor*, this is Mission Command," said the game voice. "You have been chosen for a secret mission of the utmost importance . . ."

They knew it by heart, from a thousand rehearsals: the raider force blockading this outpost moon, the desperate skip across an uncharted part of OutSide, swarming with masses, to emerge at an InField guarded by a heavy blockader—all for the sake of one passenger, the Brilliant Scientist, who, if only he could be delivered alive, would complete the Ultimate Weapon and crush the rebel raiders . . . .

Instead of listening, then, they did an imitation preflight, reading off frozen gauges and throwing switches that had not even simulated functions, that had been matrixed to nothing since these boards were pried out of a ship in the scrapyards.

It was, Obeck thought without wanting to, rather ridiculous. Being a diplomat was no less so—but that had not been Obeck's choice. This . . . game . . . was what David and Theo had chosen . . . and still, there was something about the absolute seriousness, the care and the ritual and the constant driving at longer flights under tougher conditions, that made the game something very like real.

Koleman and Norne had a gift, Obeck covetously knew, of doing absurd things without making themselves absurd.

". . . should be killed, your mission will have failed

utterly," said the game. "The best of luck to you all. For the Queen!"

"For the Queen!" they said as one. Koleman gripped his controls, and the sound and shake of turbines—audio synthesizers, pistons beneath the floor—increased. Norne read off thrusts and rates from the mathematical model that was *Condor*. Obeck overrode the TALAN trace and began plotting intercept vectors for the enemies in the statistical sky.

"T-max," Norne said coolly, and Koleman shoved thrust and thrust diversion at once, stood *Condor* on her tail, grabbed a double handful of sky, and was gone, into the black in an instant, without TALAN or ascent spiral—after all, this was an urgent mission, not some pleasure skip.

The game voice was silent—made mostly of recordings, it was the least intelligent part of the simulator. But the rest of the game played the game well. The couch cushions deflated under their backs and backsides, and the crew sank with simulated g. Stars came out on the viewround, and then appeared the running lights of half a dozen skyblack raiders.

"Got those vectors, Nav?" said Koleman.

"Got 'em, Pilot," said Obeck, and slid his charts onto the Pilot's repeater display. "New pattern—it's the Saber flanked one each, fluid."

With no Rook fortress in orbit, the raiders could practically graze air. The Saber formation scythed over a world's exit zones every few minutes; it could not be "missed," but the moment and method of lift determined the margin between hunted and hunters. Koleman had gotten them most of a minute.

"Eng, what's our status?"

"We have ion flow," Norne said. They were changed from an airship to a spaceship. "Coming up on a G-Four status . . . now." The guns were glowing, there was gas on the grids; *Condor* was armed and girded for war.

The raiders obliged. The curve of the Saber broke up, and four ships reformed at the points of a pyramid. Their blunt broad noses pointed all outward, their view arcs interlocking into a sphere. The game played fair; its pieces could not shoot what they could not see.

"Watch 'em break," Obeck said as the two outrider ships rolled sidewise. One turned end for end and pulsed thrust. They would try to pin *Condor* between themselves, wheeling round it; they would seek to force it into the center of the other formation. If that happened, the sphere would turn in upon itself—and *Condor* and crew would not last long at its center.

The pinwheelers tightened their ring, keeping precisely to opposite sides of their circle. Too precisely, Norne claimed in discussion; real Pilots, he claimed, couldn't maintain such a perfect formation, and a real pinwheel would be doomed from the first. One of these days Norne would write a book.

And Obeck, naturally, would be an Ambassador-Global, and Koleman the Admiral of the Fleet.

"Bank shot," Koleman said, "right wheel, tracking—" A firing grip, black leather and red touchpads, rotated into Koleman's waiting palm. The combat display drew lines; red, white, green, yellow-yellow. Koleman's hand tightened but did not tense.

The synthesized sound of a power gun firing began with a beep, the charge stage; followed with a click, the inertial latch; ended with a bump, latch off and bolt fired. Koleman's finger moved, and with a beeep*click*bump a twisty glowing bolt crossed the viewround. They looked away; raiders could hide in the afterimage.

Without waiting for the hit or miss Koleman turned the ship sidelong and over, and pressed for thrust. The seat cushions sank nearly flat. Obeck saw the gravcounter hit 3.8. At 7 they would black out; the controls would lock up tight. At 9 their passenger would suffer a cerebral hemorrhage and the game would be over.

Koleman said often that if anything beat them, it would be gravity. The simulator had too much of the wrong kind; 0.9 Universals straight down, no weightlessness, no acceleration vectors.

"Got a white cross," Obeck said, and as he did the scene revolved into view: the bolt from *Condor*'s gun had torn across the left-side ionizer cowl of the target. The raider was drifting at an off angle, toward the sphere formed by the others.

The hull of the remaining pinwheeler rose on the viewround, then sank again. There was a faint blue flare. "He's fired," Obeck said, and read the grid on his display. "We need more thrust."

"We're dizzy now," said Koleman, his eye hard on the grav-counter.

"Then we won't—"

The sound of a bolt impacting varied: First came a hum, as the gas flowing over the radiator grids detuned the incoming energy. A more direct hit would then screech, heating and perhaps melting the grids themselves. And if some power was left, there would follow the boom and whoosh of hull rupture, followed here only by the click of the game ending.

Hummm*Squee*—no more. "Hot grid and gas leakage," Norne said. "Gas still bleeding."

"Rate?"

"A percent per three seconds."

"Nav, how much InField have we got left?"

"About two megameters. Two hundred seconds at this vee." The game planets were always tiny, so their gravitational wells would be shallow and the battles to leave them short.

"All right. It won't leave us much gas on the other side, but we're going on through." Koleman could have ceased to accelerate and inertia would have held the shielding gas over the grids. Now they would lose it irretrievably. But they should not *quite* run out.

Koleman toggled a rear-looking camera. On black-and-white displays they could see the neat tetrahedron of ships deforming as the damaged raider intruded upon it. "They're softlining today," Koleman said. Sometimes the raiders would not fire with their own ships in the way; sometimes they would.

"Time In?"

"Eighty seconds," Obeck said.

"Eng, Outriggers down in thirty seconds."

"Doing it," said Norne.

Obeck's battle display put up a line, integrated a curve. "Bolt incoming, rear and below." It appeared, then, on the rear visual, an expanding, whirling circle of light. Behind it, lines crossed, and a red circle appeared at the junction. Obeck said, "And the one we winged just collided with his friend."

Kondor laughed. "Gas, Theo?"

"Half tanks, Pilot."

"Close the valves."

Norne turned the flow control. "Closed."

Koleman said, "When do the grids go dry?"

"Nine seconds."

Koleman pushed thrust and rolled the v-grips. The viewround spun, over and over. The gravcounter ticked to 4.5; the seatcushions emptied of air.

"I must—" Norne began, and the rest of it was lost in a hum*screeeeee* of disintegrating grids.

The view still tumbled. The ionizers whined on. The bolt had swept across a broad strip of *Condor*'s spinning hull,

THE PRINCES OF THE AIR 23

tearing up a frightening stretch of grid surface but spreading too thin to pierce the hull. "Right this time," Koleman said, and pulsed the spin away.

"Outriggers descending," said Norne.

A pair of long, cylindrical fairings on *Condor*'s underhull rolled open and gold shone from within. The Outriggers, skids half as long as the ship itself, plated with gold upon their faces, extended from the hull on fluidic cylinders. Coils and finned radiators folded and expanded out from their stored positions. *Condor* prepared to go OutSide.

But not yet: they were still in the outer fringes of the tiny world's shallow InField, the gravity flux over a hundredth of a Standard. Send power now to the geometric drive, and Out-Side they would go; but they would never come back. There would be the minutest ripple in the planetary fluxfield, one only orbital probes would notice.

Real ships were Field-safed; power was blocked by mechanical breakers from their Outriggers as long as a flux sensor read over a hundredth of a gee. In the game no such safety existed; one was permitted to make errors that cost the winning.

And the flux-01 rule was extravagant—Norne speaking again—a safety margin of ten times or more. If information were perfect, he said, a ship might well skip out sitting on the pad. Information was never perfect, of course, and its imprecision defined the InField.

Far behind *Condor*, read Obeck from his boards, the Saber-Plus had reformed into a classical Pursuit Vee—but too little, too late, this race belonged to the swift.

"Let's give 'em one for luck," Koleman said, killing ion thrust and knocking the attitude grip to the side. The cushions filled out, the gravs ticking down, and the view revolved. Stars whirled by, though Obeck's nav display stayed steady, caring only for *Condor*'s vector of motion. "Flux zero point zero two," he said.

The raiders swung into sight, their lights in echelon, two of them silhouetted against the tiny planet. Lights were missing, gas was puffing out from the ship they had damaged . . . and one other. The firing grip swung forth again, and Koleman's fingers welcomed it.

The combat display fairly sliced space into colored ribbons. Koleman's hand moved.

Beeep*click*bump.

Beeep*click*bump.

The bolts dropped behind them, bright whorls converging like the stars in view center. There were small flashes in reply, not brillant enough to be power weapons. "Raider ordnance launch," Obeck said, then: "Flux three zeros."

"Waste of good fish, then," Koleman said. "Theo, take us Out."

Norne touched pads. "Geometric drive engaged."

The starfield with its brace of ships began rising past them, and a scanning band, bright blue and staticky, appeared at the bottom of the display.

This is what it looks like, Obeck thought, as they all had thought a thousand times. But how does it feel? How does it *feel* to go beyond the Blue?

If he went to Novaya . . . if . . . then so must they. Blue hell, wouldn't he skip his indenture to follow them?

We'll find a way—

Polarizing filters rotated over the cabin lights, and they glowed again. The whine of ionizers faded. The blue band on the viewround reached its top, passed on, and they were Out-Side.

Orden Obeck looked at his hand: goggled, he saw it as gray. His blue sleeve was a darker gray, almost black. The colors of his TALAN and battle boards appeared in shades of gray. The green of Koleman's shirt, the red of Norne's robe were suppressed.

Obeck looked at the viewround. The space away, below them showed not fixed stars but colors, bands and lines and streamers of every possible hue, flowing together like sugar-candies in the sun. And above the colors was one color, roofing them, the endless plane of the Blue, shimmering bright, the shade of summer lightning.

In the middle distance the Blue funneled downward, into a shining pillar that descended out of sight: the gravity well of the outpost moon. Farther away was a thicker column, the moon's primary, and still farther off a broader funnel yet, the system sun.

There was a verse all children knew, a counting-out rhyme:

Einstein, Michelson, Sivasailam,
Put the gold on the Blue just as fast as you can.
Davis, Heisenberg, Dirac, Planck,
If you're in too close then you can't come back.
Sun Li, Schrödinger, Lorenz, Trout,
If you would go far then you must go Out!

Obeck's physics professor had lectured on the people of the verse, noting that, for the sake of the final rhyme, "if Clara Trout had not existed it would be necessary to invent her." She had also said that the jingle was not "traditional" except in its function. It had been written two hundred eighty years before, as part of a History of Science paper. Now no one remembered the paper except some people and machines who did that for a living; likewise the author; but the rhyme was immortal.

As with so much of Orden Obeck's education, he had not believed this at the time he had learned it; and now that he believed it, he had no use for the datum.

David Koleman had rotated his control stand from aerospace to Outrigger position. He put his hands on the grips, nodded to Norne, squeezed gently.

The view before them revolved, the Blue tipping over, the colorfield ascending, half a turn till colors were an analogue of sky, Blue of ground. The gravity funnels rose up forever. Koleman paused, pushed down.

The electric Blue rose a bit, and there was a slight, silent tremor as the golden skids of the Outriggers touched it.

Koleman paused again. There was no sound; the grav-counter showed zeros. Koleman pressed forward.

Colors and Blue flowed past, still silently. The Blue horizon tilted, the masstowers swinging out of *Condor*'s sight.

Koleman said, "Nav?"

"Course two-niner-four, Pilot. I read our first mass in one hundred fifty seconds."

"Eng?"

"Outriggers both in contact, running cool and normal. Our gas tanks are half full—with intermediate grid resealing, good for about one thousand grav-seconds of acceleration." Obeck, who had been taught how to read voices, could detect nothing at all in Norne's. Part of the gift of avoiding absurdity, he supposed. But Obeck knew that Norne was chafing, because real damage control was taking tools and hull steel back and fixing the plates, not an algorithm inside a games machine— done in a suit, not trapped in a couch. Simulated navigation was altogether identical to the real thing; battle—Obeck could smell their sweat in the cool cabin air—was battle. All that lacked were gravity and desperate measures.

Koleman, his hands on the grips, his eyes on the Blue, said, to no one in particular, "What we do on the street . . . that's the game. This is what life is."

Chapter 2
Compulsory Exercises

"Welcome to Novaya, Student Secretary Obeck," said the Queen. Attired in robes of pure light, her face indistinct but for her beautiful bronze eyes, she raised the scepter of knighthood. As the Service Hymn played, the rod came down, and the suddenly-shattered chains fell from Obeck's wrists—

Orden Obeck opened his eyes; only the Hymn was real, blaring to wake him up. Wristecs were beeping, beds trembling, the windowshades rolling open on an awful morning sun. The University never missed a chance.

Of Obeck's roommates, Adaly Starr—Morning Starr—was sitting up on the edge of her bed, brushing her hair, her gown donned but open and unsashed; Wixa was propped up on one elbow, tapping with her other hand on Frazer's chest, making it very hard for Frazer to pretend he was still asleep.

Obeck wondered about David Koleman. After delivering the Brilliant Scientist safely, ending the rebel threat forever, they had gotten boxed dinners and gone out to the massport, sitting near the TALANtenna to eat and watch ships lift and land. Eventually Koleman's wristec beeped, and with a great flourish he departed to meet the woman of the sangrad game— or, as Koleman put it, "to suit my lady's pleasure—tonight there will be joy."

And was there, David? That is, was there joy? I do not doubt you have a tale to tell. With all the artifice you can employ, I do not doubt you pleased your lady well. But was there that—transcendence—we call joy?

Then Obeck realized he had been thinking, half-asleep, in ELI-3. As if he had been trying to argue David's spirit into something. Worse, without being conscious of the language shift. He felt a little sick. And he got out of bed as the Service Hymn played on.

It was Gandisday, so breakfast was coffee and a slick white block of albuprotein. Never mind what the menu called it; alpro was alpro and an egg was an egg, and there was little room for confusion. Yesterday, Dyansday, was everybody's day off in ten, Cook's included, and one never knew what Kitchen left to its own electronic devices might produce. The answer this time had been stacked cakes, uniform tan and round as lasercut gaskets, resembling nothing so much as a magnetic disk pack and half as tasty. This was covered generously with a red somethingberry syrup disturbingly like human blood. The consensus was that it was an improvement over Queen's Birthday Surprise.

Oddly enough, Kitchen's coffee was excellent—probably because everybody, Cook included, had to drink it. Obeck had four cups this fine morning. Thus fortified, he went up to class.

There were forty thousand students, slightly more than half of them indentured, at the Western Continental University of Riyah Zain. Six thousand studied under the College of Society and Government; eight hundred eighty in the School of Diplomacy. Ninety percent of these were indentured. There were two hundred twelve in Orden Obeck's class, and forty in the classroom of the moment: Diplomatic History and Advanced Principles, Doctor Terrance Bishop.

Class was in session, but Orden Obeck was 9.22 parsecs away: the cleanskip distance from Riyah Zain to Novaya. Second-class fare, 4,500 marks, he thought. Nine thousand for David and Theo together. If we played the street to the limit for sixty days . . . sold everything inessential—as if we had much in that line—

"What, Scholar Obeck, is your interpretation of 'diplomacy is the art of the possible'?"

Like every student, Obeck could skip the galaxy in an instant at the sound of his name in class; like them all, he arrived without baggage. Fortunately there had been a notable quote to grab hold of. "Clausewitz—" said Obeck.

"He certainly did," Dr. Bishop said, without sarcasm. Obeck looked up. Bishop had red-gold hair—like Norne's Obeck thought—and bronze-colored eyes, like the Queen's but seen living, not pictured. Dr. Bishop was a close Royal cousin, and there was power in his look. "But epigrams by their nature require elaboration. Would you elaborate, Scholar Obeck?" Still no apparent venom; Bishop's voice was, in fact, quite gentle.

"If strength were all," Obeck said, trapping the flutter in his diaphragm, "strength of whatever kind—there would be no diplomacy, for there would be no capacity for argument. Strength would be compared, and the greater strength would triumph.

"But there is more than raw power in any confrontation: there are types of strength and qualities of power. The role of the diplomat is to understand the type and quality of the resources available, to best employ them and receive the greatest return." The flutter reached Obeck's esophagus; he shut up before it could rise to his throat.

"Nicely put," said Dr. Bishop. "Almost precisely the words I would have used—in fact, I believe I did, a few days ago. No matter—"

Obeck relaxed.

"—if you'll repeat them in ELI-Three, please, Mr. Obeck? So I'll know they've penetrated."

Obeck could feel the tension in the room, could sense the eyes turning away from him. He was suddenly alone—he and Bishop.

He had parsed 3 in his sleep—but doing it awake was harder. ELI-3 was linked to sleep-pattern, to dream-pattern. Properly used, with the rhythms perfect, it induced a mood of . . . acceptance . . . in the listener. The same experts who had designed ELI-4 for universal human use had designed 3 for very specific human uses.

Obeck despised it.

But just now it was the only way out.

"If might were all we knew, in any form," Obeck said, "what profit subtle statecraft? There would be a number on a number, and the most in quantity defined would carry all.

"But samechs see in numbers, persons not—the flesh prefers a qualitative game. And since our bargain's often out of joint—there must be clever souls to spear the point."

Dr. Bishop smiled. Obeck found his smile a beautiful thing. "Well enough done, Mr. Obeck. Philosophically inconsequential, but well done."

Obeck sat absolutely still. Heads turned back to him, and to Bishop. "My treasured scholars," the professor said, "I know perfectly well that with the Academy screening nine days off none of you has a moment's thought for this class. Not to mention that breakfast yesterday should have put us all in another world, if not the infirmary." He took his laugh. "Mr. Obeck just illustrated Mr. Clausewitz's principle of possibility by example, though he thought he was explicating it through rhetoric.

"In the best diplomatic tradition, Mr. Obeck argued that he had not been dreaming of Novaya and that he knew perfectly well what he was talking about. Since a direct affirmation of these things would have been . . . unlikely, he did so in the only possible—there's that word—fashion."

Bishop looked at his wristec. "Despite that I now have most of the attention of most of you, I see no point in continuing this session for another three-quarters—*hold your seats, Scholars*—of an hour." Bishop reached toward his desk—paused, letting the tension build—touched a series of pads.

On the indenture pins worn by every student in the room red lights went dark. The electronic hold broken, the classroom emptied in seconds. Obeck caught a departing glimpse of the professor; Bishop was looking through the narrow band of windows near the ceiling, gazing up at the empty sky.

Obeck descended to his room, traded his copy of Clausewitz (giving its cover a loving pat) for a copy of Parkinson's *Evolution of Political Thought*, and went up to the cafeteria.

> In its desire to conciliate popular feeling democratic diplomacy is apt to subordinate principle to expediency, to substitute the indefinite for the precise, to prefer in place of the central problem (which is often momentarily insoluble) subsidiary issues upon which immediate agreement, and therefore immediate popular approval, can be attained . . .

Obeck blinked, reached for his coffee cup, and found another hand stirring it. He looked up; Eva Weber, a Mathematics student, free, sat across from him. Her chin was propped on a fist, her blue eyes half open. A silver ribbon held back her yellow hair.

"Hi, Orden."

"Hello, Eva."

"Busy?"

"Getting ready for van't Hoeve. Bishop keyed us out halfway through class, so I've got a long lunch."

"Ah." She took the spoon from Obeck's cup, licked it clean. "Your coffee's cold. Want another cup?"

He looked straight at her. She looked straight back. He said, "I've got plenty of time for coffee." She got up. He closed the book.

They sat, and sipped, and watched each other, all alone among hundreds. After a long silence, Weber said, "Do you think we'll make it?"

"Make—" he said, startled, and at once knew her meaning.

"Queen's World, of course—the Academy. Not one of you Dips can think about anything else just now."

You're wrong, he thought, and said, "It's five in two-twelve. Long odds."

"You don't really think that! We figure it's among about thirty of you."

"Who's 'we'?"

"Wu Wei's Statistics group."

"I see. And am I one of these thirty Elect?"

She laughed pleasantly, showing white teeth. Obeck pressed his lips together, not tightly but to conceal.

Weber said with mock gravity, "The analysis is of University trends and patterns, not individuals." She put a fist on the table, extended a finger. "Ten percent of you are free students. Of those, half were slick-talked or parentally pressured into the Dip school." She folded the finger at the middle knuckle. "The other half are Blue-bent on a diplomatic career. That accounts for ten."

Both hands on the table; nine fingers outstretched, disappearing as she spoke. "Ninety percent indentured. Half never stood a chance here anyway—they've just put off the trip to the labor pool by a few k-hours."

"Give or take a few suicides and skipouts."

"Right," said Weber, without slowing. "Of what's left, a fourth will be cut out by their records, half the remainder by the grading curve. That leaves twenty indents, plus the free ten."

Obeck watched Weber's hands, the color of their coffees-with-cream. He had done that calculation himself, though not by chi-square and ANOVA. But did knowing the numbers make any real difference to anyone? Not really, he thought. Among the free students, the motivated ones surely knew themselves—and what did the rest have to fear?

But Orden Obeck was not free.

He had not been "parentally pressured"—there were no such people. He wore the brass because the alternative was hunger. But with the machine meals came the machine choice: the Diplomatic Corps. The machine choice: if you want to achieve, you'll achieve at what you're given—if you only want the dole, we'll give you work that needs no thought.

Weber said, "*I* think you'll get in," and again pulled him back to the world. Was she deliberately tossing double entendres at him, or was he trying to read something not at all there?

Her fingers crept closer to his. He touched the back of her hand, thinking most unromantically of the Manipool, of labor too dull for samechs, but not for slacking humans. What was Weber saying now?

"Later, Orden?"

Here they were, after all, and him without even a quote from Clausewitz. David Koleman, Obeck thought, would not be lost on false vectors. David would have kept the con.

Koleman and Norne had gone hungry and lived strange lives, but they did not wear the brass.

"Of course, Eva. Later."

"I'll see you here for dinner, then." For one moment he thought coffee now and dinner later were all she had intended; he felt greedy, unpleasant. But then she smiled and he read intent indeed. She smiled at him openly; he smiled back, closed. She got up and departed, to where he did not know. Shortly his wristec beeped, and he too rose and went; to where, the building knew, watching his brass pin. To van't Hoeve's class in Monarchical Principles, for where else could he go?

Doctor Emeritus Nathaneal van't Hoeve was an ancient, over three quarters of a million hours old, and beyond any further cosmetic or internal aid from the revi needle; if revi had come along sooner, it was said, van't Hoeve might have lived to a million. And as long as there was a Crown, went the punch line, he would anyway.

"Well, then . . . we ask . . . was Machiavelli wrong? Or Gandhi right? Is the ruler to be cruel . . . or are the people to pursue their common good?"

In the classroom some heads shook, some eyes closed tight as the students searched for a connection between Machiavelli and the Mahatma; Obeck among others was aware that, with van't Hoeve, there might not be one.

But like a spent shell from a long-ago war, van't Hoeve's questions had a nasty habit of exploding on you.

The Doctor Emeritus was looking at his lectern, not the students; hands went up, hesitantly, but van't Hoeve did not appear to see them. Finally he tilted his head up, peered over his eyeglasses, and extended a huge-knuckled finger toward Obeck.

My lucky day, Obeck thought, but the person behind him spoke: Polly Chandra, a free transfer from the University of Venus-Polar. One of the motivated ones, the free Elect.

"If the ruler," she said, gathering strength, "is cruel . . . not merely strict . . . then the people will have a common good to fight for: the overthrow of the monarch. But if the ruler is not cruel . . . then the people will follow their own, diverse interests, as Gandhi said . . . and general opposition will not arise."

Van't Hoeve's head was cocked slightly. After a moment he nodded, and said, "Quite good, Scholar Chandra. Quite a nice synthesis." Then, in a voice suddenly clear: "But of course I did not ask for a synthesis of ideas. I asked, was Niccolo wrong? Was Mohandas right?" He spoke their names as if they were old personal friends he had heard insulted. Then, abruptly, his voice became thready again. "Ah, well, then . . . you're all fretting over service to the Queen, and I can't say that I blame you. There's learning . . . but then there's romance, oh, yes . . . practice is a good lay, but theory's a seducer. Either one sounds like a good idea to me. Class dismissed."

And he walked past them, out into the hall, and was gone. Seventy minutes of the period remained. On the brass pins worn by twenty-eight of the thirty students red lights continued glowing.

"Tick-tick-*boom*," said Obeck to himself.

"What?" said Chandra, too loudly. Obeck tapped his indenture pin. "Oh," she said, giving it the smallest of glances, and sat still. After a moment she said, "Do you suppose he was just . . ." She did not finish the statement.

Across the room, the other free student, Antan Sayyid, was carefully bagging his books. Almost everyone was watching him, and he obviously knew it. He stowed the last notebook, sealed the bag, and looked toward the door.

He stood. So did some others. He took a few steps toward the door. So did they. Sayyid walked a little faster . . . and got to the door last. Two students, each with a decimeter and several kilos on Sayyid, leaned against the closed panel.

Sayyid looked up at the corner of the room where the camera was concealed. There was no way to tell if it was being monitored, though it probably was not.

"Take the physical proctors fifteen minutes to get here," said one of the blockaders, "if they're even watching. Lot can happen in fifteen minutes. Why don't you sit down, do something?"

Sayyid spoke evenly. "What do you suggest?"

"Oh, anything. What do free people do when they're bored?"

Obeck did the calculations once more. A committed free student, and one marking time. Fourteen indents who were headed for the Manipool already. And of the rest—

"Dr. van't Hoeve dismissed this class," Sayyid said, not very diplomatically.

"Yeah?" said someone else. "Doesn't look to me like he did." Red light flickered on brass in an upraised hand, then in another, then two more, six, half the class. Not precisely the statistically lost ones, but close, accounting for the achievers who were a bit radical and the losers who were a bit cowed.

Orden Obeck sat quietly, watching. Next to him were a raised hand, a folded pair of hands, a pin held high, Polly Chandra still off on a van't Hoeve vector. Obeck thought that if Chandra was lucky she would not come back until the period was ended by the Clock.

It was not a day for luck. Chandra stacked text, persec, and notepad, put them under an arm, and started toward the door, seeing nothing around her.

She nearly collided with one of the door blockers, who now numbered four. "Go sit down," one of them said, firmly but not angrily.

Chandra looked sharply up. The situation penetrated instantly. "Oh," she said, and took one step back. Then she stepped forward, reached toward the doorpad.

A large hand moved.

"Let her out," Obeck said explosively.

The big hand stopped, almost on Chandra's wrist. Heads turned. High-held pins dipped.

"Let them both out," Obeck went on. If he gave up his

momentum he was lost. "What the hell *difference* does it make?"

The student with her hand near Chandra's tightened her fingers into a fist. Obeck's stomach sank. Then the fist slammed the doorpad and the door slid open.

Chandra nodded, though not to Obeck, and walked out. Sayyid was through almost before her. Two of the students who had blocked the doorway looked long after them. Finally the door closed.

Obeck was suddenly in the center of the room, the crowd, the crowd's vision; in the raider formation, black bows and glowing guns all around. Momentum, he thought, fly or fall. "Do you think van't Hoeve just forgot to key us out? There's probably going to be a test tomorrow on what happened while he was gone."

There were grunts and snickers. Those who had stood up began moving, first toward Obeck, then their seats. In fear of the camera, the physical proctors, perhaps of van't Hoeve next session, and maybe even in fear of losing a chance at Novaya —in fear of practically anything, Obeck knew, except him— the crisis ended.

Obeck, with a deliberate effort, took out his Parkinson and flipped to the Gandhi quote—

If leaving duties unperformed we run after rights, they will escape us like a will o' the wisp. The more we pursue them the further they will fly.

—and read it and reread it and its surrounding passages, seated in the midst of tension. If I had only said—he thought several times, each time suppressing the possible concluding phrase, except one: If I had only said nothing.

And after fifty minutes the Central Clock deactivated their pins; set them all free. A little.

Obeck returned to his room in the late afternoon, finding Wixa soundly asleep, flat on her back, openmouthed and snoring loudly. The sheet was down around her hips, and an open copy of Vigenere's *Revitalization Medicine* covered her breasts. It was a large book. She didn't look at all comfortable. Ah, well, if I were Frazer, Obeck thought, his soul suddenly light. He walked with exaggerated care around her to the bathroom, slipped out of his robe and boots, set his wristec, and entered the shower.

After four minutes, forty seconds Obeck's wristec beeped over the rush of the shower jets; he hit the valve handle just before the pleasantly hot water went cold. They had plenty of heat, of course; scrubbing the used water was the costly part. Obeck pulled a towel from the wall slot, used it, crumpled and flashed it. He draped his robe over his shoulders and went back into the bedroom.

Wixa's eyes were open; her position had not changed. "Ungh-yuch," she announced. "I think spit spoils in the open air."

"I've never left it out longer than overnight," Obeck said. He took the brass pin off his gown, patted and emptied the gown pockets, and dropped it into a hamper.

Wixa said, "Did you know that muscular revies cause the recipient to taste shellfish—oysters, particularly—for two to four days after the needle?"

"Oysters? Seems I've heard that."

"While visceral revies produce a fruity taste, and neurals make you salty." She pushed the book to the floor, where it landed with a bang. She pushed herself up on one elbow, blew hair out of her eyes. "Speaking of salty, Orden—oh, great Galen, the good suit. Who's it for?"

"Eva Weber," Obeck said, sealing the gray silk trousers and reaching for the jacket.

Wixa was quiet for a moment. She said, "Her idea or yours?"

"What kind of question is that?"

"A—uh—nothing."

Obeck put down his scarf. "You say 'nothing' like it's really something." Then, more delicately, he said, "If it's that she's free—"

Wixa shook her head vigorously, brushing back her hair. "No, no, no. Look, Orden . . . do you want me to maybe ginch up a wonderful evening?"

"Yeah, Wixa, maybe I do."

"Well . . . do you know about Eva's Statistics workshop? That they're running predictions on the Dip . . . lomatic screening?"

"She told me."

"Oh . . . then you know."

"Know what? Just that? Come on, Wixa!"

"That they're all placing bets on who'll make it."

"Hell, so are we, but I . . . *oh* . . . you mean . . . your money where your . . ." He grinned. Wixa nodded. Obeck laughed. Wixa, relieved, did too, letting her hair fall.

Obeck wound on the silver scarf and sealed the dark blue jacket up to the collar. "I'm glad you told me—no, I really am. Now I know how to pick out the favorite."

As he stuck the pin on his shoulder, he wondered why in the blinding Blue he thought it was so funny.

He met Weber at the cafeteria; they did not stay there. Weber was surprised when Obeck picked out a decent restaurant some distance from the University complex; she was more surprised when he paid both sides of the bill.

"Sometimes you win on long odds," he told her. She smiled, but nervously. No more of that, Obeck thought. I'm a diplomat.

So there was coffee under imported Priman palms, beneath a full and a last-quarter moon and heat-wavering stars, and finger contact.

There was a slow walk through the dim and empty upper levels of the University, pausing at display cases and floor mosaics they had passed a thousand times each—and had not ignored, but which looked different now, as all things do when seen through two pairs of eyes. And there was lip contact.

They passed the physical proctor who sat at the entrance to the Independent Students' residences. The proctor was watching a tape of a costume drama, Shakespeare or Shakespearean. She pulled her earphone and greeted Weber by name, made an entry on her deskpad, said hello to Obeck, without any affectation he could detect, and went back to her tape. Her nighteyes and handstick lay on the desk.

Weber's room was large and cold. No, Obeck realized, not so large—slightly smaller than his own, but with only one bed, and filled with only one person's belongings (though there were easily as many things as he and any two roommates had). And not so cold, no more so than a classroom. The showers here, he knew, still went icy after five minutes; there were things too expensive to extend as courtesies. The transfers from the soggy worlds never stopped complaining about it.

Would Novaya have showers eternally warm? Novaya, it was said, had improbable things called bathtubs.

Obeck took Weber's cape. She put a hand on his shoulder, touched his brass pin, ran her fingers over it. He held quite still, permitting her.

"Did you know," he said, "that after an organ revi you taste salt for days?"

Her laugh was high, sweet. "Neural, not visceral. Did *you* know my father's the best cell surgeon in Riyah North?"

"*That* Weber?" He had known, of course. He had careful instruction in the names of the Technical Aristocracy; a Weber was the Royal Surgeon. Nor had he forgotten which taste was which.

But if she could touch his indenture sign as she did, then he could in turn probe her station a little. Though not nearly so deep, nor so well.

Obeck realized, then, what had so amused him earlier.

Clothing was unsealed, and fell, and in the dim room light (but not quite darkness) there was contact.

Obeck fumbled. He knew what to do, and to do it without haste; he knew quite a bit, actually. Between his orphaning and his indenture he had gotten along. But blue, blue hell, he hadn't gotten along very well; and Weber wasn't a written test.

That was what had struck him funny, though it was black enough humor: the lady had thought she was picking a winner.

On the night after that one, Obeck, Koleman, and Norne were dining alfresco on the slopes above the starship pads. The twilight air was pleasant; there was a scent of fuels and hot metal on the breeze from the port, but to the three of them it was perfume.

"If you keep grifting like the day before yesterday," Obeck said, "you should have two fares in sixty days."

"Sixty days, nothing, Orden," David Koleman said. "When you go, we're going with you. On the same ship."

"I have no assurance that I'm going anywhere."

"Of course you do. Don't you want it? You most certainly want it. So you'll get it."

"I'm not the only indentured student," Obeck said, feeling his chest tighten as he rose, almost unconsciously, to the argument. "They want things too, and they want out—" Obeck felt the delta-cadences of ELI-3 echo in his own bones, stopped himself short. He leaned back in the short blue grass, looked up at the TALANtenna, the darkening sky.

"Out, surely," said David, "and after out, then what? Nothing, Orden. Nothing but a climate-controlled house and lust to order. It's not your fault that from all the worlds there are to pick a destiny from, most people choose none at all. 'None but the brave deserve the fair,' Orden. *You* told me that, remember?"

"I'm not brave," Obeck said, without any strength in his

voice. He was afraid of the argument, afraid of speaking 3, afraid that he had really and completely sold his soul to the College of Diplomacy for a mess of University meals.

David either did not hear or ignored him. "And for the few, like you, who *do* want something—"

Here came the old statistical breakdown again. Obeck wondered if there was anyone on Riyah Zain who didn't know the percentages.

". . . but you've got it, Orden. You can want something enough—enough that the whole universe will bend to make it happen."

Obeck touched his pin. "Then why don't all these melt like butter in the sun?"

Koleman folded his empty dinner box between his dark hands, squeezing it smaller and smaller until abruptly it was gone, his hands empty. "Orden, Orden, don't you see? Yours *will*. Because you well and truly want it to."

Obeck sat up. A little way downhill of him sat Norne, legs crossed, spine rigid, head tilted back, watching stars and ships. He had a notebook, a pen, a tiny handlight. He was working on his book.

Obeck thought, I could almost believe David, seeing you, Theo. If I were the universe . . . I'd bend for you.

"What we need," Koleman said, "is a long-short con. Something we can pull off in one day, two at most, on the street, and bring in . . . what was the fare, Orden?"

"Forty-five hundred each, as you know very well."

"Don't stop me now, I've got a handful of sky. Nine gold cards, then. Really ten—we're going to need a bit of a stake on the Queen's World, some clothes and a place."

"And a ship?" Obeck said carefully.

"We'll manage the ship. Now, what if we—No. Or—No. Or if—"

"The Solid Gold Needle," Obeck said.

"Hmm. We've never pulled that. But I like it—oh, yes . . . Theo! Are you listening?"

Norne nodded without turning around.

Obeck stood up. "Give me a couple of days for the setup. After all, if I fail the screening—"

"Nonsense."

"I'll borrow Wixa's copy of Vigenere. And . . . I think I've got a brain to tap."

"You see?" said Koleman, who knew the brain's name and guessed the rest. "In the end . . . there is joy."

Obeck looked at Theo, who still sat working in a puddle of

light, at David, who was only a shape in the darkness. *Nothing is nonsense for you except failure, right? The book on space tactics. The Queen's Admiralty. I'll be an Ambassador-Global, I suppose. Wishing will make it so.*

Maybe it was the pursuit of the ideal: Theo's distillation of all space warfare into words on paper, David's reduction of all romance—intellectual and physical—into the person of Queen Rachel II Valeria. *How can we fall when our eyes are on the stars? How can we sink when we can fly?*

But Orden Obeck was a diplomat—it was not his choice, but still he was—and the College had taught him just where the pursuit of the ideal led. He closed his eyes tightly. *How can we live, when death is the end of pain?*

Obeck sighed. He supposed he did believe Theo and David. Even about the joy. He supposed he must, if he were to finish living another day.

Vectored from Koleman and Norne, past Wixa and Weber, toward Novaya and the Queen, Obeck returned to the Uni complex on preset course; he was immersed in thought, and his perimeter sensors did not detect the approach of the raider formation.

So when they stopped and confronted him (being far too brave to simply knock him down), there was no escape vector. Obeck would happily have run, being not as brave as they.

Obeck didn't know what this particular group wanted to beat him for. The rhetoric was standard—"arrogant kiss-up" and so forth. Maybe it was for having Bishop's answer. Or breaking up the revolt after van't Hoeve. Or having a night out with a free student. Or something he had done three years ago, or nothing at all but being alone and vulnerable—it didn't matter. Nothing did.

He spoke to them in ELI-3, the diplomatic language he hated, to vent his hate: "Strike home, thou fools, thou canst not beat me thus—" and rolled with the first punch, and the seeond, and in rage suddenly uncontrollable pounded at someone's midsection. Then he stopped, and held himself. They dared not damage him permanently, he knew, and were not intelligent enough to simply kill him and be done with it.

Go ahead, he shouted silently, *I won't fight you on your terms—and in only days I'll see the Queen. To think*—he fell to his knees, saw the brass glitter of their pins all around him—*to think I almost defended you before David and Theo.*

He was pressed to the ground, and took the blows, and won, and won, and won.

Chapter 3
Final Examinations

The carrel was a cube three meters on a side. The walls were a light sand brown, the short-napped carpet a darker brown. The ceiling glowed, casting light without shadows, and small vents drafted cool air down. The only furnishings were a chair, lightly padded, comfortable, and a smooth white console with a keyboard and three displays. The flush door had no handle on this side. There were no toilet facilities within. That, they had been made aware, was part of the test.

Obeck told himself it was foolish to be tense now; there were no texts or notes to lose his place in—they had in fact been given a change of gown and sandals and were wave-searched on the way in, indentured and free alike. All he could do was forget or freeze up, and tension would multiply the chances for both.

He did not relax in the least, of course.

His right hand was tight on his left shoulder. He glanced at his left wrist, but it was bare of wristec.

And the pin was gone.

The chains were still on, even invisibly—

The brass was gone.

He was no freer of it than in the shower; he still had to pass—

The brass pin was not upon him.

His physical grip relaxed, his mental hold grew firmer. Before him the console blinked with light, the displays glowed. Obeck set to.

The machine asked questions of form, of function, of fact. It asked for keytouches and Obeck touched; for words and positions assumed, and Obeck spoke and posed; and the answers to some questions were no answers at all—"Respond aloud to a Franconard middle-noble's comment that your hair is disarrayed." Correct response: silence.

"A Tolstoian religious anarchist attacks the concept of the Queen. Defend by appropriate means.

"Taken ill while on mission, you discover the embassy has been exposed to a biological attack. Do you notify A/the Ambassador B/the Medical Officer C/the Military Attaché?

"State at least one circumstance under which you, as a Junior Liaison-National, could individually assassinate and replace your Ambassador-Global. Machiavelli may be cited in support of but not as your case."

Obeck hastened to reply. He had not been told whether time counted for grade, so it was unsafe to assume that it did not.

Questions: The Inner Courts of the Queen and her predecessor. Key figures of the pre-Monarchic period. Titles and translations. Principalities and powers. The retort courteous, the quip modest, the reply churlish, the reproof valiant, the countercheck quarrelsome, the lie with circumstance . . . the lie direct, And When To Avoid It . . .

Obeck tried to count the passing time, but could not. Ninety minutes at least, two hours. Knock down a question, another rises. Three hours? Sensory deprivation stretched the time sense—what did overload do? Four hours? Questions growing like Hydra's heads—and were they coming faster now?

Query, answer, query, answer.

No brass on his clothing. No handle on the door. Koleman and Norne waiting, setting up for— Obeck realized that he had nearly said "the Solid Gold Needle game" aloud. That wasn't the way to Novaya. Not *his* way, at least.

The door behind him buzzed, slid open hissing. The displays before him stalled. Obeck turned and saw the Queen.

Not dreaming her—no! Seeing her, in silver satin, black stole, fifteen-jeweled golden crown.

Obeck slipped from his chair to his knees. The situation— an abrupt Royal entrance, nothing spillable or frangible in Obeck's hands, gravity present—and Obeck's status indicated a one-knee drop, hands folded on erect knee, face upturned to await Her pleasure—the posture known informally as a Jolson Six.

Obeck realized this just as he became aware that traitor muscle and faithless nerve had put him into a Jolson *Two* instead—both knees down, hands spread, palms up—a posture of urgent supplication on a Global or Metaglobal matter. And too late now to change—he might have drawn his hands in smoothly, but down his knee was and down it would remain. The reason kneeling was invented, thought Obeck in bitter recitation.

He almost spoke, in as much rage as a few nights past, but the hate this time was inward and thus the easiest for him to contain. And how would he have spoken to her except in the ELI-3 he loathed? So his hatred of 3 helped save him, keep him still.

He would skip, he thought, as he knelt and bled; they would up the grift to fifteen gold cards, and as three they would go.

No. Of course not. David and Theo were legally clean. Obeck, marked down for breaking indenture, would be a megatonne mass on their Outriggers.

Obeck looked into the face of his Queen. It was planar, wreathed in red-gold, with the bronze Bishop eyes; not finely sculpted, but strong, and beautiful in its strength. Obeck, trained in reading faces, tried to read what mercy was in this one: how much more than just Novaya he had so suddenly lost.

The Bishop eyes looked down; they were not hard. The lips, not full, smiled a little. An idea entered Obeck's mind, an impossibility, a thing he could not possibly be reading rightly —no, an improbability. Surely, he thought, hope is not always improbable. But he dared not act, lest by acting all be lost—so he held his place and his tongue.

Until finally the Queen of Nine Suns said, "I give up, Mister Obeck. What *is* so shatteringly important?" in a very familiar voice, and took off her crown and the wig beneath it. Dr. Terrance Bishop scratched his head, tugged a wire behind his ear, and his jaw sagged as the lift was released. "Sit down, Mr. Obeck. It's improper for you to kneel to me, and besides, it's awkward. No—on the floor. Then we can both sit."

Obeck sat, cross-legged. Dr. Bishop sat against the wall, knees high in front of him, his gown draped artlessly, exposing hairy shins.

"Well, Mr. Obeck, congratulations. And I mean that: when you're soldiery-sergeant to so many for so long, it's a great and shining pleasure to congratulate the few."

"Then I . . . passed." *Hell, if I did start dreaming back there, let's make the most of it.*

"Oh, your score was more than high enough. That had relatively little to do with it—you're not gaping. Good. Let's see if I can make your head spin.

"We could have asked you twenty questions, or ten, or five, for all this rote test is worth. Do you really think that we've spent all these tens of thousands of hours with you, on you, in preparation for one afternoon that will magically settle cases? Hardly. This was an acid test, yes, but of you, not your knowledge."

"You knew who would pass?" Obeck said, thinking, If Weber were here—or her professor!

"Roughly. There are always disappointments and pleasant surprises. Five go to Novaya directly. Another five, about, will be quietly transferred for another term of polishing. A few more are carefully rechanneled—for instance, Polly Chandra will probably end up a power in Policy. She proved the other day she was wrong for the field."

Obeck did not need to ask where she had proven that. "And I wasn't . . . just now . . . a disappointment?"

"*Mister* Obeck. Do you really think the Queen gives a void in a vacuum exactly how you're kneeling, if what you have to say is important—and said well? I know for a fact that she doesn't even remember the positions." Dr. Bishop picked up his crown and wig. "I know because I've *been* the Queen on a couple of important occasions, and I couldn't remember."

"You're a Queen's double?"

"And a few other Bishops. It helps greatly if you're a Bishop—the eyes, you know, the hair, the complexion. There are makeups for emergencies—even a couple of skin-tinted samechs. But Bishops are preferred, when Queens are restricted.

"But as for your present case . . . you made an error, as you will assuredly err in the future. But you did nothing awkward, which you must not, and you brazened it through, which you must. I rather knew you would, Mr. Obeck. You've got brass." Dr. Bishop paused, his eyes quite direct.

"Thank you," said Obeck, wincing.

"Glad you think that way. Brass indeed. I suspect you'll be

in the real Queen's presence before very long. Possibly pleading for your life . . . ah, there, I did make you gape a little. Sorry, Mr. Obeck.''

"That's all right, Doctor. And . . . you may call me Orden.''

"Better that I call you Novice Secretary Obeck. And you keep calling me Doctor Bishop.'' The professor stood, replaced his wig. In moments he was again the Queen.

Before the illusion could take hold of him, Obeck said, "Dr. Bishop.''

Bishop stopped with his persec out and open. "Yes, Novice Secretary?''

"You've told me quite a few things that I'd never heard.'' *Nor have many others.* "Do you expect me to keep the secret?''

"Novice Secretary Obeck, if there'd been any question of that, you'd never have gotten to this stage.'' He touched a pad on his persec. "Bishop. Pawn promoted. Release us, please.''

As the door opened, Bishop reached inside his stole. "There's usually some ceremony attached to these things. You needn't wear it any longer—but if you don't, be careful. Save yourself a beating.''

Obeck caught the brass pin one-handed on the fly. He stood and followed Bishop out, into the corridor air that, conditioned as it was, smelled fresh and clean and free.

Wings screaming, turbines howling, the liner *Theron Ware* slipped into air and was brought down to Riyah Zain. The liner settled to the pad, and all the massport types came up to it with horses and carts; seventy-eight passengers went one way, their ninety-five bags quite another.

The spacelines' excuse for the confiscation of private property they called "baggage check'' ran approximately: Since we're going to tie them down and forbid you from opening them anyway (who, indeed, knew what mischief a sock wild in z-gee might perform), you might as well just hand them over.

Once the bags were handed over, of course, they were hostage to the spaceline and no further excuses for anything were necessary.

The bags from the *Theron Ware*, after several interesting and often violent intermediate stages, slid ten meters down to a rotary raceway. (Don't ask how they got up that high.) Luggage Track 6 quickly filled with bags of every description, shape, color. There were no passengers awaiting them; all races have second finishers.

There was, however, one young man, dark skinned, in white quilted jacket and pants, who was attracted to a white leather-over-metal case bearing the Consolidated Vulcan trademark in a top corner.

A port guard noticed him all alone with the baggage and on polite inquiry discovered that he, like two hundred other passengers a day, had read his claim ticket upside down. The young man succeeded in tipping the portcracker a mark and went off in the direction of Luggage Track 9.

Before going very far, he entered a washroom, where a slightly older fellow was adjusting his scholar's gown, with its new Doctoral sash.

"Con Vulcan sample case—Xavier Grosz," Koleman told Obeck. "Home's St. Martin's Place, though his liner's in from Primus."

"He'll tip to Earth, won't he?"

"Everybody knows Primus used to be Earth," said Koleman, and stepped back from the mirror. He opened his jacket slightly, slipped a hand in, out.

"Careful what you show," Obeck said.

"Always," said Koleman, grinning, and left.

Obeck pulled his sash tight and rode the belt to Luggage Track 6. There, a blocky man in a green velvet tailcoat was retrieving the white case.

"Sir Xavier?"

Grosz turned. "Yes?" He looked Obeck up, down.

"You were told you'd be met . . . ?"

"Well, I . . . had expected Dame Patricia."

Obeck smiled. "She'll be late, I'm afraid. A storm delaying the sub-orb. You saw it, perhaps, while entering."

"Yes, yes I did."

"Well then. I'm to take you up to the Aeolus Room, for drinks—and dinner, should Medame be so long delayed."

"Well . . . " Grosz turned his arm as though to check a wristec, but did not move his sleeve. "I hate to put pleasure before business. But it was a long skip . . ."

"Precisely," said Obeck. "May I carry your bag?"

"I'd be obliged."

The Aeolus Room was in the massport's control tower, just below the control deck itself. Its deep-piled carpet was electric blue, its ceiling rainbow opal; the table settings were blindingly

white china and white-handled silver on black silk cloths.
Louvers at the tops of the high windows let wind filter
through, making soft musical sounds.

Xavier Grosz finished another glass of sparkling wine.
"Amazing, a fellow your age being factotum to Dame Pat,"
he said loudly. He said everything loudly, Obeck had discovered. "Or then, maybe not so amazing, eh?"

"I consider myself fortunate to have the position."

"Ha, yes, fortunate positions, I should think," Grosz said,
and rocked back in his chair, laughing. Heads turned nearby;
the headwaiter looked sympathetic toward Obeck and murder-
ous toward Grosz.

Grosz's eyes widened. "And what's this?" He hiked himself
up, with difficulty, put a hand beneath himself. Eyes were
vigorously averted. Grosz came up with a leather folder, like a
document case, longer and thinner than a persec.

Grosz flipped it open, and his wide eyes fairly bulged.
Within was a long fan of gold-edged thousand-mark cards, at
least fifty of them; opposite were three tape cassettes and several long, thin glass tubes. Within each tube shone a whisker of
yellow metal.

"Ho, *my*, I wonder . . . well, I don't suppose I wonder very
much, do I?"

Obeck produced a persec. "Maybe if we play the tapes, it'll
give us some idea who the wallet belongs to."

Grosz hesitated. Finally he handed the tapes—not the wallet
—across the table. "Of course, the very thing."

Obeck unfolded the persec display and plugged a cassette
into the clip. Cryptic characters appeared, definitely not in
ELI-4 script; and diagrams, apparently of a complex cage or
maze.

"What the—"

"Those are molecular diagrams," Obeck prompted.
"Organic compounds, if I'm not mistaken. And aren't
those . . ."

Grosz took one of the glass tubes from the wallet. Sealed
within was a long golden needle with a squarish hub at one
end. "A revi needle," he said.

I'll bet you're familiar enough with them, Obeck thought.
He said, "But aren't those made of silver alloy?" and simultaneously changed cassettes.

"Dateline Earth to distant worlds," said the persec in a
clipped voice.

"Earth?"

"Primus," Grosz said. "It hasn't been called 'Earth' for . . . why, centuries."

"Centuries?"

"Millions of hours," Grosz said gratingly. "May I—"

The recorded voice went on: "The rapidly developing field of revitalization medicine has suffered a major setback with the disappearance of Doctor Thaddeus Weber-Cranach, pioneer in his field. Dr. Weber-Cranach, known as 'The Man with the Golden Needles,' was reportedly close to a breakthrough . . ." The screen showed still pictures of a man in a red lab smock, examining glass vials, holding the long metal cylinder of a revi unit, needle affixed to its tip.

"Pale, isn't he?" said Obeck.

"Lot of people used to be that," said the florid Grosz.

"Oh, of course, the—" Obeck suddenly pulled the cassette and slapped the persec closed.

A man stood near their table, staring at them; he wore a white quilted jacket and his skin was very dark. His fists were clenched, and the look he gave Obeck and Grosz was startlingly intense. He turned suddenly, moved on.

Grosz opened his mouth, then turned to follow Obeck's pointing finger.

Across the room was a broad-shouldered, angular fellow in a red tunic, discussing something with the headwaiter. His skin was pale, his hair red-brown, and if not for his age he would have been the man on the cassette.

"Isn't that remarkable?" said Obeck.

"Oh . . . more than remarkable."

"You don't think—"

"A . . . descendant, perhaps." Grosz tucked the cassettes and the needle back into the wallet, signaled to the headwaiter. The man in the tunic turned toward them, approached.

"Pardon me," he said, in a very quiet voice, "but have you . . . oh. There it is. I thank you for finding it."

"Won't you sit down?" Grosz said. "Have a drink with us."

The pale man reached out to Grosz. "I appreciate the offer, but—"

"Please, Dr. Weber-Cranach."

The man's eyes grew hard, amazingly so for his apparent age; his orbits bore no marks of the needle. "I beg your indulgence . . . my name is Norne, and I am only a medician."

Grosz smiled and drew the wallet back. "Then there's some mistake, I'm afraid. We've clearly identified this as belonging to a Doctor Thaddeus Weber-Cranach.''

Norne's look went from the man in green to the scholar. "Is this so?" Obeck shrank back slightly, thinking, If only I could read your real face so plainly, and said, "We . . . read the tapes."

Norne tightened a hand on a chair back, making the bentwood creak; he relaxed it at once. His voice remained soft and clear. "Then I suppose we have some things to discuss."

"Sit down, Doctor."

"Not here. There is a . . . gentleman who may come looking for me here, and it would be best if he did not find me." He paused. "Have you seen a dark-skinned man, dressed in white . . . apparently quite young?"

"Why . . . no," said Grosz with unusual smoothness. He shot a glance at Obeck, who said nothing.

"Then if you will come with me . . . bringing my wallet, please?"

"Now wait," Obeck said, "we're expecting someone—"

"Come along, Doctor," Grosz said. "I'll tell Dame Pat it was all my doing."

"If you'll take the responsibility," said Obeck, and they went out together, Grosz carrying Norne's wallet, Obeck carrying Grosz's white suitcase.

"Not a very elaborate place you have here, Doctor," said Grosz, looking out the tiny window at the oscillating TALAN-tenna. There were a few lectras on the walls, of ships and space scenes, and some plain-ink prints; a bed and a chair; and an elaborate array of glass tubing and metal canisters in which liquids bubbled and roiled.

"The work does not require a palace. I have lived a great many places."

"Oh, I'll wager you have. What's it been, Doctor? Three hundred years Old Style? Three million hours?"

"I no longer count them," said Norne, tinkering with a series of dials. "None of my . . . patients do, after a while."

"How many have there been?" Obeck asked.

"There are things I need not tell you. And, in fact, it is much better for you if you do not know." Norne broke open a glass tube, drew out a needle that sparkled golden in the harsh room light. He fastened its hub to a metal cylinder that trailed cables and tubes, swabbed it with a blood-red solution. "The fee for treatment is fifteen thousand marks, sir, Doctor."

"Fee?" Grosz exploded.

"Fee," Norne said calmly. "You are determined to extract a price for the return of my property and your silence hereafter. Fine. I offer you something you could not have purchased for any price whatsoever. My equipment is expensive—all the more so since I must have it made secretly and abandon it frequently."

Obeck said, "My Lady Patricia would pay you quite well for—"

Norne pointed the long gold needle at Obeck's heart. "What would not anyone give for my contract? My indenture? My freedom? No. I will never serve one soul alone."

Grosz gave a very unpleasant laugh. "Nor will you serve all of them, yes, Doctor? Forgive the lad, he's young, he'll learn. His mistress will teach him. We old men—we understand."

Obeck chewed his lip. "All right. It's all I've got . . . but it sounds damned cheap to me." He produced a fan of gold-edged cards. Norne accepted them, nodded, tucked them inside his jacket. "And you, Sir Xavier? Do we truly understand one another?"

Grosz said, "Well, now, I—"

"I remind you, I shall hold the needle. A slip would grieve me; and I grieve for a long, long time."

"*All right,*" said Grosz, and fanned cards.

"Thank you both. Now, if you will—"

David Koleman crashed through the door, almost unhinging it, almost falling. He was mostly out of breath; his jacket was askew and his face was twisted.

"It's all blown up out there, Norne!" he shouted. "The crackers are coming—we've got to run—" In David's face Obeck could see the world coming apart; in his voice he could hear it crumbling behind David's heels.

While for Theo there might have been no world outside at all. Without any heat in his voice he said, "And you led them here. Idiot." He raised the revi unit with its long yellow needle. "I did warn you."

David's hand darted inside his white jacket. It came out clutching a bull-barreled pistol. "I'm not going down alone!"

Norne took a step toward him.

Koleman pulled the trigger; flame leaped. There was a crack, horribly loud. Blood spattered the wall behind Norne. Norne did not stop. The dark man fired again, and again. More blood. Norne staggered, walked on.

"I'm hard to kill," he said, and rammed the golden needle to the hub into Koleman's chest. Blue fire arced around the spot; there was a smell of ozone. A red stain blossomed on the white quilted fabric. David opened his mouth, and with the cry came blood.

Norne, still standing, his coat soaked and torn in front and demolished in back, turned to Obeck and Grosz. "I'll live . . . I've lived through so much . . ." He lost his grip on the revi unit, which was all that supported Koleman's body; it fell. Then Norne, ever so slowly, collapsed on top of it.

Obeck knelt beside them. "How could he have lasted—with those—" He poked at a ragged wound.

"His treatment, obviously." Grosz fingered the wallet. "I wonder if he might even . . ."

"The other one said the patrols were coming," Obeck said. "We've got to get out of here."

"You're absolutely right."

"Better do it separately. It will seem less suspicious—I mean—" Obeck turned to the bodies, began pushing them away from the open doorway.

"Dame Pat did hire you well," said Grosz. "I hope she'll feel like writing your bond and alibi."

"What?" said Obeck, just before Grosz kicked him in the head. As Obeck slumped forward, Grosz stepped daintily around him, reaching for Norne's body; then he cocked an ear for what might have been an alarm rising outside and shook his head. He checked the wallet in his hand for the cassettes and golden needles, gave it a kiss, and ran as fast as his thick legs would carry him out of the room, down the hall, toward the massport.

Obeck groaned, opened his eyes and was blind; vision came back in sparks and streaks. He pushed himself up, off the two bodies. "Oh, Theo, oh, David," he whispered, "only the good die young." He reached out to the crackling revi unit, flipped a switch, and the noise faded. So did the faraway alarm tone.

Norne and Koleman sat up, helped Obeck to his feet. "I'm the capper, right?" Obeck muttered. "This isn't supposed to happen to the capper . . . getting crowned."

"You can't cheat an honest man," Koleman said. "This one was just a little more cheatable than most. You noticed he didn't bother to save his sample case—or his fifteen golds, when he heard the crackers coming?"

"The case was Con Vulcan's," Obeck said, aching and annoyed, "or we wouldn't have picked him to begin with. Come to think of it, probably the money was theirs too. *Ouch.*

Thinking hurts. And besides, fifteen kilomarks *is* cheap for eternal life. Right, Theo?''

Norne reached into his destroyed jacket, produced Obeck's fan of one-mark cards, gilt-edged with the same brush that had colored the steel needles. He tossed the cards aside, produced Grosz's fifteen of the genuine article. ''He may even try to pass the cards in my wallet. If I understand him.''

Obeck took a card and pressed the cool plastic against his temple. ''Ohhh, that feels better.''

''Honors have some skill in surgery, then?'' Koleman took a card. ''I'm glad we raised the price to fifteen. I believe that ogre drank a thousand marks off our net.''

''What kind of—ouch again—roper do you take me for?'' Obeck said. ''I charged all the drinks to Dame Patricia.''

''Dame Patricia *who?*''

''I haven't any idea. But the headwaiter certainly did.'' Obeck looked at the card in his hand, its gold stained with stage blood and a little bit of his own. He tossed it into the air, watching it fly like a sleek white ship with golden Outriggers.

A tan sandy ball with small seas and scanty icepacks, Riyah Zain fell away from the starliner *Lucia G. Showalter*. Aboard ship, five new-made Doctors watched the planet shrink and spin slowly away, Riyah Primary rising brilliant and yellow-white.

''Good-bye,'' said Novice Secretary Selye.

''Forever,'' added Novice Secretary Kassim.

''If not longer,'' said Novice Secretary Hetherington, who had been free.

''Here's to ya!'' said Novice Secretary deVol, who held a bottle of cognac with a drinking valve.

''Here's to us,'' concluded Novice Secretary Orden Obeck, and from tight-belted passenger to passenger went the brandy flask, belting them all even tighter.

They had pulled three gravities in lift; now the acceleration, the rumble, the weight died away. The PASSENGERS RESTRAIN sign went dark. Hetherington, Selye, and Obeck released themselves with ease; Obeck did not miss Hetherington's surprised look, and went to help deVol.

Obeck drifted, bumped deVol's couch, drifted again. Z-gee, he thought, After this long—and soon, OutSide. He got control of himself, got deVol and then Kassim free.

The lounge was a slightly flattened cylinder, spacious, with two rows of couches. The seats were unlocking now, to swivel, and most turned to face the unbroken viewstrips along both sides of the chamber. The floor and ceiling were identically covered with a short-napped brown carpeting.

One of the samech flight attendants was distributing paper slippers with a grip sole. Obeck slid a pair over his boots, wrote thanks into the attendant's palm, and rubbed his feet against the, well, ceiling—the overhead floor, at least.

He looked down on a young man in a red gown that floated and billowed slightly about his arms and legs. His pale face, with its high forehead, was reflected in the viewport; he watched the stars with a great intensity, and his facial muscles rippled minutely in patterns Obeck wished he could read.

"Still sitting, Thorn?" Obeck said.

The head turned upward. The sharp jaw was set hard. Finally, Thorn (not Theo Norne, who had been shot to death on Riyah Zain) said, "In a moment, Orden."

Obeck smiled, nodded, walked on to where a dark fellow sat, dressed in a silver-buckled black jacket, steel-gray trousers, black boots.

"Are you still here too? Come on, David. It's wonderful."

David Kondor (for Koleman had died with Norne) snapped his belts and drifted up; his boot toes scraped for purchase and he shot up faster, raising his hands to stop the onrushing ceiling. Kondor tucked his heels up beneath him, drifted back down, rose again. He took a pair of grip-slippers from the passing samech, waved to it, and crouched quite still in the air, discovering himself.

"Well, David?"

"We should have bought skyshuttle tickets. No matter how much they cost. We should have known . . . long . . . ago."

Obeck nodded, though he knew that it was Kondor's strange life (say, rather, Koleman's, for Kondor was a newborn) that had tied him to the planet. As Obeck's brass had bound him, since he had chosen to eat the Queen's meat. And Thorn . . .

Thorn approached, walking with firm slipper-stuck tread upon the proper floor toward Kondor and Obeck afloat.

"Come on, Thorn," said Kondor, "the z-gee's just fine."

"I feel it," Thorn said. "I . . . feel it."

"Orden!" deVol said. She stood, uncertainly, on the floor; Selye, Kassim, and Hetherington stood, clutched, and floated respectively nearby. "We're going to go get the biggest plate of absolute beef and eggs this ship will serve. Coming?"

"Well, of course," said Obeck. "And do you know—" He

made introductions in both directions. The young diplomats absorbed the new two easily, even if Hetherington did raise an eyebrow when Kondor gave his profession as "soldier of fortune."

"Haven't met any of those," Hetherington said politely.

"Oh, we aren't many, and never were, and never shall be."

"And you, Mr. Thorn—didn't I see you with a Con Vulcan case at the massport? Art thou then fortune's soldier like enow?" Obeck blinked at the shift from ELI-4 to 3, but he did not comment. ELI-3, Diplomatic 3, tricky and coercive 3, was their proprietary language; Obeck was the strange workman, who despised his tool.

Thorn, of course, was in no way tricked or coerced. "I am interested in weapons, Doctor. Space combat. I have a manuscript in preparation."

And they did not laugh at that, or even smile, but nodded with some genuine awe. But then, thought Obeck, they had not laughed at Kondor either. Their gift, of being never absurd.

The seven went to the dining salon and hovered, belt-tethered, around a concave serving station with a suction grille at its well. Samech waiters took spoken orders (Obeck reached out to sign his, but did not) and returned with food, genuine food in great quantity. Selye floated a thick steak, haloed with droplets of juice, before herself with a fork to stabilize it. She took a bite from its edge. "Name of Niccolo, this is *meat*," she said, and her eyes rolled up into her head with delirious joy. Kassim took a stab at a skysaucer egg that exploded with golden yolk. Hetherington tongued a flask of z-gee beer, brewed with reduced gas since weightlessness beheaded it. Thorn plucked huge Venusian prawns from the air with chopsticks, passed them through a spin-stabilized glop of batter, then a sphere of induction-heated oil; in moments he was vectoring tempura all round the table—the catchbasin, they soon discovered. It was partly celebration dinner and at least half food fight, it was unbelievably messy, and they loved it. They were all grinning madly through egg and grease and batter—all except Thorn, and Thorn's face never showed his soul.

After dinner, after washup—water without gravity proving almost as delightful as food—they drifted, one by one, back to the lounge.

"Outside in five minutes," said a voice from a speaker. Thorn returned to his couch; they let him go alone. Kassim and deVol eased into theirs, white as samechs, their stomachs off on uncharted orbits. Hetherington put a hand in Selye's and they drifted aside.

Obeck said, quietly, "What was in Sir X's bag?"

"Oh, that," said Kondor. "Thorn went through a thermal lancet and eight picks getting it open. Had to bridge a couple of nasty booby traps. But Thorn's no booby. And . . . he well and truly wanted inside."

"Enough suspense, David, please."

"Weapons, then."

"Just guns?"

"Thorn's eyes were like supernovae when he saw them. Con Vulcan WBX wireguns, he said—*X* for experimental, I suppose. Five of them, and they were of a pattern even I could see was strange."

"I hope," said Obeck, looking out the port, "we didn't sting too big a mark." There was a rumble through the ship. Through the port the gilt edge of the descending Outrigger came into view.

"Do you think we should get rid of them?" said Kondor, but his mind was far, far from the issue.

A blue line surrounded the gold plate, and the Outrigger simply disappeared from view. Vanished into OutSide, gone to correspondence particles.

Neither Kondor, nor Obeck within his memory, had ever been composed of correspondence particles before.

"We'll . . ." Obeck said, "think of something." His feet tingled, then his legs, his spine—as if fingers danced upon it— his jaw, eyes, scalp. He checked that his body was still visible; it was. Through the port he saw a scanning band, and *did not see it*—

And suddenly, hanging above them was the Blue, a sheet of quicksilver lightning. Obeck looked at his hand; it was gray. His blue coat was black, his sash and trousers gray. The tan carpeting was gray. He put a hand to his eyes, touched just to be sure, but there were no filter goggles—not this time. The arcade game was far away, on another world.

Obeck looked out the ports, and there was color, a sea of colors, flowing, streaking, tumbling over as the ship revolved. The Blue seemed to wobble, just a little, and Obeck's heart leaped—*If you're In too close then you can't come back* (but would he have minded dying, if he could die *here?*)—and then, with a slight tremor but without any sound at all, the Outriggers touched the Blue, and with only the faintest sensation of motion the golden skids began to skim the fantastical plane, on the other side of space at thirty-five thousand times the speed of light.

Obeck looked into Kondor's dark gray face; it wavered through mist. "For the Queen," he said, very softly, and as Kondor nodded Obeck saw the water in his friend's eyes as well; they put hands on each others' shoulders, and, uncaring what anyone might think, danced a weightless step around.

"This is life," said David. "I told you it was real, didn't I? I told you we could have it . . . and now we do."

Obeck nodded, thinking that David was right: they had everything they wanted. Because what they had wanted was to go offworld, and OutSide, and to Novaya, where dwelt a Queen.

Now they would have to find new things to want. Heart's desires they had never dreamed of. Obeck knew that they would indeed find such things.

And, unaccountably, the knowledge frightened him.

PART TWO

Deeper Shades of Blue

And aloof in the roof, beyond the feast,
I heard the squeak of the Questing Beast,
Where it scratched itself in the blank between
The Queen's substance and the Queen.

—*Taliessin Through Logres*

Chapter 4
A Letter of Marque

Undersecretary-Special Orden Obeck, for eighteen thousand of the twenty-five thousand hours since his release from indenture a Diplomat in the Queen's Service, walked as fast as decorum would permit. The limiting velocity of decorum was determined by Obeck's white palace coat, knee-length and closely buttoned. On its single steel shoulderboard was a black bar, signifying Detached Service; fixed to the lapel was a red Pass-Urgent rosette. Under Obeck's arm was a lizard-leather case, with the gold shield of the Diplomatic Service, and near the lock a covered button marked DESTRUCT. A thin wire cable led from the case, around Obeck's wrist, with a pad stuck to his pulse point. If he died, the contents would burn to less than ashes.

T-pat, t-pat, t-pat went the pulser, click-click-click went Obeck's boots on the mirror-bright corridor floor. Even without the rosette, people would have made way for him. Or he would have made them make way: for Orden Obeck was on his way to an audience with the Queen.

He turned onto a corridor that was carpeted in violet for all of its fifty-meter length; the ceiling was one long skylight, and the pale winter light of Novaya Primary filtered down onto pieces of ancient furniture, art objects in the plain style the

Queen preferred, lectras and painted pictures of persons who must have been important at some time or other (Obeck had had to learn the names and deeds of quite a few dead people, but their faces were superfluous) and who, painted or enlectraed, did not seem to have enjoyed the process.

A pair of Queen's Life Guards stood before a pair of high narrow doors. There was silver embroidery on their night-black uniforms, and chromed metal, and their helmets were chased with silver; dress swords from Wilkinson of Primus hung at their sides. Then Obeck noticed their real weapons: heavy pistols with use-worn grips in black breakaway holsters and fighting knives discreetly sheathed. Obeck supposed the antique armoire nearby, with its carved figures of iron-armored knights, housed machine or power guns. Not that he doubted they could use their sabers—or their bare hands.

"Orden Obeck, Undersecretary-*Special*, on Diplomatic business to Her Majesty."

One of the Guards went to a wall panel, inserted the boss on his finger ring, opened it; the panel hid what was inside from Obeck's view, though he saw knuckle motions as on pads.

"Do you have a password?" said the Guard.

"Twenty-first hour," Obeck said, and waited. The other Guard had not stirred a millimeter from his parade rest.

"Do you have a second password?"

"Empiric."

"Do you have a third password?"

"No, I do not."

"Then pass," the Guard said. He and his companion each took a handle of the high carved doors and opened them together.

Obeck stepped through into a short corridor without furnishings. The walls were gridded, precisely like the defense grids of a starship. The door facing Obeck was similar, gasketed, without a handle. After a moment, it whirred, clicked, opened. Obeck walked on.

The audience room was large, pyramidal, almost bare. In the center of the polished black floor was a two-step dais, and on that, beside a desk with console and displays built in, sat the Queen.

Obeck stepped to the edge of the dais. He dropped to one knee, balancing the case on the other. One white-gloved hand touched the floor; the other went to his inclined brow. Obeck's long coat made the kneeling difficult. It was meant to. The pose was a Jolson Three, indicating a presentation in readiness. It was the correct posture, Obeck knew; the desk, the woman briefly glimpsed, had reminded him of screening day so many k-hours past, and the memory cut like a whip.

"And who," said the Monarch of Humanity, "are you?"

"Orden Obeck, Your Majesty, Undersecretary-Special on detached Data Unit service to the Closed Subcommittee on Clandestine Solutions, Committee on the Bakunin Situation, Department of Separated-World Relations, Queen's Own Diplomatic Service."

"You're a Queen's Own? Oh . . . a Diplomatic Queen's own, yes. And what's an . . . 'Undersecretary-Special'?"

"Undersecretary is my bracket of rank, Majesty. 'Special' indicates that my mission may operate outside of normal Service channels."

"But that's silly. They have so many channels—why would they ever need to go outside of one?"

Obeck's gut fluttered; silently, praise Parkinson. He had heard the stories, nearly treasonous, of her almost from the hour he reached Novaya . . . and he had refused them as though they were beatings. But perhaps . . . every illusion broke in time.

"You may rise, and regard."

Afraid, but not in the prescribed manner, Obeck stood. His movement was graceful, painful. He lowered his hand, tilted his head, and looked for the first time closely and alone upon Queen Rachel II Valeria.

Her feet, in woven silver sandals, were just visible beneath a gown of black fur; her ankles were crossed in token of informality. The gown had an open bodice, exposing a blouse of violet moiré silk; its collar too was open, showing silver again —mesh lightly oiled.

Blinding Blue hell, she's armored, in here.

Her forehead was flat, her chin broad, her cheekbones indistinct. Her light skin was absolutely unblemished except for small, forking wrinkles at the corners of her eyes . . . the bronze Bishop eyes. Her hair was less vividly red-gold than Obeck had expected—More like Thorn's than Dr. Bishop's, he thought—held at her temples by a ring of polished onyx, set, of course, with fifteen gems, one for each planet under her rule. Below the tiara her hair was woven with silver cord and black star sapphires, the coil resting on her shoulder, her left breast.

And they say that if that head weren't as empty as OutSide it'd flop under the weight of stones.

"Very well then, Undersecretary-Special Obeck. You're here about the Bakunin affair, and with Clan's—this must concern our request for a marque pilot. And you struck a Presentational posture, not a Supplicative, so you have a candidate to offer us and not an excuse for delay. We like that. Please proceed—and use the most informal mode that circumstances will permit."

"Do they permit the use of . . . ELI-Four?"

She smiled, and it was like the autumn sun through the leafed trees of Novaya. In four autumns here Obeck had grown most fond of those trees, of that season, that light. "Undersecretary, it is always proper to speak Four to us. When we are alone, at any rate."

Obeck knew then that the stories lied: Rachel II was no more a fool than her mother had been. Then she became truly beautiful in his sight; it was then that he began to love her.

And to fear her, for if she was like her mother in some ways, she might be like in others. . . .

He dialed the lock on his case, opened it, trying not to fumble with the cable. "There are two candidates, Majesty—"

"'Medame' will suffice, Mister Obeck."

"Yes . . . the first candidate, medame." He handed her a cassette, feeling her fingertips like a Blue tingle. "His name of record is Thorn."

"Just Thorn?"

"That is all. He is a private operator, owning his own ship, a light hunter-killer. He claims over ten thousand hours, most of them in combat."

"Where?"

"Corporate caravanserai, some Separated Worlds work." Obeck paused. The lies were beginning to stick in his throat. He was close to wishing for ELI-3; its careful ambiguities, its loose forms and cases were just suited to this sort of not-quite-truth. But he did not really want 3. And she wanted 4. So he relied on the rest of his training. He used what was always the best weapon; he switched to some truth. "Thorn is a Valerian, a distant Royal cousin, of a branch that has somewhat grown apart, not to mention having suffered misfortunes."

"One of the Riyah Zaini Valerians?"

"Yes, medame."

"Not Baron Heinrich's son."

"I do not know, medame." That was absolute truth. "It was never . . . positively established that the late Baron had any children."

"It was never positively established that our mother killed

them, either. Tell us, Mister Obeck, do you suppose our employing this . . . Thorn might heal an old wound?"

"It is a possibility that was considered. Along with the possibility that he might be a wolf seeking entrance to the fold."

The Queen nodded, examining Thorn's image on the display. "I need a wolf," she said, without looking at Obeck. "And am I a sheep? No. Nor are the Bakunen . . . *Matre mí,* he's white as a samech. . . . Two candidates, you said?"

Obeck handed up another cassette. "David Kondor. Company operator, he claims, though there is no Industrial Exchange record of the 'Kondor Marque Corporation,' nor do we have any details of his ship or ships, if any. He also claims ten thousand hours flight time, mostly combat."

"Somebody's lying, Mr. Obeck."

Obeck's heart skipped, literally; the pulser on his case flashed a warning. "Medame?"

"Either these young men are falsifying the amount of combat going on around us, or the Fleet is . . . He cuts a splendid figure, doesn't he?" She turned abruptly. "Can you keep a state secret, Mr. Obeck?"

"Of course, medame."

"I don't trust the Fleet."

Obeck laughed. He needed no permission, felt no qualm; he had been taught to laugh at a monarch's jokes.

"This Kondor . . . he isn't one of our disaffected relatives, is he?"

"No relation, medame. There is, however . . ." Obeck reached into his case, produced a letter. It was on heavy paper, written with a broad-nib pen and sweeping strokes; near the signature, where a seal might have been affixed, were three closely spaced bullet holes.

The Queen took the letter. "Beloved Majesty," she read, "my hand and my ready . . . *blade?* . . . sponge the sky—that's a nice phrase—die in your service, calling your name—oh, my . . . Your instrument, David Kondor." She put the letter on the desk, looked again at the cassette picture.

"He has no other background that we could discover."

The Queen nodded. "It seems a simple matter. The light one has the connections, he has the ship, he probably has the record—even if some of it is likely with the Bakunen themselves. While the dark one is almost certainly a rash and naïve adventurer, streetwise but not otherwise, with a 'Corporation' of paper and plastic."

Obeck was silent. This was how he had claimed to David it

would go; he had never believed her a hollow queen.

"And if we were the Fleet, it would be simple. But we are not. I need a hunting animal, true. A wolf—or, perhaps, a young eagle. When the hunt is over, can I pasture a wolf with the sheep? But I can find a perch for an eagle."

Obeck said, "Kondor's Pilot's papers may not even be genuine. We were able to trace none."

"Your 'we,' Mr. Obeck, sounds like a royal we . . . it has the self-consciousness we wish we could avoid. How many members has your Data Unit, Undersecretary-Special?"

It was the truth, but it came with difficulty. "One, Majesty."

"And you are aware, then, that you are expendable? More erasable than a displeasing cassette? Remove your gloves, Mr. Obeck."

He did so.

"Put your right hand inside your dispatch case—the Queen commands."

Obeck complied.

The Queen spoke slowly. "Now, with your left hand, press the Destruct button. Again, my direct command."

Obeck looked at the red shield over the button. He twisted it off, stared at the brass DESTRUCT stud, thinking that now he knew how like her mother she was.

He knelt, despite his coat. He waited; Rachel II Valeria, Queen of the Human Realm, said nothing. Obeck's left index finger moved toward the little brass stud, and he thought, Brass, brass, my whole life's bound with brass. Even Dr. Bishop told me I had it.

He pulled his hand from the case, put both sweat-slick palms on the leather. *TpatTpatTpatTpat* went the pulser, the destruct-upon-death.

"Can you explain this behavior, Mister Obeck?"

"I cannot . . . medame, be certain that you are the Queen."

"Our order then inspires your doubt? Then know, thou worm, that we are Second Rachel, child of she who ordered lives and dynasties incinerated as we wish thy hand."

She spoke in ELI-3, that subtly lying tongue—and Obeck thought then that he knew the truth, but he could not be certain. He said, "Yet are there many queens—in images— queened Bishops, samechs, masquers in the game of guarding she our one and only Queen. And while their ears are self and same with hers . . . their voices do not have her force of law."

She smiled, but did not laugh, and Obeck knew how lovely the smiles of cruelty could be—and then she said, "Spoken most diplomatically. Why, you've undermined our very power —you're dangerous, Undersecretary . . . Special."

"Show me a sign . . . and I will do the deed."

"Of course you would. But if you had been this Kondor, you would have on the instant burnt your right hand, and then put in your left and chinned the button. For he's an adventurer, even as you are a diplomat . . . and we are a queen. We are all in the grip of the romances of our professions, different as they may be. And I will tell you another thing that you must on your life keep secret—will you swear?"

"I will."

"I accept the oath. And tell you: if we were not romantic, just a bit, we would not at all enjoy this being Queen. Now rise, Sir Orden Obeck."

Obeck looked up. Then he stood. "I—"

"I take your oath on words—take your dubbing on my word. It will be made fully official in a day or two. We hope that your Subcommittee does not decide to erase you before then." She handed Obeck the cassettes, examined the letter again. "' . . . to exchange this poor letter for ones of righteous marque and swift reprisal.' We charge that you do that, Sir Orden."

"Yes, your Majesty."

"Remember, however, that the reason for our choice is secret."

"Of course, your Majesty."

"Then, Sir Orden . . . you are dismissed."

Obeck bowed, gathered his papers and cassettes, and departed her presence.

He walked palace corridors aimlessly for over two hours and thousands of meters; the Pass-Urgent would not expire for some time yet and gave him the freedom of the place.

He walked on carpets, bare floors of wood and tile and stone, sand in a fencing court, grass in the center of a cloister brought stone by numbered stone from Primus. There he sat down, listening to the trickle of water in a central fountain and basins on the walls, watching the sunlight from the open atrium sweep slowly across the carvings.

He thought that David would surely love the Queen his new mistress. He thought, but did not fully believe, that he himself, begun indentured, had just been knighted—spurred on the moment, as it were. And he thought that he loved her too—

but his joy was dilute; it shifted as sand. Was this one of those things he had not expected to want, that he feared the wanting of?

He left the Royal wing for the Diplomatic, surrendering the Pass rosette to a samech majordomo and signing his thanks in the white machine's palm. According to the briefcase pulser, his heart was speeding up again.

There was so very much to do.

The Chair Executive of the Committe on the Bakunin Situation sat quietly behind her desk, her delicate hands folded, her clear, blue, multiply-revied eyes flicking up and down as Obeck delivered his report. Not one strand of her white-blond hair was out of place; nothing about her seemed to move but her eyes. The office was electronically sound-damped, silent as a ship OutSide; Obeck's voice had a strange unresonant quality.

When he was finished, the Chair was still for a moment more, then said, "Apart from the Valerian matter, these two candidates have no major outside ties?"

"None, medame. They are, in fact, without any family."

The Chair nodded. "Excellent."

Obeck felt something sharp in his chest. The Queen had spoken of expendability in knighting him. He wondered, suddenly and much too late, if he had condemned Thorn to die for the sake of keeping a state secret.

The Chair said, "The candidates are, of course, unaware of the exact nature of this screening?"

"Entirely unaware," Obeck lied.

"Still, they might hypothesize . . ." The Chair looked at the console built into the corner of her desk.

"Every Pilot is presently hypothesizing a counterraider action against the Bakunen pirates."

"True enough. No purpose in wasting resources, then." The Chair looked away from the console, again at Obeck. "You are yourself an orphan, isn't that so?"

"Yes, medame."

"My sympathies. . . . The Queen values you as a resource, as well, it seems . . . Sir Orden." Her look was filled with meanings. "And so do we, of course. You're a full Secretary now. A Knight of the Realm cannot hold an underpost."

"Thank you, medame."

"Naturally, we'll have to find you work appropriate to a Secretary and a Knight." Another look at the console and at the armed samech guard standing before the closed, sealed door, its back to them both.

Obeck wondered how he was keeping so calm. But for the Queen's whim, he had almost become a discarded tool, an erased cassette; that much was painfully clear. There was, he knew, one entrance to this room—but there were two exits.

He wondered, then, just how fickle the Queen's whim was . . . and then, how much of a whim it had been. If she had meant to purchase Obeck's loyalty . . . he supposed that she had succeeded.

"You have a confirmed Royal authorization for the issuance of a Letter of Marque," said the Chair, "so you do not need ours." Once more Obeck marveled at how much was done without any trails of responsibility being left: this time at least no one had died to cover the scent.

"Axel," said the Chair, and the samech came to attention and turned smartly. "Sir Orden will be departing us now."

That would, Obeck knew, be a code phrase. One entrance, two exits, he thought, but the samech put its finger into the keyplate of the front door. The panel opened, and suddenly there were sounds again—of moving air, fingers on console pads and phototypers, printers and unflattened human voices. Obeck nodded to the guard, which saluted him, and went out.

His head hummed as if the Chair's blue eyes were power guns detuning just short of his grids.

The Production Department of the Forms Service was as full of displays as any games arcade, brighter, and a little less noisy, though not much. Laser engravers whined, presses spat sheets crackling, blades whistled through stacks of paper. There was the acid smell of new-laid papers and the stronger stink of photochemicals.

And when Obeck said what he wanted, there was the sound of heads being scratched and the smell of surprise; the whole place nearly came to a stop until Obeck was introduced to the Most Senior Scribe, whose eyes widened behind their multi-optic glasses (they were long past help from the needle) and who took Obeck with great but not exaggerated ceremony to his small office and shut the door against the rising bustle.

There was a wooden desk, an antique, with the latest model of font scanner on top of it; blocks of aromatic wax creating a confusion of heady smells; hoses leading from a pressure tank ringed by glass jars of colored inks to a multipen, its nozzle resting in thinner.

There was no paperlayer, however, though every work station outside had one. Instead there were drawers, hundreds of them, each bearing a label in elegant manual script.

Parchment, Authentic (Priman Sheep).
Index, Semigray, 150 Gm.
Origami Bicolor Red/Silver.
Eggshell.
Onion.
Rice, Edible **and** *Inedible.*

"A Letter of Marque . . . that would be two-hundred-fifty-gram semivellum, grain short, white with silver threading—has to take Royal, Fleet, and Corporate seals, you see." The Scribe turned completely around once, pointed at a drawer. He ascended a small ladder, came down with a large sheet of the richest-looking paper Obeck had ever seen. "Go ahead, sir, touch it," said the Scribe, and Obeck did: it was more like cloth than paper, smooth but not slick, resilient. His fingers did not mark it. "Archival," said the Scribe. "When tape is dissolved for motor fuel, this will exist."

"Where do I have this . . . printed?"

"Oh, sir," said the Scribe very gently, "you don't print upon this. Not with the electrostats they keep out there. Those must lay a charge on the paper, you see—and this won't take charge properly—it's thick, and there's pure silver in the weave. See it? This, sir, is for the pen's touch." Almost to himself, he added, "And they thought they'd retire me with the last impact press . . . more fools they."

Obeck nodded. "There's another thing—the paper for corporate charters. Would you have some of that?"

The Scribe looked up again. "They make that by punching buttons on those machines out front. . . . Unless, sir, you were meaning the old charter stock?"

"Precisely," said Obeck.

The Scribe spun round again, saying, "Hundred-fifty-gram English finish, legal canary with red margin stripe . . ." The incantation complete, he opened a drawer and produced a long narrow sheet of yellow paper, not so heavy as the first. He gave it to Obeck, who tucked it into his case.

"Will this take console printing?"

"Oh, yes, though . . . what did you require it for, sir, if I may?"

"We need to match a document . . . for authentication purposes. I have a photoprint of it here." He produced a sheet.

The Scribe held it between two fingers. "Sulfited garbage," he said, "not fit to wipe your . . . pardon, sir. And you needn't spend any time over this: it's ten years . . . a hundred thousand hours . . . old, at the most."

"Oh?"

"Look, sir. The curve of the descenders on *y* and *g*. The loop of capital *P*. This is Royal Serif Gothic Eight-G. The correct face, but the wrong modification. The Eight-G tape was formatted only a hundred k-hours ago, sir. And this indentation, five ems—that's a conservation measure of good Second Rachel's, Bodoni bless her. It was always seven em spaces before Her Worship."

"Fascinating, sir, fascinating. Would you mind if I kept the contract paper anyway, for . . . reference?"

"Only too happy. As you appreciate a good paper, sir."

The Scribe sat down at an angle-top table, slipped the thick silver-shot paper into a clamp. He switched a spotlight on, adjusted his eye optics, took the multipen from its holder and drew some sweeping curves on a paper pad.

"A Royal Letter of Marque . . . I haven't made up more than two of those since First Rachel, Franklin save her. It's all private privateering now, you know. They can't be bothered with the proper forms—no, some bit of magnetized plastic instead to make a machine happy. What use, what *use*, is a form," said the Scribe, staring at Obeck through his multiple lenses, "if it does not please the eye and the touch? A good script on a fine paper, mesir, and though the contents be the veriest gibberish or pre-ELI confused tongue, that document will still bear the imprint of authority. Don't you believe that, sir?" He pressed down on the multipen and in a single motion drew a huge capital *K*; then he pressed again and drew crosshairs over it.

"I believe that indeed," said Obeck, and leaned forward to watch.

The little ship *Condor*, a black-hulled hunter-killer, settled gracefully to the pad. The ship was far from new and bore welds and patchplates, the mechanical equivalent of revi marks. There were nonstandard changes to the vessel as well, some of Thorn's ideas made steel. And one more feature, unusual though not unheard-of: there was no name on the hull. There was a reason for this.

David Kondor came down the stairway, followed by Thorn. Obeck said nothing; he merely produced the heavy Letter with its Royal and Fleet seals. Obeck thought for a moment that Kondor would drop to his knees and kiss the Letter, but he only held it lightly in both hands, his eyes shining.

"And the charter?" he said.

"We're going to have to redo that. New paper, new font tape, some other changes." Obeck looked up at Thorn, who nodded and turned his back. Without a word, he reboarded the one vessel of what would, by the Queen's decision, be the Kondor Marque Corporation. He lifted gradually, up the spiral, unlike Kondor's double handfuls of sky.

There was one other difference. The ship that had landed had been *Condor*. The one that lifted was *The Pale Horse*—though the registry was the same, and there was no name on the hull to confuse anyone.

On the end of an assembly like a barbed spear, fed by oily cables, was an amber crystal, pulsing with light. Then it glowed steadily, deep gold, then straw yellow, then intolerable white.

Across black space an armed freighter trembled nose to tail. Rodwork seemed to shimmer, then to melt like sugar in hot coffee. There was, of course, no flame or sound. Flashes were visible through the freighter's ports. Cargo modules shook; some broke their fastenings and drifted. Smoky atmosphere puffed out. The interior lighting went from yellow-white to the reds and greens of emergency systems. On the underhull a beacon flashed long nine times: the signal for surrender.

The crystal glow faded.

Kondor stopped the tape camera. "Lights," he said, and Obeck dialed up the hotel room illumination, slipping his nighteyes down around his neck. Thorn disconnected the power cords to his flash-and-smoke rig, blew vapor away from the meter-long freighter model inside its starfield backdrop. He began to dismantle it, removing the pieces from their control wires and packing them carefully into a foam-lined case.

Kondor pulled the cassette from the camera, wrote KMC [PRIZE] BASILISK on the side. He put it, with some other cassettes and papers, into a small box, then wrapped the box in white paper. He put a postal sticker on the package, then a label with the address:

MR. LOAMAN STARKADR
STARKADR SHIPYARDS
VIA: QUEEN'S ROOK ONE
PRIVATE AND URGENT

Kondor hefted the parcel and tossed it toward Obeck, who looked up, startled, and held out both hands, dropping the newly printed corporate charter.

He caught nothing; Kondor produced the package in his left hand. "You see, Orden?" he said. "Quicker than the eye."

Chapter 5
A Ship of the Line

David Kondor rotated before a corner mirror, checking the fit of his flight jacket: it was of heavy gray cloth, leather patched and silver piped, with a shoulder patch showing a capital K centered in crosshairs, and KONDOR/01 embroidered in black-on-silver upon the breast. "I told you, Orden, didn't I? Want it enough, and the whole universe will bend to your goal." He laughed. "Or *Sir* Orden, pardon me. You see?"

"I'm glad it worked," was all Obeck said, having sworn never to say any more.

Thorn sat stiffly erect in a chair, a flat black phototyper on his knees. There was a small stack of closely printed sheets on the chair arm. He wore a jacket similar in cut to Kondor's but deep red instead of gray, gold for silver. His shoulder patch was a circle of six stars, his namestrip a plain cloth tape reading only THORN.

This was the third full day of Kondor's elation. Thorn had said essentially nothing about the Queen's choice of marquesman—and Obeck, watching ever so closely, would have sworn to the Queen that he felt nothing, though he despaired of ever learning Thorn's body language. "If Theo ever cried," the late David Koleman had said in private to Obeck, "the first tears would roll out black, from dust in the ducts."

With an abrupt movement Thorn pulled a sheet from his typer, stacked it with the others. He put the machine aside, went to a closet of the hotel suite and took out the white case that Sir Xavier Grosz had so carelessly forgotten so long ago. He touched the reset locks, but did not dial them. Obeck looked away.

"A problem, Orden?"

"No. Chill, I think. I'm still not used to winters." The dispatch case and its burning button were another secret he kept.

"Then I suggest that it is time to proceed."

Kondor said, "Just a moment, Thorn." He rapped a knuckle on the bar, then touched pads, and the bar filled three glasses with fluid nearly black, topped with delicate white floats. "To knighthoods," he said, passing the drinks around, "and Queen's favor, and the great enterprise ahead."

"And the smaller one," said Obeck, with a glance at the Con Vulcan case.

"Clear vectors and glory," said Thorn.

They sipped their whiskey-coffees, hot and vaporous and sweet with the dissolving cream, made strong.

When they were done, Thorn lifted the case and walked toward the door. He stopped before it and spoke without turning. "I shall be quite content to keep the present vessel for my own. Provided that it never again flies under any name but *The Pale Horse*."

"I freely agreed that you could," Kondor said. "Though it was the same ship when I called it *Condor*."

"It was of two minds," said Thorn, "and that could not long be," and he pushed the doorpad and went out.

"I never thought he could love the iron so much," said Kondor, laughing; but the laughter was quite dry.

"Just tell me what you want," said Aft Hatch Harry Doen.

"You quote me a price," said the marque Pilot in the red coat, "and I'll tell you if it's right." The Pilot lifted his white suitcase onto Doen's desk, dialed the locks—simultaneously, one with each hand—and lifted the lid.

Harry Doen gasped out loud.

Harry Grigsby Doen, a stoop-shouldered fellow with a deceptively soft and unrevied face, had acquired his nickname after he was credited with owning twelve hundred whisper-pistols and a quarter of a million steel darts to load them with. All the more remarkable about this was the fact that Consolidated Vulcan had supposedly made only one hundred of the

quiet guns, and those all for . . . Well, anyway, when asked
the source of his stock, Harry replied, "They must have
drifted out somebody's aft hatch."

Requested to turn the guns over to . . . well, at a small but
fair price, Harry responded—almost in tears, for he was a con-
noisseur of exotic arms—that they were all gone, lost, out
another unsecured aft hatch.

Charged (rather in exasperation) with trafficking in contra-
band, Harry pointed out that he had not purchased the
whisper-pistols from anyone, the law of inertia having merely
given him constructive possession; he had likewise not sold
them to anyone—where was the trafficking in that?—and
since there was no good reason to believe such guns had ever
been manufactured, Harry had never provably owned any of
them.

So goods continued to pass around Harry Doen, but he never
bought them. He never sold them. He never really possessed
them.

And now, seeing the four WBX wireguns cushioned on
white velvet in their case, Aft Hatch Harry knew that he had to
not-own them.

The guns fed charged wire from a disk magazine through
pinch-and-snap coils, spitting it out in tiny bits through six
gatlinged barrels. The spray had a terrifying effect on flesh,
and a way of finding the tiniest chinks in body armor. The
charge on the wire would pit metal and sear tissue, and micro-
grooves spiraling along the bits' length could carry a further
load of chemical or biological poison.

They were not arms for the soldier or policeman, but the
guerrilla, the revolutionary; in token, they were finished with
Con Vulcan's secret chameleon-metal process.

Aft Hatch Harry doubtless desired to ask from whom, or
what, the privateer had taken the case; he did not, of course.
That would have been absurd, and the marquesman did not
look absurd. Instead Harry said, rather hoarsely, "Twenty
thousand."

"Not enough." Thorn put a hand on the case lid.

"Forty k," Doen said instantly.

Thorn paused. Doen didn't know what to make of his look.

"Fifty k," said Aft Hatch Harry. "Look, there's only four,
and no more coming, are there? You won't do better than me,
and you could do worse. Meaning nothing hostile by that, of
course, sir." Doen's eyes, soft and moist, were still fixed on
the guns.

"I want a ship," Thorn said. "A hunter-killer, about twenty meters."

Harry did turn then, his eyes as wide as open hatches. "You're talking five mega, as you ought to know," he said.

"That's new price," said Thorn. "Not your price."

"Well, I'll grant you know how things go, but it's still ten times what they're . . . worth." Yet in Harry's eyes temptation was visible.

"I don't want a new ship. I don't care what shape it's in, as long as it can lift once and land once. It's got to have Outriggers installed, but they don't have to work."

Doen's look went from guarded amazement to guarded puzzlement. "Now, *what* . . . Thorn, eh? Should I know that name?"

"Possibly. One other stipulation. The ship must *not* be a Starkadr Shipyards hull."

"Thorn. Well. Yes, I know somebody with a ship like that. You understand that I've got nothing of the sort personally—"

"I understand."

"Right, then. You know . . . if you'd presented yourself a little better, we could have gotten to an agreement much quicker."

"I trade on hard goods and facts. Never reputations."

"Guess you would," said Aft Hatch Harry, smiling but absolutely serious. "Now could I set you up with a couple of whisper-pistols . . . ?"

Most of the Starkadr Shipyard was in orbit where it belonged, where the half-laid hulls needed suffer no strain, where weight and property taxes were nil.

But there were still a few functions best performed in gravity and unbottled ambient air; where a tool was put upon a bench, not vectored Coriolis-corrected toward a hold-down. And space labor had to be housed and fed and spun for Down and oxygenated—and paid vacuum wages, some hazards being irreducible (PLEASE CLOSE DOOR hardly seems strong enough, outside the air).

Thus, about a hundred kilometers from Crown Center/Novaya, twenty minutes' commute by maglarail, was a high-fenced compound with shippads, hangars, and workshops, all staffed with people who would rather have been in the city or, better still, the sky.

And thus the supervisory engineer making morning rounds

was not very polite to the young marque Pilot in the clean gray suit; he seemed come only to bedevil her morning, to remind her that somewhere ships lifted into the black and beautiful sky.

"Look, Pilot—"

"David Kondor. And you're—"

"Mister Kondor, I don't know how you got past the gates, but we don't give two-mark tours out here. If you want to examine the product, I suggest you visit one of our many tastefully appointed showrooms. They've got plans and lectras and models where you can take the top off, and they just love to talk to people like you."

"What kind of person am I, madame . . . ?"

"You're a privateer." The engineer looked toward the hangar roof at two workers on a scaffold at a sleek black hunter-killer. Upon its bow they were neatly stenciling the name BELLEROFON.

The engineer put a fist to her forehead and yelled, "Pee aitch, Grogan!"

One of the workers switched off his sprayer, slid his mask down. "What, Molly?"

"*P-H*, not *F*, Grogan! Bellerophon, rider of Pegasus, you illiterate duralloy-dinger! *B, E, L, L, E, R, O, P, H,* you idiot, *O, N.*"

"Huh? Oh, this?"

She raised her hard hat, ran long brown fingers through helmet-cut black hair. "I'll write it *out* for you."

"Were you classically educated, madame?" said Kondor.

"Are *you* still here?"

"Dame Molly, you spoke of my profession in a very harsh tone, when I'd said no ill of yours . . . I only wondered why."

"I'm not any Dame. My name's Molly Bajan—that's Bajan to you, Pilot. And I don't like privateers, or marquesmen, or whatever you like to call yourselves."

"And why is that?"

"If I tell you, will you go away?"

"I . . . yes."

She turned; their eyes met, hers violet, his nearly black. He smiled, she did not. She said, not so angrily as a moment ago, "Because you're shipkillers. I break my heart building birds and you break their wings. You crash them and beam-burn them and squeeze them OutSide too close and lose them forever —though I'd almost rather that than have to see the wrecks you killers bring in, and it makes less of you to boot."

"Would you rather your ships sat idle on the pad, growing dusty, rusty?"

"Isn't flight thrill enough for you? You said you'd go away."

"Nothing's thrill enough. I'll go. Will you come with me?" She stared.

"I'm here to skytest that ship," Kondor said, reaching inside his jacket. He produced a paper. "I'd be most pleased if you'd be my flight engineer."

Bajan read the sheet. "Kondor Marque Corporation? The *Bellerophon*'s under contract for a holdfast on Saavedra."

Kondor handed over another paper, this one thick and multiply sealed. "My contract to Rapal Holdfast."

She opened it. "This isn't . . . this is a Royal Letter of Marque."

Kondor snatched it back. "Pardon me—I've brought the wrong papers, I see." He cast a glance around. "You'll of course tell no one you've seen this."

She put a knuckle to her chin, looked over the first paper again. "And this appears to be a real company charter. I suppose you know how irregular this all is?" She looked out the hangar door at the blue above.

Kondor inclined his head.

"Grogan!" Bajan called upward. "Knock it off and get that rig off of there."

"What, Molly?"

"Since when did you have trouble hearing you had an afternoon off? Go and get your ears revied."

Grogan whacked his partner on the arm, spoke and gestured; in what seemed like only seconds they were down the scaffold and clearing it away.

Bajan put an interphone back in its wall cradle. She climbed into the seat of a towing tractor, clutched in its flywheels. "Well, come on, shipkiller."

Kondor got aboard beside her, and they pulled—er—*Bellerofon* out into the light of day.

Dressed in impeccable whites, a narrow blue shoulder band marking his knighthood, Orden Obeck was pressed back into his skyshuttle couch by lifting thrust. Out the window, Crown Center dropped away; first the domes, then the clusterframes hung with building blocks, then the towers, arched and buttressed. The shuttle banked into ascent spiral, and in the distance Obeck could see the stone and steel block-puzzle of the palace—no other structure (or flightpath) within two thousand meters of it by law. It stood alone in its moat—but a moat of parkland, not stagnant water.

One shadow was long enough in the winter midday to reach across the palace grounds: the Consolidated Vulcan building, a solar-gilt pyramid.

Obeck's pilot (this was not a starship, he was not capitalized) slipped from the blue into the black with acceptable skill. In a few minutes a Rook orbital fortress, almost their destination, came into view.

The Rooks were asteroids towed into orbit, powerbored, and fitted with PARdar and ring-banked beam units. A direct hit from one of those ganged power guns could punch the heart out of a large ship and flash a small one to vapor. Gas and grids did not defend against that kind of energy; what mattered was what Thorn called the Primary Shield: not getting in front of it. It was an axiom of warfare that Novaya could not be captured without first taking the Rooks; and it was another axiom that the Rooks could not be taken. On this Thorn was silent.

This was Queen's Rook One, of four that guarded Novaya from just beyond Roche's Limit. It cast three shadows: one of light, one of arms, one of vacuum. Obeck was headed for the last.

The shuttle swung round the Rook at a respectful distance, answering a broadcast challenge from it; it entered the space just behind the Rook's orbit.

Here, then, was the Starkadr Shipyard, where it belonged. This was preferred Space, swept by the asteroid of dust and debris, a higher vacuum than the surrounding vacuum. Also kept out were unauthorized craft; for this was a cradle of the Fleet.

The yards proper were an enormous open grid in three dimensions, built of rolled light-alloy foils. Work grapples clung to the framework, gliding along it in all directions, clutching panels and tubes and coils in their mechanical arms. White metal shone moon-bright; port pylex flickered ghostly; here and there were glints from golden Outriggers being mated to their ships.

Ships in every stage of genesis from spine-and-ribs to nearly complete inhabited the grid, like sandpups in their tunnels, fish in coral; so did people, in suits and cabs and building blocks not much different in appearance from those in the city frames below.

The shuttle lost momentum, nosed slowly into a dock, stopped with rather too much shock. The light near the exit hatch lit red, then turned green; the door opened.

Obeck pulled grip-slippers over his white boots, picked up his dispatch case—which did not read his heartbeat this time—and walked into a large low room decorated as a starliner: matching carpets on floor and ceiling, indirect light, deep couchlike seats. Along the side walls were strip-windows—one looking on the yards, the other on the Rook.

In the middle of the room, anchored down, was a large metal desk with a large man behind it; he was smooth and cold as hull steel. "May I assist you . . . sir?"

"Secretary-Special Sir Orden Obeck to see Loaman Starkadr."

"Have you an appointment, Sir Orden?"

"He'll see me."

Obeck and the receptionist had a brief duel of stares. The deskman was well trained, but Obeck was a professional. "One moment, please, sir," the receptionist said, a bit unsteadily, and looked below his desktop at some hidden display. He touched a concealed console. "Ah," he said, recovering himself, "I have an appointment listed for an *Under*secretary Obeck—"

"There have been changes, as thou canst well see," Obeck said in offhand 3. "And will Starkadr grant his time to me?"

The deskman smiled, touched another hidden pad. His smile vanished. "Uh . . . yes, sir, he will." He took a key from his belt, put it into a plate. A piece of the wall to Obeck's left opened. "Please take the lift."

"Thanks to thee." Obeck went to the opening, through it. He stood at one end of a long, transparent tube, rising at least twenty meters above him, a meter and a half across. There were strips of grip-carpeting along it, and bright metal handrails. Obeck took hold of a rail, pulled his slippers free of the floor; he gave one tug and rose unaided up the tube.

Loaman Starkadr's office was spherical, lit intensely by spotlights, dark elsewhere. The walls were transparent, with a system of velvet shades to shutter off any part; Obeck could see the yards but not the Rook. There was a desk halfway "up" a wall from Obeck's point of entry, a bar, the usual displays, the largest showing a cyclonic storm in Novaya South under attack by Weather Command craft. But the primary furnishing, central to everything, was a telescope rig, a complex of dark nickel, plastics, and leathers, tracked and

gimbaled to aim any direction. It mounted an eighty-centi-
meter Schmidt-Cassegrain lens assembly before a powered
operator's seat.

This, Obeck thought, was the one true fruit of success: to
never have to leave that which one loved. Probably only the
direst necessity, or a spirit of self-denial, could drive Starkadr
down under a sky that brightened. Obeck wondered, briefly,
what a home for David Kondor might look like; he could not
even imagine a home for Thorn.

"Good day to you, Secretary," said Loaman Starkadr from
his seat behind his sideways desk. His voice was big, resonant.
Obeck drifted around to face him directly and levelly.

Starkadr was a large man, blond, light-skinned (though
nothing like Thorn). He wore a shirt of midnight velvet, silver-
specked, as though he wanted not just to be near Space but to
be Space. "My congratulations on your advancement."

"I thank thee, sir." Not "Sir Loaman." Starkadr had re-
jected a knighthood for some private reason. "I trust thou
hast been made aware precisely what my mission's purpose
is?"

"You want to give me a ship," said Starkadr, his eyes flash-
ing blue as O-spectral suns. "A very unusual ship, as I understand."

"That is correct."

"But if this vessel is as special as my information indicates,
and special in these particular ways, then no sane soul—let
alone the heaven-favored Queen—would give it up cheaply. I
suppose, then, you're here to quote me the price."

"That also is correct."

"And the price is?"

"We wish to trade thee ships."

"One of mine for your . . . *'Basilisk'?* As much of the Fleet
as I build already, what kind of deal is that?"

"We mean not such a trade. We have a need— Are words
said in this room kept under seal?"

"There are no recorders, if that's what you mean."

"It is." Good man, Obeck thought, you don't trust what's
said in ELI-3 either. "Then I'll speak plainly, Mr. Starkadr.
The Queen wishes to undertake a marque operation in a . . .
sensitive area. Because of this sensitivity, the Pilot will be a
private operator working with his own vessel."

"That's plainly? You mean Rachel wants to raid Bakunen
shipping, and she's going to work blind-secret so she can keep
the diplomatic line open. With respect, Secretary."

"Yes," Obeck said, and without pausing went on: "Now, in order to keep total secrecy, we must provide the operator with an unrecorded ship. A nonexistent ship, if you will."

"So you'll give me the *Basilisk* if I'll burn the build-and-transfer records on another ship. I'm still giving you one for one, and breaking the law on top of it."

"You would burn nothing—merely hand over the records. And suppose you were to receive the marque operator's current vessel for . . . repairs."

Starkadr looked upward in thought. "And that weapon system . . . what's it called? The Eye-Lance?"

Obeck said nothing.

"The death-darting glance of cockatrice . . . keep talking, Mr. Secretary."

Obeck did.

"How does an intelligent person get to be a privateer?"

"Practice, Molly," said Kondor. He pulled back hard on the turbine grips; *Bellerofon* bucked up and reared back. Then Kondor toggled booster power, grabbed a double handful of sky, and was gone all but straight up. The white winter sky turned blue, then black. The g-counter was ticking, 2.3, 2.4, 2.5; white lines solid and interrupted shot and skewed on the nav display; the ship groaned down deep within.

"—*a first flight*," said Bajan from compressed lungs.

"Finding the limits right off," said Kondor, and rolled the ship over, filling the viewround with stars. Near the top was a thin slice of Novaya, blue fringed with light, rolling past at remarkable speed. Queen's Rook Two appeared, marker lights twinkling, glowing softly in Novayashine.

A line of digits and letters appeared before Kondor: the Rook challenging. Kondor hit a series of pads and the code blinked out. Then he banked the ship on ions, gently, vectoring straight out toward the limits of the InField.

"Eng, we're scoped clear out to infinity. Will you lock the board?"

"Locking up," Bajan said crisply, touching pads and flipping toggles. Beyond the air no vessel had an "*automatic* pilot"; that word was reserved, since no machine black-box or samech white could handle a ship OutSide.

Kondor leaned back in his couch, released all restraints but his lap belt. He looked at Bajan. Her hand hovered, stopped on the way to her belt release, as she stared at the stars. Thousands of stars, tens of thousands, white and red and gold and blue, upon black of an ungraspable richness.

Though it was not quite black, not truly. Softly, Kondor sang,

"Sing me a song of the hydrogen light,
Three degrees Kelvin illumines the night,
Three degrees Kelvin, the infrared sky,
Color too deep for the unaided eye."

She stared at him. Then she hummed along,

"Sing me a song on the hydrogen band,
Whispering low since the cosmos began,
Whispering low, as the white light shifts red,
Wavefront of hydrogen sweeping ahead."

And then they sang together,

"Sing me a song of the hydrogen wall,
Vector me out to the light bounding all,
Vector me out, in that glory to dwell,
End of the universe, cosmic egg-shell."

"Pilot, you are the damndest fellow who ever came by on a Windsday afternoon."

"It isn't me. It's the stars."

"How many ships have you killed?"

Kondor sighed. "If you must . . . none. That's the truth."

"But—you've got a Royal Letter. Are you such a magnificent marquesman that other Pilots out there surrender at the mention of your dread name?"

"Now there's a thought, Molly. One for that book . . ."

"What book? And I don't think I've allowed you to call me Molly."

"One a friend is writing . . . not a ladyfriend."

"I didn't think privateers had friends. Or knew any ladies."

"That's a cruel thing to say."

"You're right," she said, reading a gauge. "I'm sorry."

"I forgive you. And may I call you Molly?"

"Eventually, I think. Now I'm going back to check the hull." And she slipped from beneath his reaching fingers and was gone out the conroom door.

A small and badly battered ship, puffing dust and atmosphere at every seam, came round from behind Rook Two.

"Vessel, please identify," said the Rook's voice. "We are tracing you as unstable. Are you all right?"

"I am *Basilisk*, and I am in no trouble," said a voice as empty as Space, though of course Space is not cold. "I am vectored for Starkadr Groundside. I am expected, and I have a close schedule—I will keep that vector."

"As you say, *Basilisk*," said the Rook. The operator got a high-gain optical view of the ship and nearly dispatched a crash tug then and there. He did not, partly because Pilots had rights not lightly infringed, partly because of something in . . . or not in . . . the Pilot's voice.

One other thing the operator noticed: on *Basilisk*'s patched and ragged forehull was a long slender gadget, rather like a barbed lance with a glass or crystal tip. Thick oil-shining cables led away from the lance into the hull.

The million colors of OutSide flowed by above the black hull of *Bellerofon*; on rolled the Blue beneath the Outriggers' colorless gold. Within were blacks, and whites, and shades of gray, and Kondor, his mind on Bajan and the Blue.

She entered the conroom. "We went Out very smoothly," she said. *"What are you doing?"*

"Infinity figures," said Kondor, as he skated the ship between the Blue pillars of Novaya and its Primary. "A few more times around them, then back In." He checked the ship's chronometer. "Five outs and backs should be just about right."

"Do you know what happens if we slip up one of those columns, you idiot? This isn't some damned simulator—it's real."

"Funny you should say that," said Kondor, smiling.

"This is kind of unusual," said the gatemaster at Starkadr Groundside, "but it's been kind of an unusual day. Another fellow came through, a Pilot, and then he and the Engineering Super took off on a trial skip—"

"Oh?" Orden Obeck said, concealing the source of his surprise.

"Yeah. Bajan—she's the Super—she acted like she was in on some kind of plot."

"Interesting," Obeck said. "If you'll direct me to the hangars, I'll disturb you for as little time as possible."

The gatemaster pointed them out, then looked up. "Now who's *that* landing? This doesn't even look like a massport."

"If I'm not very mistaken," said Obeck, "it's a ship called

Basilisk.'' He hitched his case up under his arm and went through the gate. After two shuttle trips and a maglarail ride, he was more than tired—but there was still much left to do.

Kondor received the challenge from Queen's Rook Three, responded.

"Gannet?" said Bajan. "When we went Out we were *Bellerofon.*''

"You noticed?" said Kondor. "I think . . . I'd better start calling you Molly now."

"Were you planning to steal this ship, Pilot?"

"With you on board it, Engineer?"

"With me to help, maybe."

"What a notion! *This* ship—by no means, Molly. If I ever intended to pilfer this ship we're on, may the Blue open up and swallow me down this instant. . . . You can handle a landing, can't you?"

"A person like you should be careful about swearing."

"And what kind of person am I, Molly?"

She hesitated. She pulled the belts tight on her couch. Finally she said, "You're a very good Pilot, and you're completely out of your mind. Other than that . . . I don't know . . ."

Kondor waited.

". . . yet."

Kondor's touch on the grips was very light as he nosed the ship—whatever its name was—down into atmosphere.

The Starkadr ground crew watched *Basilisk* come in as if they had never seen a ship land before—and in truth none of them had ever seen a vessel come in quite like this one.

A wing was bent. A turbine was completely out, feathering with an awful whine. The finish was burnt and scraped down to raw metal, and most of the grids were naked. *Basilisk* may have won its last battle, but it had assuredly lost the war.

The crewmembers stood transfixed, thinking that they *really should* get the wreck gear, and just as two of them finally started for it the mad-genius pilot bent down on his diverters and crosscut his thrust, and with an organ chord and a ring and snap of steel he set *Basilisk* right down on the pad, on three unequal legs.

A skittering noise stirred Obeck, who was as hypnotized as anyone; he turned and saw a flange the size of his head go flying low past him, on escape vector from the ship. Thorn,

Thorn, he thought, we never played this sort of game before. But he had only seconds for thought; Thorn was already coming down the rickety stairway.

The ground crew had been amazed by the landing. They were astonished by Thorn—though the sum of their recollection afterward was that he had worn a red coat and been quiet. Quiet indeed: where any other pilot would have cussed out the ship, the pad, the inventors of turbine propulsion and geometric drive, and anything else convenient, this one merely said, "It's yours," pulled the title cassette from his pocket, and tossed it to the nearest person.

Obeck caught it, slipped it into his dispatch case. No one seemed to notice. Besides, there was another ship coming down.

Bellerofon landed in a rather ordinary fashion. Kondor came down the stairs, followed at a certain distance by Molly Bajan.

"Let's get this over as quickly as we can, shall we?" said Kondor, tossing a title cassette to the nearest person. Obeck tucked it into his case. Kondor said, "Where's the other ship?" just as the sharp black hull of a new hunter-killer, bare of name or numbers, followed a tractor out onto the pad.

One of the crew offered the title cassette for the unnamed ship, along with a stack of bills of sale and transfer. "Mr. Starkadr said you'd want these."

"I'll hold them," Obeck said, lifting the pile gently from the holder's fingers, putting it with the other cassettes.

"What's the crowd scene about?" Bajan said. "I didn't give *everybody* the day off."

"Starkadr's office called, just after you went up," someone said. "We covered for you, of course, said you were in Surfacing—"

"I can explain," Obeck said. "There's been an arrangement made by the Royal Diplomatic Service, which I represent, with Loaman Starkadr, to effect an exchange of ships."

Bajan looked to the adjacent pads. "*That* pile of scrap for one of my new hunters?" Her next look was at Kondor, and it could have vaporized grids.

"Not at all," said Obeck. "I'm holding a cassette of title for the exchange vessel, the *Gannet*, which should just have vectored to a rental pad in Novaya North massport. Rook Three will verify its reentry." Obeck reached into his case, fumbled a bit, brought out a cassette tape labeled GANNET, handed it to Bajan. "You are also to receive title to the vessel on that pad, which despite its appearance is of extreme interest to Mr. Starkadr." Another cassette from the case to Bajan. And another: "I seem also to be holding the title to the vessel Pilot Kondor borrowed—oh, my mistake." He took a gray box back, put it in the case, handed another to the engineer.

"And how about us?" Kondor said.

"A temporary title for the two of you." A cassette went into Kondor's hands. Bajan, one hand full of little gray boxes, appeared to be counting on the fingers of the other.

"And finally, the original records of the new vessel on the pads—those to oblivion." Obeck uncapped the brass DESTRUCT stud.

"Now just a second!" said Bajan. "Destruction of title can get you—"

One of the ground crew said, "It's all right, Molly. The Little Giant called us direct from Skyside. There was some kind of Special Secretary with him."

Obeck closed his case, pushed DESTRUCT. White light flashed from the top corners; there was the acrid smell of melting plastic, a wisp of dark vapor.

"And aren't we supposed to get a ship in for repairs?" said one of the crew. "One that we'd . . . uh, lose?"

Kondor pointed at *Basilisk*. "I'd repair that thing before I tried to stare hard at it."

Thorn said, "I must warn you that the special system is very delicate. It could burn like dry grass." That was one of the two true things said that day.

Obeck said, "Before I leave, is it clearly understood by all here that nothing transacted today is public knowledge, and the Diplomatic Service will formally deny any knowledge of these events?" That was the other true thing.

There was assent, loudest from some of the ground crew, least loud from Bajan; Thorn said nothing at all.

Obeck nodded then, shook hands in the Queen's name, and started back toward the maglarail station. Thorn supervised the fueling of the new, nameless black ship. The crew did its preflight, and the postflight for *Bellerofon*, and considered at length how they should approach the groaning, teetering *Basilisk*. (In the end, no one was hurt. A friend of Aft Hatch Harry's, a specialist in such things, had set the thermal charges.)

Kondor said to Bajan, as they stood alone on the nameless ship's pad, "If you should ever decide you want out of this job, you know . . ." and tucked a card into her breast pocket.

His hand stopped halfway toward giving it a friendly pat, and he went to join Thorn. Whistling all the way.

Calculate a vector that will take me back to you. . . .

Left all alone in the cold afternoon, Molly Bajan looked at her pile of cassettes and wondered, among many other things, which one the thin young man in the Diplomatic clothes had really burned up.

There was the buzz of a distant maglarail car, then the whine of turbines lifting; and then *Whump! Whump! Whump!* from the next pad, and the smell of a burning starship.

Chapter 6
A Message in Secret

Ten thousand hours ago, more than a Novayan year, success had separated what failure could not: David Kondor and his Corporation had made the long skip to the Separated Worlds, leaving Orden Obeck behind. Now Obeck was a Privy Consul, and he rode gold upon Blue on the Queen's business to Kondor Marque; hour by hour the gap was closing.

For the moment, though, it was steady, and Obeck could not sleep.

The Royal Diplomatic Courier *Wenzel von Kaunitz* hung motionless in plainspace, far from any star or world. Its Outriggers were retracted, shrouded; its turbines stood still. Nebulae, undimmed by nearby sunlight, glowed in shades from blue to blackest violet, and twenty thousand untwinkling stars shone upon the blue finish of *Kaunitz*'s hull.

In the dim conroom the Pilot and her Engineer slept secure in their couches. The boards around them flickered and ticked softly to themselves, set to wake crew and ship should any threat arise or after eight hours by the chronometer.

Just behind the conroom, in the circular lounge, the lights were on. Orden Obeck sat alone, five more couches empty around the walls. He picked at a meal in a covered tray; a liter flask of z-gee beer floated, revolving slowly, above his left

hand. A novel went unread on the seat display. Beethoven's
Eroica was playing for the more-than-tenth time. Obeck
wished the ship would move again.

The nine Inner Worlds, among them Novaya and the
Primus-Luna-Mars-Venus group, were mutually only a few
hours' skip or hilift apart. The same was true of the Separated
Six: Bakunin, Longshot, Periwinkle, Saavedra, Tolstoi,
Topos. But between Six and Nine was a gap of a hundred
hours OutSide—four full Novayan days. The trip could be
made in the minimum time, and was, with crews in relays. But
almost always there were stops on the way to bring back colors
and stars and the sounds of engines for a little while.

Obeck's mission was labeled SECRET and URGENT, but more
of the first than the second. So only two crew had been
assigned him; the fewer involved, went the security truism, the
better. And Pilots had to be trusted to silence; they could not
be used and used up as research Undersecretaries could.

A hundred hours had passed already on *Kaunitz*. Obeck had
slept for barely fifteen, in almost as many tries. Saavedra was
still fifty hours away, ten of them spent going nowhere in the
interests of secrecy.

Farther back in the ship, past the bathroom with its drug
locker, the kitchen with its excellent food, the drawers where
two samechs slept soundly, dreamlessly, electronically, were
two very comfortable bedrooms. No one aboard outranked
Obeck for the use of the master room.

But he did not want the drugs; he was not enjoying the food;
he could not wire his scalp to a box and shut down; and the
bedrooms seemed oppressive, airless. Obeck knew very well
that he was fighting sleep, grasping at excuses to stay awake.
But he could not abandon the fight, even if he could not quite
understand why he was fighting. There was a fear lurking
somewhere deep—but of what, of what?

He touched a pad in the seat arm, wiping the text from the
display. Another touch and a grid, eight squares by eight, drew
itself in bright lines on black; alternating squares lit white and
chesspieces flashed into place. Obeck selected a B-level game,
thinking to lose and learn a little. He was no more than a
middle-D player. The machine randomized and gave him the
black pieces. Thorn—Theo, actually—had taken black to
teach Obeck the game. But they had never really been able to
play. Thorn was a multiple-A player, and between them it was
no game at all.

Saavedra, David, Thorn, Obeck thought. Fifty hours. A

white pawn slid to King's 4. The white stars through the port did not move at all. And damn the secret interests ultraviolet, he thought, and moved a knight.

A short and apparently uninformative message crossed Saavedra's InField as soon as *Kaunitz* emerged from its final skip. When Obeck came down the stairway—having finally tricked himself into ten straight hours' sleep, enough for the instant—a closed car was waiting for him, its windows mirrored. Inside was the Ambassador-Global himself, Victor Simpson-Liu, a small, round, pleasant man. Obeck knew him slightly, which in the Service mattered more than slightly.

Simpson-Liu tapped on the divider glass, and the samech driver started the car, which was methanol motored and loud to Obeck's ears. The Ambassador switched on the car's spy shields and poured two large drinks from a steel flask. Obeck accepted one without question. "The Queen's health," said Simpson-Liu, and they drank; it was ancient brandy, Obeck discovered, and kept his swallows small.

"Welcome to Saavedra, for what it's worth," said the Ambassador. "And congratulations on your new rank . . . for what that's worth."

"Thank you, Sir Victor." Obeck knew as well as Simpson-Liu that he was a Consul solely because no lesser rank could be given such a mission. He did not know, yet, how much he might have to give in return for it.

"What were you told?" said Simpson-Liu.

"That a Special Envoy to the Separated Worlds disappeared in what was evidently a geometric-drive accident. His ship skipped out in the direction of Bakunin, and very close to the time it was expected the gradient monitors there detected a ripple."

"Right enough," said the Ambassador-Global. "But I have a Bakunen monitor operator who swears from Einstein to Trout that the pattern he detected was *not* a ship slipping away."

"Then what was it?"

"He doesn't know. Neither do the four drive-physics experts who've gone over his tapes—all of whom started out saying the operator was crazy or a liar, and finished swearing along with him. And before you ask, these are loyal people. Trustworthy."

Obeck's eye was caught by a movement outside the car; a spherical plant tumbled along in the breeze, pacing them. "So

I'm to find out what really happened to the Envoy . . . and return him if at all possible."

"Not quite. Return him if you can. But return his diplomatic pouch at all costs." Simpson-Liu eyed Obeck across their brandy glasses. "At *all* costs, Sir Orden."

"Won't the Envoy have destroyed the contents?"

"Possibly. But it cannot be left to possibility. Naturally, a verification that Destruct was executed will successfully conclude your mission."

Obeck hesitated. In the Ambassador's "possibly" was a delicate hint of defection, of treason. And in his "*was* executed"—"And am I authorized to . . . execute Destruct?" Obeck was certain of the answer, but he wanted to hear it spoken. He did have that right.

"If you cannot return with the pouch . . . it is assumed that you are unable to return." It was said without either hesitation or callousness. "I'm . . . " Obeck thought Simpson-Liu was going to say "sorry," but he finished ". . . sure you understand."

"Of course, Sir Victor. What does the pouch contain?—physical descriptions, I mean."

"Surely. There are seven cassettes, labeled only with the numbers eleven-oh-one through eleven-oh-seven. There are also three documents in the usual white folders, bearing plain wax seals without impressions."

Somebody had had an absolute fit of anonymity. "The ship?"

"A courier with one gun, the *Montjoie Two.* Starkadr *Scroop*-class."

"I know them. Now, Sir Victor . . . who is it I'm looking for?"

Simpson-Liu sat up. "You weren't told *that?* No, that'd be like them, with their single crews when we may have no time at all. . . . The Envoy is Dr. Terrance Bishop."

Obeck said nothing. He took a sip of the relaxing brandy and thought on defections and treason.

"That's one reason why you were chosen. You know him well—he knows you. And you've shown a certain . . . aptitude for unusual operations."

And, the thought intruded, because this is big enough to expend a Knight on? Obeck was absolutely awake again. "I don't suppose," he said carefully, "that I can be told the nature of the Envoy's mission."

"No." The Ambassador took a large swallow from his

glass. "Not even which planet of the Six he was headed for. And I'm sorry. But I can't, Orden. If you find him—and that pouch . . ."

Simpson-Liu looked out the car windows at the gentle green hills rising around them. The sun, yellow as Outrigger gold, was huge and high in a magnificently blue sky. "If he's not . . . gone . . . you may be the only means to find him." The car topped a rise and there was a sudden vista of exposed stone, a meadow, and open fields rolling on forever. "Look out there. The Free Zone extends five hundred kilometers from the massport. Beyond that, it's all holdfasts. Even the rail lines end, though some of the holds have their own—do you get the idea? We couldn't go out there and search by brute force if we had nine divisions and Fleet support. And this is only one world of six—and by far the most loyal to the Queen." The last words were spoken with a great weariness—almost desperation.

Obeck realized, then, that Simpson-Liu was expendable as well, Ambassador-Global or not. He was no more expected to keep Saavedra under tight Royal rein than a gradient monitor kept ships from being lost beyond the Blue. He could only read the signs and try to interpret them and hope that his reports did not upset any carefully wrought theories.

The bureaucracy consumed people like a fire consuming wood. If one were usefully talented—a stronger stick—the process would take a little longer. But in the end only ashes were left. To survive one had to be not wood at all, but less, or more—stone, or metal.

"I'll need a Pilot," Obeck said.

Simpson-Liu nodded. "I'm taking you to David Kondor." He turned back to the window, toward a private OutSide. "He's the best, you know. He's been teaching the Bakunen raiders just where their freedom ends. When we lost Terry Bishop, I went straight to David. He said that if Bishop could be found, he'd find him, and I believe that. . . . He also said that he needed your help. . . . That doesn't seem to surprise you, Privy Consul Obeck."

"Oh—I'm just . . . rather tired, Sir Victor."

The car entered the fringes of a large town with broad streets, low buildings with sunscreens and wind turbines on roofs. The car passed people in cloaks, jackets, gowns, tunics, of fabrics and leathers in every color. There seemed more variation in skin tones than on Novaya, though where natural tan ended and solar began Obeck could not tell. It seemed he saw a young man on a streetcorner, surrounded by a small crowd, selling jewels from a velvet cloth; but the scene passed by and he could not confirm it.

The car stopped. To the side was a plaza, not large, tiled with copper and roofed with the interlaced branches of slender trees. Banners were hung for shade and pretty motion in the breeze. Shopfronts stood around the plaza on three sides.

"There's a caffe here called the Eye of the Moon," said Simpson-Liu. "Pilots like the place. David will be there."

"Thank you again, Sir Victor."

"No more than my job." The Ambassador-Global drained his glass, then looked at it with evident regret—perhaps for how full it had been. "There's a room for you at the Embassy tonight, naturally. The password after sunset will be *Manzikert*. The night staff is small—this is a highly dispersed Mission—but adequate."

"It sounds very nice . . . but I imagine David will want to get under way very quickly."

"I rather suppose he will," said Simpson-Liu from some distance away. "Give him my—well, you know."

Obeck nodded and left the car. It moved away growling, its windows reflecting sunlight and the tops of buildings. Obeck turned and went into the plaza.

He was wearing a Scholar's gown with sash, such as he had not worn in a very long time, and no signs of knighthood or Royal Service. A few heads had turned when he got out of the government car, but very soon he was part of the crowd.

Around him, people stared through shop windows, ate from their hands, sat playing chess and skytale. Two dancers wove themselves between red cords held by their partners, two more making music with flute and polyharp; all six wore wood-soled shoes that rang on the copper tiles. Light between leaves overhead cast geometric patterns.

There was movement without bustle, ease without idleness. Obeck knew it would infect him if he allowed it. He wished he could allow it.

A hanging sign showed a white moon with a startlingly realistic pupil and iris peering from a crater. There was no written legend. Obeck went through the swinging doors.

The caffe was dark, with softly luminous lectras of stars and sky around the walls, and what looked like ship's conboards but were really collages of glass beads and light, artistic imitations. The customers' dress was varied, with no insignia flashed or flaunted; anyone there might have been a Pilot, or everyone, or no one.

But the man in the distant booth, who got to his feet and flew a clear vector across the caffe floor, could not have been anything but who he was.

David Kondor gripped Obeck's shoulder, pushed a coffee mug into Obeck's hand; he said, "Welcome to Saavedra, Orden," and there was no for-what-it's-worth about it. Obeck nodded, tightening his fingers on the hot mug and Kondor's strong dark arm in its gray sleeve. He was not struck speechless. As a Diplomat in Service he could always find something to say. But there was no wish to—no need.

They went to the booth, sat. Kondor pulled an opaque curtain across the entrance. After a moment, the back wall began to slide upward, without a sound.

Beyond the wall was more booth, more table. And Molly Bajan and Thorn.

Bajan wore a coat like Kondor's with BAJAN/02 on the breast; on the table before her were a persec and a portable navplot unit. She had a meat pastry in one hand and was calling off grid numbers to Thorn between munches. Thorn's red robe was open, the hood thrown back, revealing his red flight jacket beneath. The jacket was much worn now, the gold trim fraying, the patch with the six stars half unsewn. He held a small silver stylus in his pale, thin fingers, and his hunched shoulders made him seem to have grown even shorter and broader.

They both stopped their work and turned. Bajan swallowed, said, "Hello, Orden. No tapes for me this time?"

Thorn said, "Close it, David. Hello, Orden."

Kondor touched Obeck's arm and they slid to the inner booth; the wall lowered after them.

"The matter is puzzling," Thorn said. "The sound hypotheses do not fit the facts, and the truth may be stranger than our guesses." He sipped his coffee. Obeck did as well; it was strong with whiskey, sweet with heavy cream. Bajan drank, and then Kondor, and the company was reformed.

"None of the significant Bakunen pirates or smugglers have bragged about a take like this one," Thorn said. "The best lead seems to be some strange comments—jokes, almost— about Blue anomalies."

Obeck nodded. Pilots did not joke much about Blue anomalies. Thorn's robe shifted, and below his jacket's loose nametape Obeck could see a medal pinned: the Bakunen Black Diamond, given by the mining syndics for service at the risk of one's life.

Bajan pointed at the starchart. "These areas are the places *Montjoie Two* could not have been taken through—under observation by Fleet or others we trust."

"Do you trust the Fleet?" said Obeck, surprising all but Thorn. He said no more. It was a state secret.

Kondor said, "There are leaks—"

Thorn said, "Everyone talks but the samechs. And we don't have many samechs out here. Understand very well, Orden: this is the Too Far Six. The Tolstoians and the Bakunen are only the most visible parts of a great invisible flux. Here the monarchy is thin."

There was a moment's pause. Obeck looked at Kondor, who watched Bajan, who watched Thorn.

Kondor said, "But there seems to have been no leak concerning the Envoy. If anything, his presence was discounted—what, a professor recalled to duty? We believe, then, that Dr. Bishop was taken on speculation—maybe even by accident. And the fact that nothing has been said since—not even a ransom demand—implies that they still don't know how important he is to the Service."

"Or that he was too important to leak news of," Thorn said. "Or dead, of course."

Obeck nodded. Nothing was said of the nature of that importance.

Kondor said, "And that's all—until you, Orden. It's known that messages have been sent, but Simpson-Liu knows who in his courier pool can be trusted. And you were seen getting off the *Kaunitz*—yes, we knew before you drove in—but who are you? Who knows?"

Obeck looked around at his friends' faces. "Only you and the Ambassador . . . David, you know Simpson-Liu, don't you?"

"Reasonably well. I think he's a good man."

"Does he usually go to bed early?"

Bajan's eyebrows rose. Thorn turned his head. Kondor said, "In fact, he does, Orden," and had to stifle a grin to speak.

"And is he quite understanding?"

"Where Kondor Marque is concerned, he's learned to be."

"Then he wouldn't be too upset by a midnight visit from the Royal Inspector-General?" Obeck was quite awake. He knew he would remain so for a long time now.

Kondor took a long pull at his whiskey-coffee, wiped cream from his upper lip. He turned to Bajan. "I told you he'd do it, Molly. Just like the old days. And this time—you can play along."

"Manzikert," said the man in the white coat and high black hat, and the samech at the Embassy gate opened it. Little sparks jumped around its white dielectric fingers. The man stepped through, followed by a woman who wore a hooded white cloak and a shoulder satchel. Both had dark eyevisors—though it was 0010 in the morning, with barely any moons and a sky as black as the man's silk stovepipe. After the samech released the gate, the man signed a message into its palm; it saluted and handed over its handstick.

One of the two human guards had two of his opponent's men on bar and was about to turn the doubler when a heavy black handstick came down with a *Whap* dead center in the gameboard; it folded up halfway and *all* the pieces slid onto the bar.

The other guard started to rise, reaching inside his tunic, and the tip of the stick jabbed first the back of his hand and then his chest just below the breastbone. With a great exhalation he sat down. A white-gloved hand probed where the guard's had tried to go, came out with a double-barreled hideaway pistol.

"*Back*gammon on *du*ty," said a voice like the peal of Doom; the guards realized that that was the exact truth. "Left the *gate* with the *sa*mech; carrying a *non*standard *iss*ue *weap*on—which the owner could not properly em*ploy*—are you *get*ting all this, Undersecretary?"

The woman's fingers were dancing on a shortform phototyper in her right hand. "Verbatim, Inspector."

The guards looked at each other with expressions of disaster.

"You may *add* the anno*ta*tion that the samech showed more native in*tel*ligence than *both* these two. And *prob*ably plays a better game of *back*gammon." The Inspector turned back to the guards. "I wonder if you two would care to *sal*vage your worthless repu*ta*tions?"

They nodded.

"*Ex*cellent. Then *guard* that gate and see that *no* one enters or *leaves*. Am I clear? *No* one."

They hastened to the gate, took up posts by the patient samech.

"Here's where we part company," said Obeck. "Can you find the junction center?"

"Can you find the bathroom?" Bajan said.

"I deserved that." He checked his wristec. "I'll meet you here in twenty minutes. Give it ninety seconds after that. And turn your cloak."

"Got you." She flipped it to its black side, seeming to draw on invisibility.

"Twenty from now."

"Nineteen forty," she said, and was gone.

Obeck bypassed the Embassy garden by the covered sub-rosa walk all such gardens had, slipping through shadow with the step of a student out after hours. He touched the light wire, hidden by his bushy hair, that turned his dark glasses into nighteyes: an invention of Bajan's.

A sheet-metal door appeared. Obeck took another device from his pocket: a small box very like a cassette, with a rod sticking from its side. He pushed the rod into the door's keyplate. It rattled a bit, made some soft whistling sounds, and the door clicked open. Light spilled out.

Ducking to clear his high hat, Obeck stepped through. White enamel and bright metals shone; the nighteyes stopped down.

Three young people in kitchen whites were sharing looks at a mildly sensational cassette and pulls at a bottle of clear liquid. At the cooktop, a samech in a butler's coat was warming a glass of milk. The humans held quite still, one straining to swallow. The samech reached for the buttons on the interphone panel. "Manzikert, apse seven spades," said Obeck, and it went back to its milk.

"As for *you*," said Obeck to the staff, "*shirk*ing, *dally*ing, *drink*ing—" He held out his hand for the bottle, sniffed the contents, took a sip—and spat it into the sink. "My *apo*logies for accusing you of drinking this—you must have been cleaning the *sil*ver."

Bajan walked around crates and racks, sidestepped loose cellar stones and puddles of condensation. A depowered samech, missing one arm, leaned forlornly against a wall. Tubing and wires and a large metal bushing protruded from its shoulder stump. She took a pad and stylus from her shoulder bag, wrote a note, and pinned it to the machine's torn, oil-stained coat. It read: THE REALM'S FIRST AND BEST LINE OF DEFENSE.

A few steps further on she came to a double metal panel labeled DANGER—POWER JUNCTION PANEL. A handtool opened it in seconds, exposing breakers, wirenets, chattering relays, and a starfield of solder points.

Pulling on insulated gloves, she applied a tiny clip to a connection, then another, another, and a small box with digits on its face to link them all together.

She read her wristec. Sixteen minutes plus ninety seconds.

From the kitchen Obeck moved up the carpeted halls, pausing to leave notes: THIS MIRROR IS SMUDGED, CLOCK TWO MINUTES SLOW, ANDIRONS TARNISHED, and several GUESS WHO?s. He met no one but samechs, and a whisper and a palm-scribble sent them about their work.

He climbed the grand staircase (tagging a loose carpet with SOMEBODY'S GONNA BREAK HIS NECK) and sidled down the upper hallway. He felt a sudden, wholly irrational desire to cause some real damage: to smash something. To destroy—

He stopped, dizzy, leaned against a bust of Kissinger in an alcove. This is a game, he thought very clearly, but the Service owes me more than a game. They owe me— Obeck closed his eyes, tightened his fists, feeling his heart swell with rage at himself and the Service and the whole unbending universe. There was physical pain to go with the mental.

He knew then what it was he wanted to smash and destroy, and he was afraid. Aren't I always? he thought with cooling passion, and stuck a note on the statue's glasses: I WAS HERE. WHERE WERE YOU?

He had only a little farther to go.

Bajan made the last of her connections, pushed buttons on all the little boxes. They began counting down. On her way out of the cellar, she had a thought and took something with her, tucking it in her bag, leaving a WHAT IF THIS HAD BEEN A FLEET CRUISER? note in its place. Seven minutes plus ninety seconds were left to Obeck's deadline.

Obeck checked his wristec and cursed his stupid fit. He worked a door handle, very gently, stepped through.

A man at a desk, reading under a spotlight, turned to face him. "Who in blue hell are you?"

"Manzikert," said Obeck.

"Yeah, fine. Now who *are* you?" The man reached for the interphone, and with great regret Obeck gave him the handstick in the chest and, as he gasped, a spritz from a spray can. He folded up in his chair. Obeck propped him up comfortably with a note in his pocket reading PROMOTE THIS MAN—INSPECTOR GENERAL.

The room was lined with metal racks and bookshelves. Obeck took one each of three sizes of dispatch case, nesting small into large. He then selected several books and papers, tucking them in as well.

He snapped out the reading lamp and went on to the next room, being more quiet than ever; once through it, he realized that he need not have worried so. Simpson-Liu was a very sound sleeper.

Bajan's nighteyes showed her the Embassy gardens brightly, but in false color, skewed responses from the micromultiplier phosphors making the plants seem strange and rare. Kondor had told her the Force rhyme:

> Roses are purple and coffee is red,
> My buddies are ruddy but look like they're dead.

The gate came into view; the samech did look healthier than the human guards, though perhaps that was to be expected. Bajan crept a little closer. Thirty seconds, then ninety. She waited.

At ten plus she swept her cape out and reversed it to white. The guards, flesh and plastic, turned.

She hoped Obeck was on time.

Obeck nearly didn't make it.

He stared out the bathroom window at the ground. He had the clamp fixed to the windowframe, the rope through it and ready.

And he thought, as in a dream, about falling. Cracking bones, breaking organs.

Obeck knew now what he wanted to destroy. He had just seen it, nighteyed, in the bathroom mirror.

Why here? Why now?

When better?

Seconds went by.

If he failed, there was no question of returning in disgrace. If he failed, he was dead—and so would be David, and Molly, and probably Thorn, because Obeck might say anything under the right pain. Not to mention Dr. Bishop. . . .

And if he succeeded, they would send him out again, and again, until he did fail—

He pushed up the window, looked at the pavement. Only five meters, he thought. Not far enough. I can't even succeed in that.

Obeck knew he was a coward, had long known it. But which did he fear more, the dying or the pain?

He took off his white coat, draped it over his shoulders, and fastened the collar clasp. The night wind in his dark hair, he grasped the line and put a boot on the windowsill.

Bajan took a step toward the guards, and they took steps toward her. Their handsticks and one service pistol were out; they had had a third of an hour to wait and think and plan.

"No one's to leave the grounds, you understand," said the one who had been winning at backgammon. "The I.G. was very specific, wasn't he, Hermie?"

"No one at all," said the other guard. They took more steps. Bajan flexed her knees slightly, relaxed her spine, hoped again that Obeck would be on time.

He was. The weighted rappel line fell from the window with a snap and down it slid Obeck, his coat floating on the air. He touched ground almost silently, bowed from the waist.

The guards turned, mouths open. Bajan hardly blamed them. She walked up to one—Hermie—and chopped her hand down on the wrist with the handstick. It fell. He started to yelp, but the heel of Bajan's hand slammed his jaw shut. Elbow, knee, elbow finished the job, and she turned to the other guard—found herself staring down the enormous black hole of his gun barrel. His nighteye-greenish face was very flat.

Then his eyes bulged as the samech's fluidic fingers closed on the back of his neck and lifted slightly. The man stood on tiptoe; the gun fell from his fingers. Obeck gave him a shot from his spray can and he went quite limp, still supported at the end of the samech's arm.

"Thank you, Max," said Obeck to the machine. "I'm glad somebody around here knows whom to be loyal to." He wrote in the samech's free hand, and it saluted and held the salute. And the guard.

Obeck and Bajan, their coats fluttering white in the darkness and new moonlight, ducked out the gate and got into a car parked nearby; Bajan engaged the quiet flywheel and they were off, without lights for several blocks.

When they were comfortably away, Bajan asked, "How did

you know that samech's name? And what did you tell it when it saluted you?''

"It was a Master-Max Three," said Obeck, "one of the best designs Consolidated Vulcan ever turned out. And I told it to hold the guard for Simpson-Liu himself. It was quite pleased to, of course."

"Oh, I'm sure."

"I'm serious," said Obeck. "Do you know what meta-programs are?"

"Sure. Programs created out of lesser programs, without being explicitly written."

"Well, samechs contain a metaprogram that causes them to feel . . . something *like* satisfaction at doing a job well, and something *like* disappointment at failure."

"Who designed *that* in?"

"No one did. It seems to have been a side effect of the job-recognition and order-hierarchy programs—and those are about five generations removed from human writers."

"How does a diplomat know so much about samechs?" She glanced at him. "Though I suppose, knowing David and Thorn, I shouldn't ask that."

"When I was at the University, I took my nonfield elective in sapient-mechanism theory. I don't really know why. I'd . . . my family never owned a samech, and the University used mostly Manipool labor. I guess I was curious . . . they're really extraordinary machines, for all we take them for granted. Not one person in a thousand can write samech-sign, you know . . . maybe that's why I do it so often. Maybe that's why I took the course: to know something that nobody else did." Obeck smiled, feeling painfully awkward—though perhaps not quite suicidal.

"You were an indentured student, weren't you?"

"Yes."

"And you wanted to know what the other kinds of slavery were like."

"I—" It came out a squeak.

"It's all right, Orden. I wore the brass too. On Tacante. And I would have gone into the Tacante Manipool if Loaman Starkadr hadn't bought me." She ran fingers through her black hair; Obeck saw that it was no longer helmet-short, but held back with steel rings. "That looked like . . . well, then . . . but it was just a longer chain."

"Until David," Obeck said.

"Until David. But he doesn't know," she added, "and you

won't tell him . . . please. Thorn knows, of course—Thorn knows everything, I think—and I had to tell you. Since you'd been there.''

"I won't tell," Obeck said, thinking, What would you like me to swear by? Knowing finally what David had seen in her, and wondering without much hope if he would ever be that brave. "None but the brave deserve the fair" played over and over in his head, with a band—a brass band.

The lights of the massport appeared in the distance, the rocking TALANtenna cradling a rising moon.

Ninety seconds after Obeck and Bajan had gone out the gate, every light in the Embassy blazed brilliant. Music blared over the interphone system and elevators ran up and down to the beat.

Ambassador-Global Sir Victor Simpson-Liu was awakened by sound, light, and a dozen alarms at once. He grabbed the interphone by his bed, dialed all the channels, and got "March of the Samech Soldiers" on all of them. He let the handset fall, stood up, and staggered into his bathroom in search of a drop of analgesic.

The night air rushed in through the open window, from which a rope dangled into the courtyard. Realizing in the cold draft that he was well lit and quite naked, the Ambassador-Global shoved the curtains closed, only briefly glimpsing the tableau of guards below.

He turned to the sink. Upon it was a high silk hat, a pair of white gloves perched on the brim. On the mirror above was a message, written in scented soap.

DEAR MR. AMBASSADOR:
THANKS FOR THE OFFER OF BED AND BOARD, BUT THE MAGIC SHOW IS ON THE ROAD. IF THIS PERFORMANCE DOESN'T ATTRACT A CRITICAL AUDIENCE—NOTHING WILL.

OO & CO
P.S. PLEASE WASH MIRROR AFTER READING.

The Ambassador did, just as the news—and notes—began to arrive from around the Embassy. As things began to settle down, Simpson-Liu realized that he would never get to sleep again that night.

Then he noticed that he no longer needed the analgesic.

Chapter 7
A View from Space

"Saavedra Control, this is QSC *Cordell Hull*," said David Kondor, "requesting lift clearance immediately upon TALAN green trace."

"*Cordell Hull*," said the tower, "reason for request?"

"Control, this vessel is a Diplomatic Special Transport carrying an . . . important passenger on urgent Royal business."

"*Hull*, will you clarify?"

"Control, negative." There was no immediate reply. "Suggest you get in touch with the Embassy, Control . . . after you clear us, please?"

Bajan, at the Engineer's board to Kondor's right, said, "Point five of lift thrust," and the tethered turbines underscored her.

Obeck, in the left seat, read his displays and said, "Deep trace is clear long distance. TALAN still amber."

"Saavedra Control," said Kondor, "do I have that authorization? The sun's up and your sky's empty."

There was a pause, and a different voice from the first said, "Uh . . . 'firmative, *Cordell Hull*."

"Thank you, Control," said Kondor.

"Green light," said Obeck.

"Lift thrust," said Bajan, and on the instant Kondor took the grips; *Cordell Hull/Condor* roared and rose.

He took no double handfuls of sky this time, because all of them, including the ship, were playing parts: Kondor actually climbed the ascent spiral. Though from the ground it looked more like he executed a horizontal inside loop around the TALANtenna, then broke for clouds at a remarkable angle. There was a purpose: to stay in view a little longer, to assure that they kept their carefully attracted attention—while not signing Kondor's name in the sky.

Out of the blue, into the black, stars by hundreds lighting up around them, Kondor backed off thrust and the gravcounter ticked down. *Condor/Hull* tumbled, ionizers gimbaling, to put the gravity synthesized by their thrust normal to the floor. Z-gee would have been pleasant, but on a skip of this length thrust was more in keeping with urgency.

"Lock us up, Eng," said the Pilot, "quarter-gee."

"Quarter-gee."

"Quarter-gee, onward," said Obeck, securing his boards and releasing his belts. Kondor was already up; he took Bajan's hand and they stepped lightly from the conroom. Before following, Obeck had a look through the Nav-Main display at retreating Saavedra. At the center of the image, outlined brilliantly by machine overlay, was the Free Zone like a dented wheel; all around lay the Holdfasts, marked with travel cautions in all severities, a quilt seamed with luminous lines.

In the lounge Bajan was opening a luggage bin, while farther down the corridor Kondor worked the kitchen. He returned with a tray of cold beef sandwiches; Bajan had recovered her shoulder satchel and extracted a bottle with a gold foil seal.

"Don't tell me," said Kondor. "You bought it at the import-free shop."

"Even *I* know they don't have those in the Six," said Obeck, and looked close. "That's a Chamonix-Palace-Reserve . . . where *did* you get it?"

"The Embassy basement," Bajan said. "I left them a note."

"Well, in *that* case," Obeck said.

"It's white wine," said Kondor. "Does that go with roast beef? Is it a good year?"

"It's a C-H one forty. That's supposed to be a terrific year," said Bajan.

"The one forty A is," said Obeck, blowing dust from the

bottle, "but there are two seasons on Chamonix, and the one forty B is awful."

"Is this A or B?"

"Or," Obeck said thoughtfully, "is it the A that's vinegar and the B that's choice? I took Food Protocol so long ago."

Kondor had produced three stemmed glasses from the kitchen locker, crystal of indestructible viewport pylex. Bajan tore the gold foil with a fingernail—"Hey, I think this is real gold!"—and twisted at the cork beneath.

Kondor looked up. "I just had a frightening thought—this isn't a sparkling wine, is it?"

"The way *you* lift?" said Bajan as the cork came gently free. The white-gold wine poured slowly in the quarter-gee, drops bouncing high. They touched glasses.

"For the Queen," said Kondor, and Bajan said, "In that case, this had better be the good season."

It was.

The car that crossed the beaten zone from Free Zone to Pykos Holdfast at dawn had open sides and a canvas top; it carried one man and had no room to hide a second. But rifles tracked it from the moment it left the Government Road, and when it reached the Pykos gate a Consolidated Vulcan swath-gun was leveled on the vehicle and another on the driver, and the man in bulletproofs who went out to ask the driver his business went with his pistol in his hand.

It was harvest time in the North of Saavedra—time for reaping.

As the guard made the signals to permit the car to pass—which involved lowering a spiked mesh curtain and deactivating two belts of mines—he nodded to the driver, but made no further apology. Thorn did not expect or require one. He nodded in reply and drove on, toward a group of buildings, round roofed, set into the soil.

Martin Pykos and his linkwife, Rowa Latimer, met Thorn at the largest building, which directly abutted a hill. Ag-crawlers, mounting harvesting equipment of frightful aspect, stood around the sloped steel walls. A shadow passed over, with a rush and whine: an airskimmer up on recon. There was a handgun on every hip, not omitting Pykos's and Latimer's, but no heavy weapons were in evidence, and only one uniformed guard. There were quite a few people out in the morning sun, all brown, no white plastic.

"Fine morning, Thorn," said Pykos. "*The Pale Horse* is on the pad, all but ready—but so is breakfast. Will you cut bread with us . . . inside?"

"Of course, Martin, Rowa," said Thorn without hesitation.

They went into the large building. To either side of the path were dust-wrapped bales of grain stacked ten meters up and twenty down; the warehouse was gridded in three dimensions, like a shipyard or the hold of the hugest freighters, with the same sort of roving handling gear. The walkway was made of plates laid from gridrail to gridrail, with low curbs and the lightest of handrails.

Past the bales were cargo cubes of kernels, seed, and flour, and more goods, food, supplies, fuels in a firefoam enclosure, machine parts—heavy guns and organ-rockets made to fit the crawlers and skimmers outside. Last of all were small arms, rifles, rockets, grenade strings; and just beyond them, neatly stacked, boxes very much like white metal coffins, but stenciled with the Con Vulcan trademark and the legend:

SAPIENT MECHANISM
MYRMIDON-2S/MILITARY
DEACTIVATED—STANDBY MODEL
FRAGILE—DO NOT EXPOSE TO VACUUM

The building ended, the hill began somewhere, but from inside it was hard to tell just where. Cables ran in all directions; steel walls shone in the dim light. They crossed a last long walkpanel over the dark deep grid—a drawbridge, of sorts—and passed through a valved and gasketed door into a bright, pleasant, furnished area, full of the sound and smell of steaks and eggs cooking.

Some distance from here was the main house, large and fine; it was no dishonor to be asked to a meal there. But this was Martin Pykos's keep, his fast of fasts. An offer to dine within was not lightly made or refused.

Korit Pykos and his sister Leila were collaborating on the food (she whacked his wrist when he tried to salt the steaks on the grill). Meia and Jehan, infant and toddler respectively, were waiting more or less patiently at the table. Only the two oldest children were missing.

"Lev's in the skimmer?" Thorn said. Pykos nodded. "And Avis?"

"Here," said a voice from even deeper within the hill. Avis Pykos was stripping off work gloves and a shop coat heavy with white dust. "I was buffing the ports on *The Pale Horse*."

"Asymmetric pattern?" said Thorn.

"Practically Gaussian random," she said. "What do you take me for, Thorn? I know about pattern refraction. And I know how you feel about other people working on *Horse*."

Thorn nodded, possibly in agreement. Lev entered then, his mother covering his flightsuit with a duster, and they sat down. The bread, of the holdfast's own grain, was passed to Thorn with a long silver-handled knife; he sliced the loaf and the meal began.

Midway through, Martin Pykos said, "Thorn . . . will you do something for me?"

Thorn put down his knife and fork. "If it's a thing I can do," he said—and his face was blank but his meaning was clear, "then of course, Martin."

"Well. It's harvest, you know. We haven't been hit really hard, these last few seasons . . . but Rapal's just linked with Jaravellir, and there's blood and territory in their eyes."

"You want a strike sortie flown against them, then? Preemption?" Thorn's tone was level. Around the table, Rowa was quiet, Lev intent; Leila flew orbits with a coffeepot, Korit salted his steak and pretended disinterest; the smallest children stared directly at Thorn, their faces no plainer than his. Avis crossed her silverware and fiddled with her napkin.

"Nothing too hot or too heavy," said Martin, not hastily. "I don't want a blood feud. I just want to tell them where the boundaries lie . . . and that they lie deep."

"You understand I've already a mission today."

"Funnel wind, not today. And you needn't at all," said Martin, meaning it. "You don't owe any of us, after all you've already done."

"I do owe you, Martin, risk for risk. And I'll do it. Understanding that I'll do it alone—and that your concern's not the tactics I use but the results I get?"

"Naturally," said Martin. "Your way."

"Do you guarantee results?" said Avis suddenly, and her eyes met Thorn's, but only for an instant. Martin Pykos looked hard at his elder daughter.

"Service," said Thorn, "but never results." He drank off a glass of juice, and the rest of the meal was eaten in silence.

Powerbored tunnels, lit by green betaglow strips, wound from the cavern apartments into other areas within the hill. Some branches led nowhere. Some led to traps. Thorn, Pykos and Latimer, Lev and Avis emerged from the maze into a very large room with sloping walls, a natural cave smoothed with powerbores and poured stone. Down one gallery were three airskimmers; in another, heavier aircraft. In the center of the room, on a slightly raised pad, was *The Pale Horse*, its midnight-blue finish glistening under the lights, its ports clean to invisibility.

"I'll be leaving now," Thorn said.

"You'll be back, though," said Martin Pykos. "And when the Split finally comes—"

"If there's a Queen forever, you're still welcome here," said Rowa Latimer, who bound Pykos Holdfast to Latimer Holdfast by body, blood, and bullet.

"Do you want me to fly split-cover for you, Thorn?" said Lev, a little too eagerly.

"Not this time, thank you, Lev. And, Avis . . . the ports are fine."

"Next time, true random, I promise." Avis smiled.

Thorn nodded, turned, went up the ship's stairway. The others retreated behind a small ground-control console. Avis and Martin tapped pads and radars came to life; pylex-windowed blast doors closed before the console area and the ship galleries. The wall beyond *The Pale Horse* opened: past it was a dark, broad tunnel, marker lights strung along its walls, leading out to one final door, sod covered, search screened.

Thorn lifted on minimum power, barely audible behind the doors. The ship turned, headed down the tunnel to daylight. It reached the hillside opening, passed through—and dropped from view, vanishing as well from the console radar.

"He's pancaked!" cried Lev, and Martin's hands froze above the console.

"He's done no such thing," said Avis Pykos calmly, and touched a pad: an outdoor camera showed *The Pale Horse* flying cross-country at barely treetop height. "He's below the radars. He told me this ought to be possible—"

"*Ought!*"

"—and had me mount the camera. Now you see why he didn't need Lev flying cover."

Lev stared at the deep blue ship and its life-sized black shadow. "Why," he said, off on a new vector from his sister, "doesn't Thorn challenge the Dark Condor?"

"You don't win battles with duels of champions anymore, son, no matter what you may have heard," said Martin Pykos in an old, old voice.

"I'll bet Thorn knows who the Dark Condor is, though," Lev went on. "And I'll bet Thorn would win the duel. Wouldn't he, Avis?"

Avis, then, was driven onto a variant course as well. "It wouldn't be a draw, that's for sure. Someone would go Out-Side . . . forever."

The Pale Horse left the camera's range, and then the air, and then the world.

Condor called *Cordell Hull* settled to the surface of Periwinkle and sank beneath it.

There was nothing on the world but ocean and frozen ocean; the nearest land was fifty meters below water. There were floating towns, and a city on the southern icepack, but the life of the planet was under the sea. So the ships that could —most of them—and would—a lesser number—closed intakes and submerged.

There were thuds and thumps as water passed *Condor*'s hull. The water surface shone above like a Blue in a monochrome OutSide. Shortly, lights appeared below, and the spheres and cylinders of Peri Prime became visible. A Remora subtug pulled alongside *Condor*, latched on by suction. The tug's pilot was a semimer, working dry inside the glass cabin but with gilltubes visible on her bare shoulders; two true merfolk, their gills fully internal at the expense of their lungs, swam alongside.

Condor locked down to a seapad, and the merfolk sealed a boarding tunnel to the hatch.

Obeck, in full formal whites but without any badges or bands of rank, tucked the largest of his "borrowed" dispatch cases under his arm and waited for the hatch light. "See you in ninety minutes," said Kondor; that, according to Simpson-Liu's Intelligence report, was how long Dr. Bishop had spent off the *Montjoie II* here; its crew had never left, so neither would Kondor and Bajan.

Obeck checked his wristec as the hatch flashed green. "I hope it's you I see," he said, smiling but not really joking, and went through.

They were, just now, flying through dust with instruments out: Dr. Bishop had, said Intelligence, spent his ninety minutes at the Embassy—but with whom? Not the Ambassador-Global, who was at Peri Polar. And *what* was he doing? The report was unstrangely silent.

Obeck took a chair from a public rack, unfolded it and sat down on a passenger belt, and waited for something to happen.

He tried to like Peri Prime, but he did not much succeed. The corridors were confined and ugly, with exposed pipes and valves everywhere and constant mechanical noises. There was only a low-speed belt, no expresses. Out the ports was no sky, no starfield, just blue-green hydrosphere with a vague light filtering down, and no terrain but some rough rocks and sand, more barren than Riyah Zaini desert—and dimming to nothing a few meters away. Occasionally a swimming creature fluttered by, but none stayed to let him look, and all seemed quite drab. It was rather the same with the people he saw: few and unexceptional, even the semimer. . . .

He passed a sealock labeled with street directions, and it showed him the vector to the truth: this was only a tiny corner of Peri Prime, the dry corner. Ninety percent of the city, of the population, lived in water. The true mer, who had built this city as the first here, had built it for themselves; the air swallowers—and even the semimer, who had to come up for two-thirds of their time—had to make do with the back doors, the cellars.

So when Obeck found that the main hall of the Embassy was a pylex dome, he had to wonder if the merfolk watched from the sea outside, staring at the unmodified humans in their atmospherium.

And he wondered what Dr. Bishop could have done here.

Obeck was met by the Undersecretary for Dry and Surface Affairs, a semimer in sandals and a loose robe that showed his gilltubes. The scar where the pinvalves and sensors entered his chest and pulmonary artery was brown, old.

And he had never personally met Dr. Terrance Bishop in his life, if he was not lying. There could be little question of assumed names or mistakes for a Queen's-side Bishop with bronze eyes. The USecDry was friendly, though he did speak to Obeck in ELI-3 exclusively.

"Of course, we have an entry in the book that some time past an Envoy did appear. But what he may have done, with whom he spoke—of those things were no records kept, I fear."

Time to lie, thought Obeck. "It does not matter, if he's truly gone. The Service finds a way to carry on."

The Perian did not react. This was no receptionist overconfident of his power; this was a professional of Obeck's own Service. And semimer, where the Global breathed only air.

Obeck talked on, learned no more. He was offered a samech escort back to *Cordell Hull*, which he politely refused; he had not seen a single white machine on the trip in and was at once very suspicious of the offer to mark him. Or was it to protect him from a genuine danger?

He left the Embassy thinking of icebergs that were mostly concealed underwater. A huge, gape-jawed, spiny fish hovered near a corridor port, but Obeck had no time to leave the belt and watch it. Mer swam by. Finally, standing in the tunnel before *Condor*'s hatch, a bubble of fear rose in his lungs: a dreamlike image came of the door opening and a wall of water rushing outward, flooding the tunnel, drowning him before he could make a sound.

Molly Bajan, however, glass of Ch140 vintage in her hand, was all there was on the other side, and the dream was broken and the bubble dissolved, if not quite burst.

"How did it go?" she said.

"I think they smelled the bait," said Obeck, "but no strikes," and she laughed and seemed to see nothing terrible in his look.

A pair of Remoras took them to the surface, and in minutes they were out of the green and into the black. The next point on the itinerary was Bakunin . . . where the trail would end.

As they were leaving the board-locked conroom, a voice echoed tinny and loud through the whole of *Condor*.

"Your attention, please. This is to inform you that an explosive device has been affixed to the underhull of this vessel. Should you not comply precisely with the instructions to follow the device will be detonated and the vessel will be destroyed without survivors."

"Where's it *coming* from?" said Obeck.

"Leech speaker on the hull," Bajan said, and went into the conroom, calling back, "I'll try to find it on cameras."

Kondor said, "So where's the following instructions?"

"There will now be a pause to allow you to organize your thoughts and to verify the existence of the device, which is located on the right central underhull."

"I see the . . . thing!" Bajan shouted.

"Naturally, any attempt to disarm or remove the device will cause it to detonate, as will this vessel's entering an atmosphere or the transmission of any messages. When you are

*ready to receive our instructions, please stamp firmly on the
floor near the device; this will also confirm the existence of our
antitampering sensors."*

Obeck thought Kondor might stamp his foot right then, but
he only clenched his fists and teeth. "A mechanical hijacker,"
he said tightly. "One that talks like a cabin steward on top of
it. Really a comedian, isn't it?"

Bajan said, "If you find a fusion bomb stuck under your
backside funny. Come in here and look."

They saw a disk, about a meter across, against the black
hull. Atop it were the unmistakable radial cylinders of a fusion
imploder.

Bajan said, "Probably attached during all the underwater
hull-banging. The boarding tunnel would have hid it when we
were down. . . . Looks like a Con Vulcan Cleanfire-Eight with
the usual modifications."

"Usual?" said Obeck, and then did know he was in the
Separated Worlds.

"I'm fairly sure. Wish Thorn were here—he'd know."

They were all quiet a moment, thinking of Thorn; he was to
follow and assist "on the off chance we need it," though they
had all known that if help was needed its arrival would be a
question at best.

"But no question about 'no survivors.' "

"None at all," said Bajan. "What do we do now?"

Obeck said, "Stomp on the floor, I suppose," and went to
do it.

*"Your instructions are as follows. They will be repeated,
once only. You will take this vessel OutSide in the normal
fashion, and proceed as to Bakunin. However, you will not reenter plainspace but will instead proceed to Longshot, and
only then reenter. You will be met there in sufficient force to
destroy you—"*

Kondor slammed a fist into a palm.

*"—Again, any attempt to disarm or remove the explosive
device will cause its instant detonation, as will entering an
atmosphere, broadcast of any message, or deviation from the
course instructions. Should you prove hesitant, the device will
also detonate automatically in twenty hours."*

"They think of everything," said Kondor as the instructions
repeated. "Well, now we know what happened to *Montjoie
Two*."

"At first, anyway," said Obeck. "But what happened Out

around Bakunin? Did the device under *Montjoie* go off . . . or . . ."

Bajan said, "If you're interested, we're out of the InField."

"Blinding Blue hell, yes," said Kondor. "Till we figure out the game, we've got to play it . . . right, Orden?" His rage seemed to have diminished a little; Obeck was glad.

"Right," he said. "It'll be quiet, we can think. . . . Will going OutSide shut that thing up?"

"No. Only geometric-drive gear goes silent."

"Too bad," Obeck said. "It couldn't have heard us coming, if . . ." He said it idly, an unfunny joke, but suddenly ideas were adrift in his head. "By all means, let's go Out. Don't you see? OutSide they can't blow us up."

"They can't?"

"No. *They* can't. Only *we* can."

"You mean . . . no one can deliberately trigger the thing while we're Out. It has to go by booby trap."

"Unless they've come up with Blue radio—and if they're that far ahead we may as well quit now."

"Then we can disarm the thing!" Kondor was triumphant.

Obeck looked at the display, at the flat spiky bomb. Little lights shone from it. "If we can get past the traps, and if . . . we go OutSide and then leave the ship." He looked at Kondor, who was pensive for what might have been the first time in his life, and Obeck felt cold. "Better we play along, David, as you say. Taking it apart would be a risk in dock. In a suit, *OutSide* —you *can't* want it off that badly. They're intending to kidnap, not kill—"

But he read the desire very clearly in Kondor's eyes.

Airlocks were not much use on starships. Docks had boarding tunnels; to abandon ship the hatch was faster, and any feelings of confinement during a trip would not likely be relieved by a stroll in a pressure suit. *Condor*'s one lock, manually operated, was on the left side just behind the wing, leading from the engineroom annex.

Obeck closed the inner lid, turned the wheel, hearing a grate of metal and the squeak of gaskets mating. He knocked on the curved lid, got an answering rap. Then there was a series of bumps, elbows and boots along the meter-wide tube, and a hiss and rattle as the air within was valved out. As the air to carry it bled away, the hiss diminished; the rattle went on a little longer. A warning lamp lit—a little unnecessarily, since

Condor's internal atmosphere held the lid down with thousands of kilos' force.

More sounds of metal conducted through metal. Obeck drifted a few meters to the other side of the room, cranked open a blast shutter between two plates of pylex. A white-gloved hand covered the small port. Then the hand showed a thumb-up, and the mask of a helmet moved into view, a curved band of gilded pylex across the eyes.

"Jack in," said Obeck, exaggerating the lip motions, "te-le-phone." Samech-sign would have been useful, but just now he could only talk to himself with it.

The hand came up again, holding a plug, then moved down. Obeck turned away. To his side was a mesh screen, and beyond it the rings and plumbing of the engines. Below the screen at waist height was a console with inset displays. Obeck picked up a headset and clipped it behind his ear; he touched pads until he got outside/OutSide view of a suited figure, stark white on black hull, fixing a cable to a cleat near the lockway. The camera was mounted looking forward, and just behind the white suit the black wing split colorfield from Blue. Arms and legs moved only two meters from Outrigger coils, four from the rushing Blue.

The ship could travel on a single Outrigger, if one were damaged; that indeed was the reason all ships carried two. What the shock and disruption of touching the coils might do to the toucher was another matter. And if any part of the body —if anything not golden Outrigger—should touch the Blue, that was another matter still.

There was no way to measure the "speed" of a ship under geometric drive. There were no references; the Einsteinian light-beam experiments did not work—it was doubtful that "speed" had any real meaning OutSide.

But the energies of Blue contact were very real. If a hand, a foot should touch the shimmering plane, it would stay while the ship moved on; and something would be torn apart to leave it—cable, or hullplate, or if necessary muscle and tendon.

Obeck watched the figure cross the underhull toward the waiting bomb, paying out cable, barely touching the hull lest the bomb hear the trembling, the Blue so near. Obeck wished, then, that he had said nothing, had, just this once, failed to provide Kondor with a brilliant plan on the spot. Let talking bombs lie, he thought, and realized his hands were cramp-tight on the edge of the console and the headset wire. Very gently, so as not to startle, he said, "Reading me, Molly?"

"Clearly, Orden." On the display, she reached up to lightly touch the hull, and hung between black steel and Blue, regarding the bomb. "It's a Cleanfire-Eight, all right. Eight pulse lasers around a tritium injector. Can't just take the core out— that'd set it off for sure. So we get the guns."

"All eight?"

"It'll detonate with five, and it might go with four. So we have to knock out five of them. They're probably all tamper-triggered, all in different ways."

Obeck said, "You don't have to do it, Molly," and almost added, "Please."

"Then who will? It's a little out of your line, Orden. And I want David's hands on the controls, thank you."

"I meant . . ." But he knew she knew what he meant.

"Pick a number from one to eight."

Obeck thought a minute, then read the time from his wristec. "Six."

"Six it is." Bajan opened a pouch of tools on her left thigh, reached for her helmet spotlight. "Suppose there's a white-light switch? But it's pointed at the Blue, so there probably isn't." She snapped on the spot.

Obeck had not even had time to tense. He wound up the magnification of view till he was practically looking over her shoulder, watching the shiny tool in the gloved fingers, the machinery below. Or above—the Blue was below. Bajan's breathing was loud in his ear.

He reached to the wall interphone, opened a link to the conroom. Kondor had promised to keep his mind on the smooth Blue run, not Bajan at work. He was probably not keeping it. Or perhaps he was; his voice came soft from the wallpanel.

> "I am OutSide on the Blue
> With the grips beneath my hands.
> Though I'm wishing I was In,
> Though I'm dreaming I can land,
> There is nothing else to do,
> Silent on the silent Blue."

"Got it!" Bajan said, snapping Obeck back. One of the lasers, a busy-surfaced tube of metal and crystal, was cradled in her hands, free of the bomb. She took a small hammer from her toolkit, smashed the end-stage optics, and settled the gun back into position. "We don't want it to look too disarmed, right?"

"Right," said Obeck. "Did you have . . . trouble?" Silly question about a bomb, he thought.

"That one was easy. The mounting bolts were reverse threaded, with a pair of open contacts. Twist the bolt left and the buttons touch. . . . But the clod who put it together marred the boltheads with his torque driver; clear as buffed pylex to spot. Pick a number, Orden."

"Two."

"Two it is."

> *"Though my skip's gone on too long,*
> *It is surely going fast;*
> *Though I feel a little pain,*
> *In an hour it will have passed.*
> *Only instruments are true*
> *Out upon the silent Blue."*

Two was even . . . easier: a radiator fin slid in a groove, with a feather-switch beneath it. Silicone sealant stuck it in place. Number Eight had hairlike wires wrapped over the mounts, waiting to be broken; they were bridged first. Number One had a pin riding in a crooked keyway; Bajan sprayed insulating paint over the contact surfaces and pulled the cylinder free.

After it trailed a thin black cable.

"*Molly,*" cried Obeck uselessly, but someone else was watching: *Condor* was already turning on its Outriggers as the laser fired, the bright pulse missing Bajan's shoulder by centimeters and the right Outrigger's coils by less. Bajan's hands opened wide, her gloves smoking; she groaned in Obeck's ear and swung down on her cable like a pendulum, away from the Outrigger, the laser, the bomb, toward the Blue.

Condor turned again, sharply; waves of light flashed around the skid Obeck could see, and for the first time ever OutSide he felt inertial force, a strange and uneven drag. Kondor had stopped singing, and the only sound was the hard breathing in Obeck's earphone—and his own chest. Bajan crumpled into a ball, three meters from the Blue, then two, then one—

The ship leaned into its turn, compressing the Outrigger fluidics, and Bajan's right arm snapped out. There was a brilliant flare, and he thought that her fingertips had touched it —but there she still was . . . swinging rapidly back toward the hull, propelled by Kondor's swing of *Condor* and her own toss of a tool.

Swinging back toward the bomb.

And again Kondor leaned on the grips, but there was no time. As Bajan tugged grip-gauntlets over her ragged gloves to stop the outgassing, her left shoulder collided with the bomb frame. It trembled; an edge, its glue overstressed, shifted.

"You've forced us to this," said the cabin-steward voice, and four lasers flared at the tritium core.

Holding laser and tool gingerly, Bajan snipped the black wire to the dangling fifth gun—the one short of detonation—and pushed it back into place. "That's called a spite wire," she said. "Setting the gadget off is one thing—but that's just *mean.*" Her voice was very light; Obeck suspected pain and some shock. He looked at the pressure suit in his size in its case on the wall; but when he finished looking she was already at the lock, with a boot hooked to turn the handwheel.

> *"Someone's waiting on some world*
> *As my mem'ry of her dies.*
> *Can't see the color of her hair*
> *Or the color of her eyes.*
> *She might even have been you*
> *Here upon the silent Blue."*

The damage to Bajan's hands was minor, her gloves having taken the worst; Obeck sprayed her fingers with Amnifoam, gave her a mild jolt of TraumaStat and a drop of analgesic, and in moments she was floating. Obeck draped her flight jacket over her shoulders and guided her to the conroom, vectored her into the Engineer's seat.

"You said . . ." she told the back of Kondor's head, "you weren't gonna watch."

Without turning, Kondor said, "Once you called me a ship-killer."

"Y'are . . . but only of other people's ships."

Obeck drifted toward the conroom door, knowing that again he had survived but failed.

"We're coming up on Bakunin OutSide," said Kondor. "Wonder if that damned Sixer speaker is going to remind us not to stop?"

"If it does, I'll go back out and smash it," said Bajan, quite clearly. "Bust all their triggers, nearly get shot by a cheating spite-trap, and *then* have it detonate because their *own lousy glue* was loose. I hope the gashead that built it is in our welcoming party, because I'm gonna kill him with my bare"—

she flexed her fingers, winced—*"feet."*

Kondor turned in his seat then, very gently raised one of Bajan's foam-slick hands, very gently kissed it.

Obeck paused in the doorway, no longer feeling the intruder, no longer having won to lose; the relationship was now defined. They were all players in the same game. He began to feel that—early in the day as it was—there might even in the end be joy.

And then the Blue rose like a wave around them and the universe went mad.

Chapter 8
A Masque of Anarchy

As the floor tilted, Obeck dove for the Navigator's seat, pulling the lap belt tight. Bajan pressed herself back with knees against her console. Kondor's back muscles tightened visibly as he pulled the grips, touching pads for more fluidic assistance.

The Nav displays blinked to life before Obeck and showed him absolutely nothing of use: impossible angles and values, the main display just tumbling an empty horizon over and over. The gravcounter had ticked past 19 and was still going, though there was no weight at all; a high-gee alarm beeped shrilly.

Obeck turned his head to look past Kondor out the viewround. The Blue dropped away before *Condor's* nose, as if the ship were raised on a pedestal in the plane; then they were skidding down its side. Again there was torsion, like acceleration inertia but uneven. The Blue rose like a wall ahead and another alarm sounded furiously, signifying nothing.

And then the . . . ripple was gone, the Blue flat as always; Obeck touched for the rear-looking camera, saw only the pillars of the Bakunin system. The Nav boards were dark and quiet and stable, showing zero gravity, zero velocity, zero anomaly.

Kondor's eyes were locked dead ahead, his hands like ebony carvings on the grips. Bajan leaned her elbows on her boards, her knees still raised, shaking her head to clear it. Her hair floated in the z-gee.

"That was a *ripple?*" she said.

"It was nothing like a ship lost Out," said Kondor.

Obeck did not need to ask why he spoke so assuredly. "But what *was* it?" Obeck asked, and there was silence.

After a few minutes, Bajan asked Obeck for another drop of analgesic. He stirred it into the last of the Embassy wine. She drank it, said, "Wake me when the war starts," closed her eyes, and was instantly asleep. Obeck fastened her belts loosely and was suddenly very tired himself; he went back to the bedrooms, leaving Kondor alone with the vector and the con.

Obeck fell, or was thrown, into deep water. It was the color of water, at any rate; a warm fluid, very thick, dragging on the limbs. Crushing against the chest.

He reached up to the surface, which was so bright it hurt his eyes, touched it, pushing fingers into it.

But not through, for the surface was solid, like glass. But stronger than glass; he pounded it with both fists, making only faint sounds, barely feeling the impacts. His hands were gray, in gray sleeves. He moved close: the glass had a crystalline pattern that broke the light from above into rainbows. Radial crystals, six pointed.

Ice.

And Obeck knew why he moved so slowly, why he felt so little; he was numb and freezing to death. He hammered on the ice again, and his fists froze to it. With nothing to brace against, he could do no more than wait, suspended, for a breath—

"Orden," said Kondor from the interphone, and Obeck awoke. He floated facedown in the cushioned cylinder of the bed, his hands pressed against the plush. He touched the small phone. "Yes, David."

"We'll be In in fifteen minutes."

"I'll be there." Obeck touched the catch and opened the side of the bed, drifted out. He took off his sleep-rumpled whites, tore the wrap from a fresh set.

He opened a flat, thin case. Within was the twinkle and sheen of metal and silk, bars and ribbons of rank and Royal honor. Their brilliant colors were absent now, of course, but it did not matter; the Service heralds had designed the patterns to be readable In or Out. Prominent in the jewelbox was a brooch with linked copper ovals, set with a fire opal, and a copper ring with a matching stone. Obeck lifted them out carefully. They were the dress metal of a Privy Consul, and he might have only this one chance to wear them.

"Red ruby *light*, Orden," said Bajan as Obeck entered the conroom.

Kondor glanced back. "You look like one of Molly's boards in an alert. How much of that hardware is real?"

"All of it," said Obeck. "This one's for being from Riyah Zain. This one's for knowing samech-sign—"

"For *what?*"

"The Human-Samech Communications Ribbon. Most of them are on that level. It's not considered proper to attend a social function with your chest bared. You've got to look for quality, not quantity."

Kondor shook his head. "And we thought *we* played games." He reached down on his control stand, touched pads. "Here we go. Heard much about Longshot, Orden?"

"It's not a good place for a summer home."

"Word does get around."

Obeck said, "Since you mention it—how have these people managed to stay ahead of us? First talkative bombs and now an ambush party. They . . . haven't *got* Blue radio, have they?"

"They're using couriers with the flux-breakers pulled," said Kondor, "dragging high gee all the way. It saves better than an hour and a half at each end of the skip—and three hours' lead is all they need. For 'anarchists' they're damn well organized."

"Sounds like a chapter from Thorn's book."

"Who else?"

"You mean he—"

Kondor pulled back on the controls, and the Outriggers made their only sound—the long, low note, as of a bass viol, of the gold pulling free of the Blue. Without a pause *Condor* revolved, putting spine to Blue, and the scanning band wiped down the viewround. Obeck tingled, scalp to spine to soles, and then space was black again.

From behind Obeck came a whining, scratching sound. "It's talking again," he said, and went back to listen.

The bomb, no longer tight against *Condor*'s hull, spoke

with a handicap. It was saying: *"—no resistance, and will follow them down. Again, you will hold station precisely here until these vessels—"*

Through the port Obeck could see stars that moved and blinked: marker and formation lights. Away, above, hung Longshot, gibbous, brown and blue; it flashed too, with lightning. Obeck closed the conroom door, flicked imaginary dust from his sleeve, and leaned into a couch to await capture.

Three ships approached: a blocky freighter, an open-framed construction carrier, and a bat-winged scoutship mounting three power guns and two rotary pods of killerfish—a home-made pocket destroyer.

There was a clang beneath *Condor* and Bajan's voice on the interphone: "Our noisy friend's just separated. I think they're going to show off a little more for us."

They did. One of the scout's guns glowed and fired; there was a flash of light from not far below *Condor*.

"Were they scared of a heroic gesture?" said Bajan. "And I was so careful with it." Obeck heard Kondor's voice muttering in the background, away from a phone, and the interphone pinged off. *Condor—Cordell Hull* again—began to move on ions.

There was a palace corridor saying about Longshot to the effect that the Realm contained fifteen inhabited planets but only fourteen habitable ones. It was as true as any such saying ever was. Luna had no air, Periwinkle no land, Aschpunkt no resources; Longshot had all of these—but uncertainly. The world was young, stormy, hot beneath its crust, and unstable. The weather was beyond the normal storm-control methods, and the earth shifted by the hour.

The ships—*Condor/Hull* at the center, the armed scout over its spine—skimmed into air, above dark clouds. Obeck watched from the port, then unfolded his seat display and got a repeat of the radar trace, watching rain and turbulence and the other ships.

Together they banked. Cloud wisps blew by the side ports, then they entered dense cloud illuminated from within by lightning strokes. Rain sprayed the pylex.

A flash on the radar caught Obeck's eye. Jagged lines ran down either side of the display, jittering by: cliffs. They were in a valley less than a thousand meters wide, its sides and floor completely invisible. Obeck thought about going back to the conroom, to his Nav chair. But he did not. He was not playing a Navigator's part this trip—just as this ship was not *Condor* and its pilot was not David Kondor.

They dropped below the clouds and the cliffs could be seen: black rocks, sharp, though sponge cake would have been as deadly in a crash. The end of the valley was visible, barely five km ahead, in a box of cliffs and clouds; landing strobes flared through downpour, and the radar showed pad markers but no TALAN system.

Kondor did not need TALAN, even in darkness and lightning and rain—still, he wobbled a bit on landing, playing his part. The other ships set straight down, though a gust caught the freighter and it settled off-center to its pad. People in raincapes ran from a shelter, fixing cables to the ships' legs.

Obeck stood, feeling the drag of gravity returned, walked slowly across the lounge. As he reached the port opposite, the valley was lit up end to end by a lightning stroke. Blue-colored light showed fissured rock, scrub lichens contorted by wind, a stream that looked like black glass. Raindrops were strobe-frozen in midair. And bleached white were clustered building blocks, without a mainframe to hold them together, raised off the ground on struts. The architecture of quake and flood.

Behind Obeck the hatch clicked; he turned. Standing in the opening was a person in an electrostatic raincape; it flapped in the wind, showing wool trousers of a tartan plaid tucked into black boots. A battered helmet and visor hid most of the face. In the hands was a metal device, pointing prongs at Obeck, probably a tool and certainly a weapon.

Two more people slipped past the first, scouted out the lounge. "Where's the crew?" said one, loudly but not unpleasantly.

"In the conroom."

One of the armed group went to the conroom door, tapped the wall interphone. "For now, we only want your passenger. You can stay here if you want—but if you try to slip off, or lift, we'll slice you." He turned back to Obeck. "You're coming with us."

"Yes, I'd rather supposed that."

A raincape was unfurled and tossed over his shoulders, and they went down the stairs into the storm. The cape fluttered, throwing off drops so that Obeck walked in a cloud of fog. He had only a light hood, no helmet, and water blinded him—which might, he realized, be intentional.

Shortly they were under a metal roof that roared with rain,

and Obeck's vision cleared enough that he could see the stairs leading up to the building block—and, to one side and many meters away, a ship that was definitely a courier of *Montjoie II*'s class.

A door opened for them, closed behind them. The raincapes were removed and hung up to recharge. More doors, then—some with raised thresholds and gasket rings. There was a tremor through the floor and one of Obeck's escorts looked up sharply; but it passed.

Obeck noticed small details like the guard's twitch, the way the door controls operated, the small black-handled knives the people wore in their boots. He supposed that it would be useful to know all this when the time came to escape, but that was not why he watched so closely. He did it because he was terribly frightened, of the storm and the weapons and the prospect of pain and death, and the watching and noting kept him away from panic.

The guard in front of Obeck put a key in a hole and stepped to one side as the door opened, motioning Obeck through. He thought only after taking the first irrevocable step of what might be waiting beyond. The door closed.

He was in a square room, six or seven meters on a side. In the center was a large trestle table, bare, lit by spotlights. The ceiling was too dark to see. On one wall was a window, multiple panes of pylex, with an awning outside; it looked down on the pads, toward the open end of the valley. The other walls were hung with dark cloths, like blank tapestries; a bit of white peeped above a fold, and Obeck saw it was a map, curtained off. Something I'm not supposed to see, he thought, and if they were just going to kill me that wouldn't matter. But he was not much comforted, because of the room for pain remaining.

A door opened in the far wall; three persons came in. Two hung back in the semidarkness. Obeck could guess why; he could see their rifles. The third moved into the light. He wore brown woolen robes in three or four layers and a helmetlike cloth cap. Not a Longshooter, then; a Bakunen. His face was old, marked by the revi needle around the eyes and on the right cheek, which was flatter than the left—some old injury. Bakunen used up their capacity for revi younger than all but the vainest youth.

A large hand went to one of the table spots, twisted it into Obeck's eyes. "Copper," the man said in a coarse voice. "You know what we call copper, where I lived, Queen's-man?

Copper's our piss. Silver's our bones, gold our blood, radon our breath, and we piss copper." He moved the light down. "I am Arich sankt Efer."

Obeck knew the name, from his time as Data Unit for the Bakunin Situation Committee; it was not a reassuring name to know. Sankt Efer was a Bakunen Active, committed to independence for his world by "any reasonable means," which for sankt Efer meant simply "any means." There had been some incidents, some deaths, some cries in the night. Eventually the Bakunen themselves had exiled sankt Efer. He claimed that the syndics had been duped and coerced. In truth they had become frightened of him, and Bakunen did not frighten easily.

Not nearly so easily as did Orden Obeck.

"My time is limited, diplomat," said sankt Efer, without feeling of any sort. "I will ask a question. You will answer and you will not lie, or I will kill you. Do you understand?"

"Yes," said Obeck, not certain that he did.

"The first diplomat I took had some tapes and papers. He hid them from me, on his ship. I would like to be spared the trouble of searching for them. If you have duplicates of these documents, give them to me and you may go."

"In the event of capture, a Destruct would have been executed on any—" Obeck's ELI-3 was unsteady, imperfect.

"The documents were not destroyed, of course. You either did not know this or did not think I would. I give you one more chance: tell me where the documents may have been hidden, and if they are there I will let you go."

"There's no such place—I mean, no standard place, except the vault, and that's not secretly located." Thoughts of defection and treason again intruded. Was sankt Efer testing his loyalty? He had, Obeck knew from the files, little enough respect for it.

"They are not in the vault. Bakunen children could open your vaults. That is all your chances, diplomat."

Obeck's throat tightened. "Are you going to . . . torture me?"

"Of course not," said sankt Efer. He reached inside his outermost robe and drew a large-caliber pistol, its satin finish shining in the direct light. In a voice suddenly rather soft he said, "Did you want me to?" and pointed the gun at Obeck's heart.

Too afraid to close his eyes, Obeck stared at the gun, the hard metal making him think of *Condor* outside. Would sankt Efer try to kill Bajan and Kondor? He won't do it as easily as this, Obeck thought. Or would he let them go, ignorant of who and what they really were? David Kondor would not leave his ship behind. While he lived.

And nothing, *nothing* I could have said could have made any difference at all, thought Obeck, awaiting the bullet. If I jumped aside—came down on his arm—what's the worst that could happen? I could get killed?

But he did not move.

The door behind sankt Efer opened and a man stepped through, carrying a mechanical assembly. Sankt Efer turned; the light showed the newcomer to be broad shouldered, wearing a lapped and pleated jacket of red leather. His face and hands were almost white in the light. Obeck nearly cried out in joy and relief.

"On the table, Toranaga," said sankt Efer, and the man put the machine down. Obeck tensed to move; then he saw that it was not Thorn.

The chin was too broad, the hairline too low, the fingers too thick; the walk was wrong, much too stiff. Obeck looked on for a moment, hoping to pierce a brilliant disguise. But it was not Thorn, and the fear came back like a cresting wave. The lining of Obeck's white gloves rubbed unpleasantly against his sweat-wet palms. He did not want to be afraid; how better to die than in the Service, gallantly? But he did not feel gallant. Just afraid. Now that the game was over.

Wasn't it?

Sankt Efer was muttering to Toranaga; the gun was still in his hand but no longer leveled on Obeck. The wave of fear broke, and in the trough was cool, calm anger . . . and more thoughts beside. He's a mark, Obeck thought. Play him. Play him, dammit!

"A starship is a most complex machine," Obeck said, "with myriad spaces under and between; and if one searched unsure of what was sought one might explore for weeks, uncovering naught—and if it were in subtle hull's disguise, might one discard, or yet destroy the prize." The ELI-3 rhythms, controlled this time, had caught sankt Efer's attention—better than Obeck had hoped; he saw the dilation of sankt Efer's pupils. Toranaga's eyes were in shadow, but his body was rigid; he was unmoved. Still, still.

It's not hypnosis, Obeck had been taught, not nearly so. It's only a persuasion technique. Still he had hated it, as counterfeit coin of communication. And now that he had the coin spinning on the table, how would it fall, and what would he buy?

"You want a word pried loose from someone's tongue," Obeck went on, before the spell could break. "Yet what the drill and prybar can't achieve a slow erosion can. Do you believe that truth is played on harps that are unstrung?"

Sankt Efer tapped his pistol's barrel against the device on the table. "Later, Toranaga," he said. "And send Calhoun here." The man in red nodded and shuffled from the room. Sankt Efer turned to Obeck. "You think he would tell you?"

Obeck said nothing; it was time for the stall, to let the mark con himself a bit. He took a glance at the gadget. A metal plate on its side read MASPAC XP 4. There were lights on the side as well, small lights . . . Obeck thought of the base of the talking bomb; one of these might have fitted inside, showing its lights.

"Are you an investigator, diplomat?"

"I have been." *So you were watching.*

I have a report of an investigator and causer of disturbances. There are a great many holes on this unpleasant world, diplomat. If you cause a disturbance, I will throw you down a hole, and when it closes there will be nothing of you to find."

There was no useful answer to that.

"Very well, diplomat. I will put you together with your colleague. And I will listen for good news . . . but not, I warn you, for anything else."

Obeck was escorted to a door. It opened on a dark room; a long rectangle of light, split by Obeck's shadow, fell in. The edge of a table seemed to float by itself, and something moved in a corner of the room. A rifle touched Obeck's back and he crossed the doorway. The door closed behind him with a multiple clank of bolts.

There was a little light inside: a bluish betaglow strip, and a window, too narrow to possibly crawl through, showing the rain and the lightning. In the white flash Obeck saw that the movement in the corner was a man in white clothes.

Dr. Bishop sat on the floor with his back against the wall and his knees elevated, just as he had in another locked room many k-hours ago; but this time Obeck was the one in costume.

And Bishop was the one hungry. The light had shown his Royal eyes sunken in pits, his cheeks hollow. The next bolt showed the table bare, the toilet a sandcloset, and no sink or faucet. Suddenly Obeck knew what sankt Efer had meant by *not listening*.

"Full Court glitter, I can see . . . Consul's copper? Well. If we had a Secretary and a files clerk we could open a Mission." The voice was unquestionably Dr. Bishop's, though it was no more than a whisper. "Who are you, then, Consul?"

I only wish I knew, Obeck thought, but said, "I'd hoped you would recognize me, Doctor."

"I can barely *see* you. No lights here. And no food . . . but do you know, I don't think he's being cruel. I think he just can't be bothered."

Obeck knelt, wrote CAN YOU READ SIGN? on the taut, papery skin of Bishop's palm.

"Can't understand, sorry. Should have learned that. Too late—" Lightning flashed again; in the too-white light Bishop looked like a skeleton in shrouds. "Mr. Obeck . . . isn't it? Sir Orden, I believe, now."

"Yes, Doctor."

"Knight . . . somewhat errant, aren't you? Or did someone appoint a Special Subcommittee for Suicidal Rescues?"

Obeck smiled, but that was all he could do.

"I suppose you were sent after the pouch. It's hidden, of course. Sankt Efer won't find it." Bishop shifted position, then moved back, his joints audible. "Not even you would find it . . . unless I told you . . . and you escaped, of course."

Obeck felt sick. He looked up, but no pickups were visible —only darkness. He could not play any further. He had no plan now—not even to stay alive. "Sankt Efer's listening, Doctor."

"Metternich's ghost, I know he is." Bishop paused, working his jaw, trying to raise moisture. Obeck chewed his tongue, but he had none to give.

Finally Bishop whispered, "So let's pray, and sing, and tell old tales, and take upon us the mystery of things as if we were gods' spies. . . ." Thin fingers circled Obeck's wrist, and he was afraid of his teacher's madness until he saw its method. Or thought he did, or hoped so. He picked up the quote: "And we'll wear out in a walled prison, packs and sects of Bakunen that ebb and flow by the moon."

"Listen carefully, Arich sankt Efer, thou Bakunen clown," said Bishop as loudly as he could manage. "This is one of my students, a rare good one, and I'll make a bargain with you for him. Let him go, and I'll tell you where the goods are."

"You *can't*, Doctor," said Obeck, wishing his heart were more in it.

"Nothing's worth an infinite amount. The Lost Order wasn't what whupped Bobby Lee, was it?"

"No, but—"

"Houston Chamberlain told the truth, didn't he?"

"He—" Obeck was lost. He did not recall the reference, but Bishop's look said it was important; he was being told tales under the jailer's nose, and he must interpret them correctly, even if they took him no further than the tapes and DESTRUCT key.

Obeck stood as the guards came in. Dr. Bishop did not; he could not. A guard slung his rifle and carried the Doctor out.

When they reached the map room, sankt Efer was talking to a woman in a flight jacket—Calhoun, Obeck supposed. "The Patron is generous but he is not a spendthrift," said sankt Efer, and brought his hand down on the MASPAC XP 4. "And that applies especially to *these*. I do not care how nervous you may be—these are not to be destroyed without my express—" He turned as the guards came in. "Enough, Pilot."

Calhoun said, "But I know I've seen that ship before, and I—"

Obeck's heart jumped. He had to revector the conversation before it led to *Condor*. He cleared his throat in the manner normally prescribed for large treaty conferences—Dr. Bishop smiled approvingly—and then the floor trembled again, rocking all the buildings on their sprung struts, shaking the lamps. Bishop's eyebrows rose.

And sankt Efer said, *"Later*, Calhoun," and turned to the diplomats. Calhoun, who had clutched at a doorframe during the tremor, released it, pulled at her cap, and left.

"I'll have a sip of water ere I speak," said Dr. Bishop. He was given a glass, drank part of it, with difficulty. "Now put the young man back aboard his ship, and I will show you where the parcel is." Only a short speech, through a dry throat, yet Obeck felt himself nodding to the rhythm of the ELI-3 as spoken by a master.

Sankt Efer was quiet, with a puzzled look. "I am not such a fool . . ." He shook his head. "No, only a fool would return the situation to its former state." He seemed to draw strength from the possibility of foolishness. "I will . . . kill you, Envoy. Yes," he said, gathering momentum, "I am going to kill you, as an insulting, bad diplomat. So if you wish to insure the safety of your student, you must tell me honestly where the documents are, and when I find them, I will let him go. But . . . he will stay in your apartment until they are found. I hope you understand."

Dr. Bishop opened his mouth, but only coughed, and then twisted in the guard's arms; the water had knotted his stomach.

Sankt Efer went to Bishop, put out a hand, and gripped the

Doctor's shaking head; Obeck started, and was touched in warning, but there was no violence in sankt Efer's hold. There was even a perverse tenderness. "Tell me now. Before you cost the young man his life."

Bishop waved to Obeck, and he moved close, ignoring the armed guard and trying to ignore sankt Efer. Close, in the better light, Obeck realized how much he had overestimated Bishop's age; they were less than a hundred k-hours apart, a dozen Zaini years, but it had seemed three or four times that.

Bishop said, "Don't forget, ever . . . the class the Gautama put us in . . . and how few we share it with." He touched Obeck's wrist, then spoke to sankt Efer. "The vault."

"The vault is empty."

"The *inner* vault. Key the control . . . R-two-V-R, then the OPEN bar three times."

"R-two-V-R. Rachel the Second Valeria, Regina," said sankt Efer. "I never said you were not clever, in your parochial manner." He looked at the tartan-trousered man who patiently held Bishop. "Now take him out and throw him down a hole. But shoot him before you do."

The man walked away with his quiet burden. A hand tightened on Obeck's shoulder and a rifle pressed his spine.

"Do not cause a disturbance," said sankt Efer. "The mother of our child voted to bar me from my home, and what can you say that will hurt me any more? Bakunin will not have me back until I overthrow the Brazen Bitch, so what can you do that will deter me from trying? There are only two things that will stop a soul cold, diplomat: death and shame. That is why your teacher is dead, and you will be let free as soon as the documents are recovered. I can afford it. Because, you see," he said without malice, "should anything untoward happen, I will surely confess who offered to pry the secret from the late Dr. Bishop . . . Would you like this before you go back to the room?"

Sankt Efer held out the half-full glass of water.

Obeck lay on the cell floor, on his side, knees against his chest, back close to the wall. The storm had stopped, the window was dark; the betaglow strip was unaffected by the occasional tremors.

He wore a belt, but there was nothing to suspend it from. The pin of his copper Service brooch was long enough to reach his heart, barely; but he did not think he could push it through. More likely he would stop halfway, pull it out when the pain began. Maybe if he fell prone upon it. . . .

The thoughts were serious, yet abstract; had he a real weapon—a knife or a gun with a single shot—he thought he could fight. No, that was wrong. He could not fight. But surely he could die well, if there was such a thing.

There was, of course; so died Terrance Bishop. Obeck thought of R-2-V-R OPEN times three and smiled.

A heavy tremor shook the room; Obeck was the only loose object within. He wedged himself into a corner. If the window shattered it would be no help. But suppose the door sprung?

The rumble ended, and the silence began again.

The door clanged open, and the awful light and the human shadows split the room; Obeck edged away, then scrambled to sit up. He could at least die on his feet, if not well. "You should have closed the vault first," he said, unevenly.

Hands lifted him, a man's and a woman's. In the light he saw the broad shoulders and red coat and wondered if sankt Efer might be dead and Toranaga risen, and if Toranaga would shoot him before throwing him in a hole.

"Blue hell, Orden, *come on*—his eyes, Molly—the shits haven't hurt his—"

"I'm all right, David," Obeck said, meaning it more than ever he had, "Molly. Thorn." He had no water for tears.

"Do you know where the documents are?" Thorn said.

"Microphones—"

"Not anymore. Only emergency power."

"Then yes, I think I do. There's something else—I think it's related to our Blue ripple." He briefly described MASPAC XP 4.

"It is of secondary importance," Thorn said.

"It sounds well worth stealing," said Kondor. "We'd better split up anyway—feel like making a side stop, Molly?"

"For *that*—around the moon."

"Go then," said Thorn. "I *must*—" He broke off.

Kondor nodded, said, "Take care of Orden," and left with Bajan.

"You weren't really Toranaga—were you?"

"Who's Toranaga?"

Obeck told him.

"Perhaps I'll be mistaken for him. Good." They left the cell. A moment later, they rounded a corner and confronted two Longshooters: one carried a rifle, the other a stack of books.

"Tor—" said the armed one, then clutched his throat.

Obeck turned and saw a whisper-pistol in Thorn's hand. He pulled the trigger again; the gun made a sound no louder than a throat clearing for small Committee sessions and the man with the books fell, burying himself under paper. He bled slightly, down the cheek.

Obeck took a step toward him. He looked at Thorn. "Was it necessary to—"

"Yes. Come, Orden."

They went through a door. Inside, before a chart table, stood the Pilot, Calhoun; she was lit from below by a table lantern, giving her sudden smile a demonic aspect. "*Thorn?* What are you—"

The whisper-pistol leveled and spoke. Calhoun stood for a moment, a hand where her right eye had been, then shook her head slightly and folded to the floor.

"She was very good," said Thorn, and took Obeck's wrist, pulling him to a trapstair across the room. He lifted the door and pointed down, keeping the gun on the room door.

"You knew her?" Obeck demanded.

"We flew four patrols."

Suddenly Obeck understood. Thorn's carefully constructed identity was in danger, here, now, and anyone who saw him in this act must never speak of it. Obeck was angry with him then; why had he come, knowing he must kill and kill and—

Because he said he would come, he thought, turning the hate again inward, where it had begun. Because he thought it was worth the risk.

It was time, Obeck decided, that he should risk something.

"Thorn. Is *The Pale Horse* nearby?"

"You must go with David."

"That's not— Look, if I don't get the papers off—no one gets them."

Thorn said simply, "How long do you need?"

Obeck looked at his wristec. "If I don't have them in fifteen minutes, I never will."

They went down the spiral trapstair. Thorn reached under his jacket and produced another gun, a black rocket pistol. Obeck took it with thanks but no pleasure, put it in his coat pocket. The coat, far from crisp, sagged out of line.

On the ground the wind was up, and people were running; an alarm had evidently been raised. *No surprise, with corridors full of blood*. Thorn pointed out *Montjoie II*, touched Obeck very lightly on the shoulder, and then was gone without sound of footstep or breeze of passing. Obeck moved on.

The stairway to the ship was unguarded. Gun in his pocket, Obeck climbed it.

The ship was a ruin inside. Carpets were torn up, plates pried back, lectras slashed and leaking inks; the couch cushions were taken completely to pieces.

In the central corridor the vault door was open, half off its hinges, unclosable. The fittings around it were twisted, covered with white ash; the control pads were molten. Obeck smelled burnt hair. R-2-V-R OPEN-OPEN-OPEN, this thousand hours, was the sequence for CRISIS DESTRUCT; and with the vault door *open* . . .

The class the Gautama put us in, and how few we share it with. Any student of Dr. Bishop's who did not recall that Parkinson reference would have ended in the Zaini Manipool.

The Indian rules of warfare enjoined the soldier to spare the timid, the intoxicated, the insane, the negligent, the unprepared, the aged, women, children, and Brahmans. To this list Gautama is said to have added ambassadors and cows.

Obeck paused before the kitchen and dialed a glass of milk. The delivery unit clattered and thumped—and delivered a dispatch case on a tray with dinnerware and paper serviette. With a cry of joy, Obeck took it from the chute. It was cold, fresh from the cooler. He tucked it under his arm, turned.

Arich sankt Efer stood, blackened and terrible, in the corridor. There was no hair at all left on his face, and the skin was white with blisters; his eyes were bloody. His wool robes had burned, as had the hair on his chest and arms. His fingers were black talons.

He took a step; Obeck took a step backward, and thought, No way out that way.

There was a roar of turbines overhead, and they both looked up; Obeck realized that he needed only stall for a minute more and he would win. He would die, but well.

Sankt Efer put a hand on the case. Obeck saw and heard burnt flesh cracking; clear fluid leaked out. He flinched, and the case came free. Sankt Efer said something unintelligible through his ruined lips and turned away from Obeck, carrying the case.

Obeck's sagging arm brushed the pistol. He drew it, and hesitated, as sankt Efer staggered toward the door and Thorn's engines whined.

Death and shame.

Obeck fired.

Sankt Efer's step faltered as the rocket hit him and exploded —*Blue heaven, Thorn!*—but the Bakunen was now literally beyond pain.

Obeck fired again, wildly; the little warhead went *pam* against a wall. He gripped his wrist to stop his trembling and fired. Sankt Efer's left knee went *pop*, red and white, and the man fell down.

Obeck's wristec gave him eight seconds to live, seven when he finished reading it. He ran to sankt Efer's body. Six. Pushed at him. Five. Grabbed the case. Four. Stepped through the hatch. Three. Looked up, and, dizzy, lost balance in the downdraft and fell down the stairway, two, one, zero.

One hand still on the case, he lay on the pad, illuminated by *Montjoie*'s stairway lights, realized Thorn could see him. See the case. Was holding his fire.

A shadow cut into the hatchway. Arich sankt Efer, dead twice, risen twice. *What can you do to deter me?* Obeck groaned and began crawling, knowing how slow and white and visible he was.

The Pale Horse released an armed killerfish without igniting its motor; it dropped straight down to *Montjoie*'s spine and detonated. Yellow light flared from ports and hatch and splitting seams. Arich sankt Efer, any last words quite lost, fell within, and collapsing hulls enclosed him.

Thorn's turbines went very quiet off hover, and in a moment his deep-blue hull was lost to sight. Obeck stood; nothing seemed broken, though everything hurt. Clutching the case in both arms, he loped toward *Condor*, knowing that he had the papers and the mission and his life, and knowing that they had all cost too much.

PART THREE

The Knight on the Cross

Alas! How should you govern any kingdom,
That know not how to use ambassadors?

—*Henry VI, Part Three*, IV.iii

Chapter 9
Blind Chess

There was no pain, that was the strange thing.

Eight stainless-steel clamps held Privy Consul (Detached) Orden Obeck immobile but for his head. He could tilt it enough to see the colored wires that ran over and around him and most of the forty needlepoints piercing his skin. Then gloved fingertips—not samech fingers but as cold—pushed his head back, and flipped a latch, and then all Obeck could see was a bit of the corner between the ceiling and the wall.

Not three thousand meters away, in another part of the palace, Obeck knew the Queen was giving knighthoods, and David Kondor and Molly Bajan were there to get them. (Thorn was gone again, back to the Sixer anarchists who thought him their great red hope.) But Rachel II had already done that for Obeck, and so now her people did this. . . .

The Security officer's uniform was gray-green and plain, without even a badge of rank. He didn't need one. He was Royal Security, and that was all anyone needed to know. His face was young, handsome without prettiness. His hands were large and muscular and tough as lizard leather.

"The committee recommendation, Sir Orden," he said, "is that you volunteer for physical debriefing." Obeck read unconcern in his voice and terrible things in his hands.

"Am I—" said Obeck, thinking, Delicately, dammit, "under suspicion?"

"Naturally not."

"I've given a complete account." *Down to the glass of water and the things Bishop said that I still can't understand.* "There are no gaps or lapses in my memory."

"Naturally not." The officer paused, thoughtful; déjà vu, perhaps. "They would have inserted gaps only if the intent had been to discredit you. No one believes that was the intention." Then, with rising enthusiasm: "Gaps are rather obvious. Better technique is to insert slightly skewed memories that may even pass the first filters. And with selective refocusing . . . " The officer stopped, finally aware of himself.

Obeck thought, Right, man. I could con you out of the keys to Rachel's bedchamber, and said absolutely nothing.

After a beat, the officer reached below the bare desktop, tapped a hidden pad, produced a paper form. Obeck noticed it was indelible paper. The Security man said, "This is the consent for PD. Sign here and here."

"I returned the pouch, you know," said Obeck, staring hard at the paper.

"I don't know about that," said the officer. Then, quickly: "That is, I don't know the details of your mission. The report I read said it was concluded with relative success, but that you were imprisoned by the Bakunen. Tortured."

"Not—" Obeck stopped. How explain that he had not been, when he was not sure himself?

"By sankt Efer himself, on Longshot," said the officer to himself, a little dreamily. He was staring at Obeck's hands, which lay tensed in his lap.

How, indeed, explain anything to this officer, who was not a soul but an appendage, the speaking part of a committee organism? Once, during his life, Dr. Terrance Bishop had said, "A committee cannot be wrong—only divided. Once it resolves its division, then every part reinforces every other part and its rightness becomes unassailable."

Obeck looked at the paper, making no real effort to read it. It did not actually matter what it said. Only his name upon it would mean anything. And everything.

Physical debriefing . . . Obeck knew brave souls who were afraid of that phrase, and though he knew no one who had actually been through it, he was afraid of the general fear. "You said 'volunteer' . . . ?" he said weakly.

"PD was considered the most likely method to validate your record and return you to active duty," said the voice of the committee, "but physical debriefing is always voluntary."

Of course it was, Obeck knew; that was the most elementary semantic distinction. If it was involuntary it had some other name: Neural Probe or Pattern Interrogation or . . . the wires were the same. And the needles. And the steel.

"I'm not a spy," Obeck burst out. "I'm a diplomat, and—" A Knight of the Realm, he had almost said; but Security were not made Knights. Obeck suspected they enjoyed doing this to Knights, and the flicker in the officer's eyes proved him right. Carefully, Obeck said, "I had thought some consideration would have applied."

"Considerations did apply," said the officer in a changed tone, as if a different head of the beast were speaking. "The committee's decision was made very much under consideration." His head turned slightly, and Obeck knew in what direction. Toward the Queen, without whom they would not have considered at all what to do with Obeck.

Without her . . . Yet I wasn't silent, Obeck thought. *Qui tacet consentire;* silence gives consent. Thomas More had said that, at the end of his silence, before they took off his head. And him a knight as well.

Or had someone only said More had said that, in a play? Dr. Bishop again—"Are you puzzled, put off, offended by these forms, costumes, this language? Mask and buskins, that's what they really are. Ever since Shakespeare, theater has made better history than history has. Our history is only a masque of the past . . . just as diplomacy is the masque of government, and terrorism the masque of anarchy." And him a cousin of the Queen.

Something flashed light in one of the strong hard hands, but it was only a stylus, and the fingertips of the other hand were easing the form toward Obeck.

Obeck seized them and wrote. It was only his name he gave them, after all. They already had his life; he just ransomed a little of it.

There was no pain, though there should have been, between the needles and the steel. Then one of the PDTeam said something to another about enkephalin levels, and Obeck understood: acupoint needles were triggering his enkephalin system, loading his blood and brain with the chemicals of paradise, blocking and destroying pain.

Physical debriefing did not involve questions and answers. In the state Obeck was entering he might give any answer to any question. PD was an analytic examination of the neural pattern, a kind of search for signs that someone had been there to alter and cut and patch.

Gradually and from all directions Obeck was enveloped by a warm fog, supernaturally pleasant, not the sharp stressful thrill of physical ecstasy but a relaxed upwelling joy. Borne up by angels, he was not frightened anymore by the fear of others.

"Inducer running," said an angel from the fog. "REM state in twenty seconds."

REM sleep? Dream sleep. *"To sleep, perchance to . . ."*

It came to him, then, just faintly, what he might have to fear, whether or not there was pain to accompany it; but the enkephalin wave submerged all action. And then the sleepstate inducer put him into REM, in which all voluntary muscles are disconnected from action . . . the reason why, in a dream, one cannot run away, or even scream.

There are places where the night is endless. Waiting without hope for morning, the senses are paralyzed, so that sight lacks color, sound resonance; time is warped and communication impossible. And outside the fragile walls is a midnight landscape of emptiness, and desolation, and moons and stars that do not care at all.

The place could be a transit stop in an unfamiliar town, or a ship skipping the Blue OutSide, or the mind of a useless man.

Consul (Unassigned) Orden Obeck sat in an all-hours caffe, looking through the window at the thousand lights of the palace, diffused through a light rain. A maglarail streaked past, cometary, silent. High above, an orange flare and violet aurora were a weathercraft steering the winds.

Obeck's wristec chimed: the second hour of Novaya's twenty-five. He had come here in the last minutes of yesterday; so the time was really passing and dawn would come, no matter how it might seem.

He looked away from the black sky, at the tabletop, his persec and notepad upon it, his wrist and the wristec digits and the sleeve of his jacket. The sleeve was suede, brown, not white. Not white for many days. Still bearing the blue stripe of knighthood, however; they had not found enough to take that from him.

They had not found enough to do anything except give him a meaningless lateral promotion.

The caffe was dark except for the spotlit tabletops. Obeck could see or hear no one else. All around were wooden louvers, and dense green ferns hanging below dark skylights, and long window bands like a ship's, with the city lights outside as blurry stars.

He looked at his notepad, picked up his stylus, and wrote two words at the top of the page, underlining them to make column headings. The words were RESTRICTIONS and FREEDOMS. Under RESTRICTIONS he wrote:

> No active assignments
> Level 4 files access
> No audience with the Queen

He paused, took a sip of coffee, moved his hand to the FREEDOMS column, and held the stylus poised.

He put it down and drank more coffee. After the cup was empty he put the stylus away and folded the pad. He knew what word went there and he could not write it. Rain spattered the window, making little supernovae of the palace lights.

Obeck's head hurt. He reached to the order board for analgesic and a vial came up; he refilled his coffee cup and tapped in a drop.

And another.

And a third.

He rolled the vial over in his fingers. There was nothing on the label but a brand name and a maker's mark. No warnings, no dosage directions. Was there anybody who hadn't taken a drop? Was there anybody who had ever died from it?

Seven more drops and the vial was empty. Obeck stared at the rippling dark surface of the coffee, wondering. He could order another vial. He could order a dozen. Or . . . was some kind of alarm set off if one ordered a dangerous quantity, however much that might be? Did Emergency Medical come to pump out the stomach—and wash out—the bloodstream—

Obeck twisted as if his soul had touched the Blue. His arm swept the table and the cup went flying, trailing coffee, to crash and spatter five meters away. Obeck pressed back into his seat, totally tensed, all needles and steel, thinking, *no, no,* and nothing at all. Smooth cold fingers touched his forehead and he shuddered and tried to scream, but his lungs were voided. His eyes snapped open.

A samech was touching him with fingers as white as its uniform; it held a sweeper in its other hand and smiled pleasantly. Obeck's eyes flicked around, but no one human was watching.

He groped for the samech's palm, which was obligingly turned up. He wrote, SORRY—ACCIDENT—FELL ASLEEP, BAD DREAM.

The samech nodded as if it understood the whole message, which was doubtful, and signed, ANOTHER CUP, SIR?

NO, Obeck signed, not trusting his voice with even one syllable. THANK YOU. The samech nodded and stood still. Obeck, his way blocked, tensed again; then he slid a five-mark card into the pay slot. The samech smiled broadly and went to clean up the mess.

Obeck gathered persec and pad and went outside, stepping hesitantly away from the building. The rain was cool and gentle on the back of his neck; it lightened his mood in an instant. He began walking, loosening his jacket collar to let the rain run in, and as he walked his tension evaporated. He passed transit stop after transit stop, only taking to awnings and covered ways after his hair was thoroughly wet. After an hour he reached the edge of the Grounds and decided not to hazard the wet grass; he caught a car in to the General Apartments Block. On the way he plastered his hair straight down all around in a fake helmet-crop, so as not to startle the nightwatch.

He keyed the door to his rooms, went in, and without touching on the light walked to the window. The view from the forty-third floor included the white stone gridfront of the Trade and Commerce subbuilding, a stretch of the Grounds, and in the city proper the slender golden pyramid of Consolidated Vulcan, samech-makers, gunsmiths. Beyond the hundred-fifty-story tower, the horizon was beginning to lighten. Dawn was coming, as it would come every day until the end of the world.

Whenever that might be, thought Orden Obeck, and put his fingertips against the cool glass, looking straight ahead at the sunrise, not down at the hard ground below.

The Files Carrel had Obeck's name on its door, and except for the Master, his was the only key. As he closed the door, for a moment his body shielded the lock from view; in that time a small metal pin went from between his fingers into the mechanism. Obeck flipped the latch. It was not a heavy nor a shielded door, but now his really was the only key.

He tapped at the console, opened inquiry lines. After hesitating for a few seconds, glancing at the corners of the small room (there only *might* be cameras), he tapped PHYSICAL DE-BRIEFING, stared at the words as they stood on the display, then called for a global search: every reference mentioning or relevant to the topic. Feeling suddenly less bold, he delimited the search to sources released in the last twenty k-hours.

Not that his account had anything to fear. He had not been too surprised to get the assigned carrel he'd asked for—but they had additionally given him an unlimited disbursement of time. The carrel had a kitchen slot and a toilet; if not for the floor being cleared at 22:00 he could have lived there. He was not sleeping anyway.

All the computing power he could spend, in a private . . . locked . . . closed box.

He had filed four petitions against his removal from duty without firm evidence on formal charges. The first was ignored. The second was referred, which was the same thing. The third was politely but firmly refused.

The fourth returned with a statement from a Plans and Actions Superintendent, saying that if Sir Orden was idle, it was Sir Orden's own fault . . . and the clear and inarguable meaning was all that free machine time, just as the words *own fault* knelled their double meaning like a brazen gong.

Obeck's fingers drew back from the console. He looked up at the displays, wondering how long the search would take— hours, perhaps.

END RUN, said the display, and below that were three strings of words. NO MORE FOLLOWS or PARTIAL PRINT or EDITED. Just three titles.

Obeck touched the OFFPRINT bar. The paper slid out. Three titles. He hit FULL DOC, OFFPRINT again, and snatched the sheet from the bin.

PAGE 1 OF 1 PAGES
TEXT BEGINS:

1 **PROCEDURES FOR REQUESTING AND CLEARING** *PHYSICAL DEBRIEFING*
2 **Royal Security Intelligence Circular 108:14**

3 *PHYSICAL DEBRIEFING:* **AN EFFICACY STUDY**
4 **Munchner, Krone, and Wu Wei/Special Report to Royal Security**
5 **[This is a Acc Clear 4 Edit. Original is Acc Clear 7.]**

6 **SILVER VS. GOLD ELECTRODES IN** *PHYSICAL DEBRIEFING*

7 **Munchner/Journal of Electrochemical Medicine V620 #8 P67**

TEXT ENDS

NO MORE PAGES

Obeck was about to relimit the search, to everything published at any time, and then realized that there was no point. The phrase in the middle of the print said everything: *Original is Acc Clear 7.* When Obeck was a free soul—And how damnably brief that was, he thought—he had been only an Access 6. There *were* only nine grades, and Blue knew if Rachel II was a 9 herself.

No one would talk to him. There was no help. Everyone was either Security or terrified.

With great care Obeck tapped in the title of the Special Report. He knew very well how PD was authorized, and he hardly cared for the color of the needles.

READY TO PRINT, said the display. Obeck touched the bar and the pages spat into the bin, a plastic band binding them down the side.

It was a twenty-page pamphlet, though the last page was numbered 268; he held the ghost of the echo of the iceberg's tip. There was no Abstract, no Contents page, no graphs or charts (in a paper by the statistician Wu Wei?) and no results of the "Efficacy Study." What there was, in a tatter, was a raw description of the machinery—not much more than you could tell by being in it—and an outline of the purpose of the technique.

Obeck closed the pamphlet. He gripped the edge of the table, then turned sharply, rising, knocking his chair over, staggering to the toilet and vomiting until nothing was left—not long—and then a little longer.

He *had* to clear his mouth, and so got back to the kitchen slot and touched for charged water. He rinsed and spat. Then he dumped the cup out, crumpled and flashed it, before it could remind him again.

He looked at the slot, thinking on all he had learned lately about analgesic: five drops would stop the spasms. Ten would make him sleep without dreams. What would fifty do, on the emptiest of stomachs?

Not here, of course. Here they would find him—break down the door and take him out and *ask*—

He cleaned himself up with paper towelettes, took off his stained jacket and threw it over an arm. Before departing he cleared the console, shoved the report down the flash slot, and pulled the trick pin from the lock.

The floor secretary looked at Obeck closely as he logged out, but said only, "Day t'you, sir." Obeck nodded and walked, stiff as a ten-mark samech, to the elevators.

And waited, watching his blurred reflection in the metal doors.

And waited, mouth slimy and knees weak.

And watched the world snap-roll and the floor slam against first his knees, then his shoulder, then the side of his head. He was asked by someone if he could rise, but could not speak to say that he would be just fine. Then someone appeared in a doctor's coat, with an injector. Since he could not ask not to be made to sleep, he could only hope beyond all reason that the dose would be dreamlessly heavy. And he saw one more thing, but it was a memory, and so he repressed it.

He awoke and saw the memory again, and could not make her vanish this time. So he said, "Hello, Wixa."

She looked at the bed display, touched a pad, and said, "Well, you're that well oriented. Hello, Orden. Or should I call you Sir?"

"Only if I have to call you Doctor."

"Hey, I went to school a long time for that. You drive a hard bargain."

"What do you think *I* learned in school?" It was not so hard to be playful with her; it required no honesty. It could have been a nice and amusing interlude, until she spoiled it.

"Orden, how long have you been trying to kill yourself?"

He was silent, but the bed display betrayed the *blipblipblip* of his heart. He ran his tongue over his lips, tasting fruit.

"You're malnourished," she said, "your fluid and electrolyte balances are a mess, and you've been taking analgesics like the Kitchen used to salt the broccoli. Your kidneys had begun to fail, did you know that? We had to give you an organ revi . . . someday you'll want that revi, Orden."

He closed his eyes and turned his head.

"Furthermore, you're—" Her tone changed suddenly. "Orden, what's wrong?"

"There's no way I can tell you."

"I did finally get to be a doctor . . . but you never were much of a secret sharer, were you, Orden. Is this a state secret?"

He almost laughed; if it had been someone else, someone he had never known, he might have. Instead he said, "How long will I have to stay here?"

"Since you live in the Center, only another day or so."

"It couldn't have been so bad, then."

"Orden, you collapsed a hundred hours ago. This is the first time you've been above twilight sleep since then."

A hundred hours. And there had been no awareness, no memories—just a rather obvious gap. He wondered who had watched him while he was lost—

"Orden." She touched him, and he recoiled and rolled away from her with a shallow groan. "Orden, I'd like to help."

Obeck spoke very evenly. "Will you please go away? If you're through as a doctor, that is."

"Yes," she said, "but I'd still like to help."

"I appreciate the thought."

She took a few steps toward the door, paused. "If you should appreciate it enough, call me."

And she left him alone with his wretchedness and desolation.

Obeck sat on a bench in the green Palace Grounds, speaking to the persec open in his lap. ". . . but of course I can't appeal directly to her. The truth, David, is that . . ."

Obeck pressed STOP, pulled out the message cassette; then he replaced it and pressed the ERASE key. No point in it, he thought. David can't understand; he never would have gotten here. Thorn might understand—though how do I know that? —but I can't reach him. Molly's David's lady, not mine.

And being compromised, I risk compromising all of them.

Obeck looked up at a maglarail station some distance away, watching the train arrive; he thought.

There were fences guarding the tracks, but Obeck was an old fence-climber. He had calculated the time between departure signal and motion, the acceleration and braking distances, and knew just where and when he would have to jump so as to strike the coils and be struck by the train at the same time. And then all the Queen's horses and all the Queen's men—

Who taught me that verse? No matter. It was necessary that he not merely break, but be broken. He could not answer any more questions. *Not as long as I live—*

He felt quite calm and perfectly reasonable. And the reasonableness of it terrified him. He got up from his bench and walked by the station. He had been walking a great deal. When they released him from the hospital, a doctor had told him walking was healthy; Obeck had laughed out loud.

He wished they would make it rain.

The sun began to set behind the palace; the light caught the Con Vulcan tower, making it molten gold. It was a hundred and fifty floors, four hundred fifty meters high. An object falling from the fiftieth floor in Novaya's standard gee would hit the ground in five and a half seconds, traveling at fifty-four meters per second. From the hundredth floor, eight seconds, seventy-seven meters per second. From the peak, nine and a half seconds, ninety-three meters per second, three hundred thirty-eight kilometers an hour. Faster than a maglarail at full speed. Fast enough to answer all questions.

Below his feet were power conduits, multiple kilovolts sheathed in liquid helium that could make flesh crack like glass.

The elevator to his apartment had an escape hatch in its roof, and there was space for a man between the car and the shaft wall.

Obeck pushed his door closed and latched it, then leaned against it and sank to the floor. He put his face in his hands.

Some small-sound, real or imagined, made Obeck open his eyes wide to stare at the bedroom ceiling. The room was still, cool, darkened to shades of gray. Obeck lay twisted in the sheet, his legs bound by it; his right arm was pinned beneath him, his left stretched straight. It had the makings of an unspeakable dream.

He freed himself and tried to lie quietly but could not; in any position tension soon became discomfort, and discomfort pain. He had been strictly forbidden more than two drops of analgesic a day, and those were long gone.

Wixa had made him promise that . . . what had he said, to her or anyone, in the time he could not remember? A hundred hours . . . he had been assured that it would not further prejudice his position.

He had been told the PD would clear him.

His right fist tightened and he slammed it into the bed, millimeters from his outstretched left hand. The sweat was cold on his naked back, and he pulled up the sheet to be covered, but it slipped to the floor and exposed him.

His wristec read 02:36. It was the next day, he decided, and he could have two more drops.

He got up and went from the bedroom, not into the bath but the living room. He stopped beside the desk, reached under its top, and touched concealed keys in order. A piece of the side trim opened, and Obeck slid out a shallow drawer.

Within, upon the gray cloth lining, was a black L shape, very black indeed, the blackest thing in the world. It was the gun Thorn had given him, that despite best intentions had so far failed to kill anyone.

Here I am now, he thought, and the only wonder in the thought was that he had taken so long to arrive.

He reached down and touched the weapon, and the cold metal sent a shock up his fingertips so that he jerked away.

He touched the desk lamp on. A shadow crossed the drawer, but the gun was still there, black in the black, waiting. No one living had waited so patiently for him. It had been one of his few comforts these past days, knowing that it would be there when he was ready.

He was ready now.

He looked out the window at the night and the lighted windows. Other people were awake, of course. Others kept late hours. The world was round; somewhere someone was always awake.

But none of them was waiting for him. He reached for the gun. His hand revectored in flight, though, landing on the desktop by the call terminal. Tucked under its corner was a tiny white card with Wixa's name, a number, and the words ANY TIME.

He looked outside again. There were really a great number of lit windows. He lifted the handset and put a hand on the drawer. He touched the numbers, and the drawer did not close.

"Hello?" Not sleepily. If he broke circuit now—

"Hello?" again. Courtesy demanding some answer, even wrong number—

"I—hello, Wixa."

"Orden?"

"Yes."

"Orden, are you . . . do you want to talk, Orden?"

"I, ah . . . I'm sorry I bothered you, Wixa. Good night."

"*Orden!* Are you at home?"

He stopped, thinking, What does she know? What can she? What did I tell her? "I'm at home."

"Orden, stay put. Don't go anywhere and don't *do* anything. Do you hear me? I'll be there as quickly as I can."

"Alone?"

"Yes, of course alone. I want you to do two things, right now, Orden. Unlock your door, and then lie down, do you understand? Lie still and don't do anything else until I get there."

Obeck nodded to the blind handset and broke the connection. He went swiftly to the door and without hesitation unlatched it. *If this is all a . . . if Security comes through, not Wixa . . . well then, I'll know, won't I?*

But I don't believe that. To believe that, I'd have to be insane, and if I were insane . . .

He went to the bedroom, closed the door without latching it, lay down flat on his back.

If I were insane I might want to die, and I might want to live—but I wouldn't want both at once.

After a little while Obeck heard the swish of the door and a light footstep. "Orden?" came a voice, and then a small gasp and a metallic sound. A weaponish sound.

Obeck wound his heaviest robe around himself, pushed his feet into soft shoes, and opened the bedroom door.

Wixa had the gun out. She was working the manual feed, so the rockets fell one after another on the carpet. *"Don't—"* Obeck said, and took a step, and she held the gun back from him and scattered the spilled rounds with a toe.

"—explosive," Obeck whispered, pointing at the rounds, and Wixa's look went from determination to horror.

"Oh, my . . . " She put the gun down, behind herself. "I didn't know you had—"

"It was a gift from a friend," said Obeck, and hoped that Thorn would forgive him.

"Will you tell me now what's wrong?"

"Is that what you came for?" said Obeck quietly, for if she insisted on that he was lost.

"Not necessarily. If you want to talk, I'll listen. If you want to listen, I can talk. If you want to trade favors, you know how I feel."

"About sex or me?"

"Both. Orden—"

"Go away, Wixa. Please. I'm sorry I woke you."

"You didn't wake me."

"Go away, Wixa . . . *why* do you want to be so damned *kind* to me?" He stared at the floor, at the bullets, wondered if he could set one off between his teeth, and then the rage

twisted him as if he were a tangled marionette. He could not see Wixa then, only the past, and he clawed at his eyes.

She pulled his hands away. "Tell me what's happened to you, Orden. *Please*."

"No. I . . . can't." *If fear is all the strength I may have, very well then.*

"I won't leave until you do."

"Then stay the night," he said, and the brass bell of double intent tolled intolerably loud. Her hands on his were work-hard, but skilled and very gentle.

"If you need me to," she said, and he knew he did, though he did not want her at all.

Which was a lie too. He wanted her till it hurt.

"Physical debriefing," she said.

He stopped dead still, staring, thinking, Oh, no more.

"It was in your medical file. Orden, nine PD subjects out of ten kill themselves—that's what the manual says. But it doesn't say *why*, Orden. Tell me why. Tell me what happened."

"I *can't* . . . don't you see?"

"How can I? Then tell me about what happened."

It was impossible, he knew. And then he thought of a way it might be done—to pile hate on top of hate. "*All right . . . all right . . .* Our memory's an iceberg, floating deep, of which only a fraction is disclosed. But sometimes fragments surface while we sleep, assembling into nightmares when exposed."

He pulled away from her; she let him go and said, "Go on."

"What, then, do you recall of what you've done? The kind-nesses, the hates, the rage and love? Not you—nor I—Blue hell, not anyone remembers all the things that we're made of." He took a breath, pulled his robe tighter. "But now suppose that there is a machine that brings those lost things back, picks neurons clean."

She looked at him, light dawning.

"And if you'll that, then this: this tool should be entrusted to a single-minded few who did not care, forgot, or never knew forgetting is forgiving—*do you see?*"

"Yes," she said, awed, shaken. "All your memories in a single bad dream . . . but only a dream, Orden. Can't you wake up?"

"Only the *truth*," he said. "I *am* awake, and I can't go to sleep again."

"Were you such a bad man as that? I don't remember—"

"*Exactly*. You don't remember—but I do, *I do!*"

"Memory can be dredged up but not fixed . . . surely you must have forgotten things again. Who can remember a dream for a whole day?"

"Does it help to know the monster's gone back into hiding? . . . Please, Wixa, I've told you now . . . go away."

"You want me here, don't you?"

"No."

"Orden, I remember that—how you'd wait until you were about to explode, never saying a word to me or Adaly or anyone—and when someone finally got to asking you, you'd be so ravenous that nothing would really be satisfying."

He closed his eyes. She went on. "But great Galen, you weren't *wicked*—clumsy, yeah, and selfish, we're *all* that, but that's got nothing to do with evil."

"You *have* forgotten."

"Damn it, will you open your beautiful gray eyes and *look* at me, Orden Obeck? How much pity are you going to waste on yourself? I remember you very damned well—I had some pretty selfish fantasies about you too, you know. Do you really believe that people have to forget the truth before they can forgive one another? Because if they *do*"—and her voice fell to nearly a sob—"then there's not enough forgiveness to survive on."

Obeck thought of all the tales of thievery and lies and abuse he could tell her, if only he could find the courage. "I was a coward," he said. "Somebody died."

"Yeah," she said, and looked at her hands; she made a needle-into-skin motion. "Me, too."

Much subdued, he said, "I didn't accept what was happening."

"Who does? That comes later."

"I hurt, and I shut it out."

"Nobody suffers voluntarily."

"Volun*tarily*—" Obeck gasped, and then the boil burst and the vileness flooded out. "No one but masochists and heroes," he said in a grating voice, and closed his eyes tight and knew why love was done in the dark.

"No," said Wixa harshly. Then: "No," again, much more gently. "No one takes the pain willingly. Masochists least of all—they're slaves to it. And heroes . . . heroes are just as forced—it's *what* forces them that makes all the difference."

Obeck sat down on the floor, arms around knees. Wixa knelt next to him.

"What am I going to do, Wixa?" he said in a tiny voice.

"I don't know, Orden. What do you need to do?"

"Need—? I . . . oh, yes, there's something I need to do. Something important that I never finished."

"An old debt?"

"Old class assignment, you might say." He smiled; he thought he had forgotten how.

"Do you suppose," she said, touching him, "it could wait till morning?"

"It has to wait till the Files floor opens," he said. "But . . . there's something I'm going to do right now." He stood, went to the callterm, touched numbers. He looked at where she sat. She looked puzzled. She looked beautiful. All the hours by thousands they had lived in the same room, and he had only just realized how beautiful she was.

"H'lo?" said a dazed voice from the handset. "Weather Control Command."

"I *know* that, mister," Obeck growled. "I called you, didn't I? Now, you snap to and scramble, or you're gonna be flying snow patrol on Longshot, you understand?"

"Who *is*—uh, yes, *sir*. What can I—"

"Rain," said Obeck. "A nice light rain, with a moderate wind. And some lightning for show. But I don't want some Blue-stuck hurricane, now—do I make myself clear?"

Wixa was shaking her head in bewilderment.

And watching the sky.

Chapter 10
Knight's Gambit

Doctor of Applied Philosophy Sir Orden Obeck stepped from the long blue hirecar onto the doorstep of the Consolidated Vulcan tower. Obeck handed a hundred-mark card to the driver, catching the morning sun on its silver edge, and waved the car on without collecting change.

The samech doorkeeper observed this scene, then bowed politely to Obeck, who signed THANK YOU as he passed. The doorkeeper removed its braided cap and bowed more than politely. Obeck smiled and entered the building. Two weeks ago he had called down the lightning and the rain; now he might do anything.

Obeck wore a frock coat of deep blue velvet. On the sleeve were the blue band of knighthood and a crimson doctoral knot; on the left breast were several badges, including the Human-Samech Communications Ribbon, a Royal Academy bar, and the buffed-gold coronet that indicated at least one audience with Rachel II Valeria Regina.

He was, once more, entitled to everything he wore. He really was a Doctor and a Knight who could talk to samechs and had talked to the Queen. Obeck was hardly responsible for how others might assemble that information.

Similarly, the fact that he wore a bit of makeup around his

eyes, jawline, and wrists might lead one to conclude that he covered revi marks with it, though his only needle bruise was in a place that Isoroku Daisho would not see.

Daisho. Obeck had used his computer time to assemble an algorithm, a Diophantine equation of people and events. Fill in the right blanks and the machine would answer some of the rest. And if it was short some bit, it could ask for enhancement or clarification.

SEE ISOROKU DAISHO, the algorithm had said, and though Obeck hardly needed to ask who *that* was, the machine noted CHIEF EXECUTIVE CONSOLIDATED VULCAN. "I know, I know," he had told it aloud. *But how can I . . .*

He sat at the machine, thinking, and in a short while he knew. *Not me, then. Someone I might have been.*

The black crepe soles of Obeck's half-dress shoes squeaked faintly on the hallway floor, which was bronze tile chequy buffed and blackened. And aside from a slight movement of air, that was all the sound there was. Shortly he came to a reception area, a low-ceilinged, round room with a desk at its center, and discovered the reason why.

The receptionist was a samech. So was the switchboard operator nearby, working with its fingers jacked into the board. So were the two security guards, who wore nighteyed helmets but no other armor and carried pistols cabled to their wrists.

He handed across a calling card (300-gram white Perlex Bristol, the papersmith in Documents had said, selecting it for Obeck like a jeweler setting an emerald), wrote messages back and forth for a few moments, then received a plastic rectangle and instructions where to pin it to his coat. There were no visible markings at all on the badge, but as Obeck turned it in his fingers a diffraction rainbow flickered across its face. He wondered what he would read there, if he saw in digitized color like a sapient mechanism.

He was directed down a short corridor, past a samech hand-polishing the blondwood paneling, then by two humans in blue coats like his own; they stopped their conversation to trade a greeting and seemed rather startled to see him.

An elevator door opened for Obeck. There was no operator inside, samech or otherwise, and only two control pads. He touched the upper one. The door closed and the car began rising.

The floor plate, belt rail, and ceiling panel were dark bronze; the rest of the car was glass, or pylex, with a dark brown smoke tint. The other side of the panels would be plated, as was all the building, with gold. Whenever it was made to rain, a thousand marks was washed into the sewers. Someone had once asked Isoroku Daisho if he were aware of that. Daisho had answered, "I could not have come to the top of a golden tower without knowing such things. I could not live in a golden tower if I cared about them."

They made half the weapons in the Realm, and *all* the samechs, because all other makers were Con Vulcan's licensees. And Isoroku Daisho lived in a pyramid of gold.

And, Obeck thought, they make Cleanfire-Eight fusion bombs with strange modifications. And stranger bends in the Blue.

A hundred floors had dropped past. Obeck was on the shadow side of the building; he looked out and saw the Palace Grounds from the height of a shuttle but closer than a shuttle might approach. The shadow of the building, three times as long as the structure itself in the early light, cut a deep dark wedge into the Grounds, reaching nearly to the Palace itself.

The car stopped. Obeck turned as the doors opened; he stepped through, his shoes silent on thick, figured carpet.

The room was square, with walls that sloped inward toward the ceiling; all four walls were of half-gilt glass, and Obeck realized that the room was the entire floor.

There were one hundred desks, set in a precise grid ten by ten. At each desk a samech sat, steel-rail straight on a backless stool, reading sign from vibrating pins with its left hand, keying a console with its right, its eyes motionless, facing a flickering screen. There was no more sound than in vacuum. Less—in vacuum you could hear your own breathing.

Obeck was suddenly aware of a standing figure at the opposite side of the floor, silhouetted against the windows. It was as still and silent as any sapient mechanism but was not shaped quite right for a samech. Obeck took a few steps; there was no answering word or motion. Obeck walked on.

Isoroku Daisho seemed built out of blocks with their corners rounded off. Large muscles showed through the sleeves and shoulders of his long tunic, which was of a gold brocade that somehow did not seem extravagant on him. His very black hair fell down all around the sides (and corners?) of his head in a helmet crop. The eyes in the flat face were flat and dull, giving out nothing.

As Obeck came close, Daisho turned sharply and started up a spiral staircase. His movements were deliberate, as if each part of the motion were being considered, but there was no hesitancy or lack of grace there. Obeck read immense energy under absolutely rigid control. He thought quite naturally of Thorn, who had the same sort of mass and power—but Thorn's control was never a visible effort.

Obeck followed Daisho up the spiral stairs and before he reached the last tread felt them retracting upward beneath him. He was propelled the last few centimeters up and shortly was standing on a bronze rosette set flush with the floor.

The office was the pyramid's peak: trapezoidal walls of gold glass sloped up to a dark point with a sunburst lightsource hung within. A pair of tracked rods, a lift frame, came down from the dark. Unlike Loaman Starkadr's private rooms, where everything had been subservient to the telescope seat, there was a great clutter of objects in the room, things of a hundred varieties representing a thousand interests.

There were ancient, yellow parchment maps of Primus when it was *the* Earth. Within a large bell jar on a blondwood base was a brass six-sided clock with a different face on each side and a frighteningly intricate assembly of levers and gears below. Books with brown hubbed spines and gold-edged pages lay racked and stacked and open. There were three computer consoles, all live. On the golden sand of a wargame table, Romans faced Carthaginians in miniature ranks of figured bronze, while on an accessory table were fifteen scale models of Con Vulcan's amphibious combat vehicle, the *Hardraade III*, so new Obeck doubted there were fifteen real ones in existence.

There was brass, gold, bronze, amber, topaz, tigereye, yellow diamond, blondwood, golden oak. Midas, thought Obeck, is home.

Near the western wall, facing the Palace, was a round, raised platform, and upon it an enclosing sphere chair. Daisho ascended the dais and stopped, facing away from Obeck, his right hand on the chair. The platform began to revolve.

To one side of the chair, between windows, Obeck noticed a full-figure portrait lectra, much larger than life. It was of a Priman Old Roman, in red and gold breastplate, scarlet cloak, high-laced shoes (not sandals; Obeck recalled from a Clothing Protocol class that respectable Romans wore shoes in public). In his hands was a white rod with gold fittings . . . and a conical flash-hider, a rectangular magazine, and the Con Vulcan trademark. Obeck looked up to see that the laurel leaves circled the blocky head of Isoroku Daisho.

"You noticed. Good." Obeck turned back to the spherical chair, where Isoroku Daisho sat with hands on knees.

And stood at attention beside himself.

The seated Daisho reached to the standing one, wrote in its palm. It signed a word back and went to a wall alcove; a panel closed over it.

Well, of course, thought Obeck. But at that range—the motion, the skin tone! The Queen's doubles were not made so well.

"Caesar is the best, I think," said Daisho. "But there are others." He moved a console before himself, touched a key. The lectra faded and one on the other side of the chair lit up. It showed Daisho in golden armor, carrying a shield with the company mark and a pi-crystal combat wand instead of a sword. The lectras flickered around the room; Daisho as a Mongol, a Samurai, a Mayan drenched in gold, a German general of the Priman Ground Wars, a Venusian clearsman, a Longshooter clan chief—always armed with the finest money could buy.

Or steal, Obeck thought, because the Longshooter portrait had carried a wiregun.

And then he realized that he had voluntarily turned completely around, directly in front of Daisho and whatever sensors were in his chair. *Have to tread carefully.*

Daisho said, "I am told by my Division of Sapient Mechanisms that you have an important thought. They further say your credentials for having this thought are very good."

Very carefully, Obeck thought.

Daisho paused for a moment. His eyes moved to something behind Obeck; Obeck was careful not to turn. Daisho's eyes were shadowed, but they appeared just as flat and dead as his samech double's had been.

Fear rose up grinning, then, and danced in the boneyard of Obeck's mind. But he caught it, and held it, and exorcised it with the knowledge of the task.

The machine had told him to see Daisho. Here he was. He would not run.

Finally Daisho looked back to Obeck and spoke. "And all important ideas are brought to me, for *ultimately* . . . it is I who decide what is important and what is not. Come around." He moved a finger and his chair turned away, back toward the window. Obeck went around the platform.

He saw Crown Center laid out like a woodblock model. He saw the Palace, its size and scope not really diminished even from here. And he saw the severe angle of the tower's shadow, black across the Grounds.

"Motivators," said Daisho suddenly. "Something about motivator circuits. You worked with Fluellen, didn't you? Before he retired to teach."

"Yes," said Obeck, referring to motivator circuits; he had not been born when Dr. Fluellen had gotten out of samech design . . . but he had aced Fluellen's course.

"Terrible thing about his deafness, of course," said Daisho.

Without a blink Obeck replied, "What's happened? Pardon me, but I don't recall—"

Daisho waved a hand. "No. There is no deafness. Just a little game." He indicated the panel where the double had gone. "Like my twin. You understand, of course? I think you are a little worldlier than the average."

"I understand," said Obeck. He had heard the bridge cracking, but for the moment it held his weight. "My theory—"

"Your theory." Daisho turned away, looked out the window. "About motivators. Proceed, please, Doctor."

Obeck nodded, glad he would not have to face those dead eyes while he spun whole cloth. He had hoped to learn something before events reached the lying stage—something in Daisho's look, his manner, or his office, since the interiors of offices so often matched their owners' minds. But the look was dead, the manner neutral, and the office contained too many things to sort. *Maybe the mind does too. Why am I here? Because the machine said so.*

Obeck began. "I became interested in the concept of disobedience by samechs. There were several types recorded—priorities violation, trivial self-preservation, orders by an incomp—"

"I know all the recorded types," said Daisho, very intently. "Did you find any examples of true contrary action?"

Time to choose, Obeck thought, the truth or the lie.

The complete truth—that he had discovered Daisho's interest and found a good hearsay case—was out of the question. The partial truth might get him thrown out, with or without benefit of elevator down. He would certainly be thrown out hard if caught in the lie—but that could not happen for a little while at least.

"Yes," Obeck lied.

Daisho leaned forward. "In what model? A Myrmidon? Or the Hussar?"

"Actually . . . it seems almost silly, saying it . . . it was an Epicurus-Four." Obeck waited. Daisho did not react. Obeck went on, "It seems the restaurant owner and the samech cook disagreed over the proportions of cream, flour, and salt in a certain pastry—"

"Equerry's hackleberry tart," said Daisho, and of course Obeck did not dispute him. "I warned Equerry—please, Doctor, proceed."

"Well. The samech prepared the pastry in what the owner considered an incorrect fashion. Told to start over, it repeated the action. The third time it was allotted only the . . . correct . . . quantities of ingredients. It then refused the preparation order completely. The order was given vocally twice and by sign three times."

"By sign . . . you're certain of that?"

"Absolutely," said Obeck, suddenly concerned; he was lying himself a tangled web, with unexpected knots in the weave. Best end the tale. "Finally, the samech refused all commands. Shortly, it collapsed."

"And they found the motivator had burned up, didn't they?"

"Fused to glass and solder," Obeck said heavily.

Daisho touched a pad and his chair tilted slightly, setting him on his feet. He walked around the dais—his gait was the same as his samech's—then stepped down to the carpeted floor. He walked past Obeck, ignoring him, went to the sand table and examined one of the tin legionaires. After a while he said, "But what shall we make of this?"

Obeck waited, unsure he was the one spoken to. Then Daisho's head turned slightly, an eyebrow rose. His eyes had changed, as if tiny lights had come on within them. Obeck said, at least half improvising, "The temptation, of course, is to be anthropomorphic . . . to assume the samech, caught between duty and commands, burned out its module through an effort of will . . . broke its heart, so to speak."

Daisho said, "Resisting that temptation . . . what do we have?"

"Perhaps only a defective motivator."

Daisho pounded a fist into the sand, disordering the hastatii. "*What* is that, Doctor?"

"I meant no criticism of Consolidated Vulcan product quality—I—"

"To the deepest circle with product quality. I know my product's quality. I know to the last decimal how many moti-

vators fail, and how, and why." Daisho advanced upon
Obeck, seemingly locked upon a vector of final approach.
Obeck wondered how he was to stand his ground, when he had
no real ground to stand on.

Daisho halted, his kinetic energy going into an upward snap
of his head. "You come to me," he said, his voice losing its
terrible edge, "with the most important news since the first
samech awoke, and you lay it to a *malfunctioning part*." Except for the last two words, Daisho was now completely controlled again. He looked at the figure in his hand; he had
destroyed it between two fingers. He let the twisted bit of
metal fall into his palm and closed his hand over it.

"I am sorry," said Obeck—he had almost used ELI-3, before realizing how it could betray him. "I was only being
cautious."

"Of course," said Daisho, and looked straight at Obeck; at
the height of his outburst there had been a bright spark in his
eyes, but it was gone now, leaving no more feeling than
buttons on the linen face of a doll.

Obeck looked down. Daisho's closed hand, with the figure
within, was white knuckled and rigid; Obeck looked up again
instantly.

"Of course," said Daisho again, and stepped up to his
chair. There was a faint sound from outside the building, like
approaching thunder. "You are cautious in your ivory tower.
While I prefer a golden one."

A shadow passed across one wall of windows, and the sound
from outside grew louder—a helicopter or a small ship on
downthrust, hovering around the peak of the building. Obeck
thought about anarchists and bombs and took an involuntary
step away from Daisho.

Daisho touched his chair console. "I will have to ask you to
leave now, Doctor. I thank you for your information. If you
would like a research grant, it can be arranged. Just call the
Samech Division." He looked up. "Possibly you'll want to
study cases of motivator failure."

"And if I discover anything, should I report to—"

"The Samech Division. You'll be welcome there. I seldom
receive anyone twice, Doctor. Very few people have two things
to say."

Overhead there was the sound of a door and rushing air. A
square of light appeared in the dark apex of the room, then
was partly blocked; someone was descending on a lift panel.

Daisho touched a key and the spiral trapstair opened. "Goodbye, Doctor," he said, looking upward.

Obeck looked upward too, for just a moment. Then he turned and hurried down the stair while it was still unfolding, hoping that he had not been seen by the figure on the lift, not sure what it would mean if he had.

This time there was no skintint, and the face was as white as any samech's; but the face, and the build, and the red leather clothing, were unmistakably those of Toranaga, who had carried the infernal device to sankt Efer, on Longshot, in the Too Far Six.

Obeck returned to the palace, conscious all the way of the Con Vulcan tower over his shoulder. He went to the Files floor and inserted new data into his algorithm, but the conclusions were obvious.

Arich sankt Efer had spoken to Toranaga (revise that: to *a* Toranaga) about a "Patron." Anyone could buy samechs and deal in guns. But there were some very unusual qualities about the Toranaga on Longshot—providing he hadn't imagined them.

No. He had not. And the MASPAC XP 4 was not an ordinary rifle for the rebels, and he had not imagined *it*.

All right then—suppose Isoroku Daisho was providing arms and more exotic things to the Bakunen Actives. Why?

As Obeck thought of the tower's shadow, that seemed the least necessary question of all.

He composed a brief, with references and notes, tactful but inevitably pointing a finger. He tabbed it with Urgent notices and launched it to the Department of Separated Worlds, up through channels toward the Queen.

It was inadequately referenced, he knew too well—rather, it was too often corroborated by the testimony of a Privy Consul named Obeck. That vector added into another straight-line resultant; he had to produce some evidence.

Not facts from the file, either. Someone would have to go into Con Vulcan and come out with something concrete—or plastic and metal, more likely.

And now where was Thorn? David? Parsecs away, days by the straightest of skips—and they were Royally chartered, on Queen's business. He did not have the authority to call them back.

Obeck realized with a major shock that he *did* have the

authority to send out Clandestine operators. As a full Consul (and they had made him that, hadn't they?) he could pull a team from the pool, requisition a Pilot and a ship, and—

But that was not true. It was indelibly recorded that he *might* do such a thing—but—

What he could do was call a committee. The full members had to be of his own rank, not low-grade aye-sayers or high heraldics brought in for prestige and by blackmail. He would be Chair, and preside, but he would not really be in control.

He had not forged enough links. He should have been able to pick up the callterm and collect a committee out of friends and debtors. He should have had a whole whispering network under him, trailing down to Riyah Zain. But he did not. What he had was a high office with no visible means of support.

What links did he have? A doctor. A paper expert. Some privateers who were a long way off. And the Queen, which had been a very good link until it got broken.

Why is it, he thought, uncomfortable in his brown coat with its brass badges, that whenever I wake up—I'm alone?

He had an anxious, breathless feeling of being out of time, that it was too late for anything.

He looked hard at the computer displays, at the work he had yet to do, and quite deliberately thought, Not too late till we're dead. Nor all alone.

He put in a message tickler that would alert his persec if anyone called about the Daisho file. Then he left the floor and made a call from a public booth.

Finally he went home and called Wixa.

"I can't stay," she said. "I'm on ten-minute response tonight, and I'm stretching that by coming here." She indicated the light on her wristec, dark now. "It's almost like, sometimes . . . you know."

He did. They both knew all about red-lighted jewelry that commanded attendance. "You didn't need to come. We could have—"

"I did have to, though. I had to tell you . . ." Her voice dropped. "That I can't stay."

"Where are you going?"

"I'm not going anywhere. And I didn't say I'd never be back. But I won't be back soon. Or often."

"What did I do?" said Obeck hollowly.

"Do?" She smiled. "Nothing. Except . . . except come back from the edge."

"And was that it?" Obeck was hurt, angry, but more confused than either. "Now that I'm well you can go on to the next case?"

"Orden, I—" Quietly: "If you want to think of it that way . . . yes."

"Well, I don't! After all this time, do you expect me to think of you as a doctor?"

"I don't see why not, Orden. I *am* a doctor."

That struck him like a blow. He took it and kept going. "I'm just about to do something very important. Can't you wait until after it's done?"

"No."

"After a couple of more weeks—just a few more days—" *I called down the lightning for you.* He was at once aware that he was pleading, and checked himself.

"That's half of it, right there," she said. "A few more days, and a few more . . . forever is just one day after another, Orden."

"But after this thing is over . . . things will be settled. Maybe I . . . won't need you as much."

"I know," she said, nearly whispering, "that's the other half of it."

He held her, kissed her. She agreed to it. But after a few seconds there was a small, rapid, mechanical sound, and she pulled away firmly. Her wristec was signaling. "Ten minutes, Orden. I have to go, right now." She went to the door; he followed. She paused in the doorway. He reached toward her; she said, "It means someone's dying, Orden," and he let his hand fall. She said quickly, "I'm glad you found something important to do," kissed him very lightly, and was gone, running down the hall. He watched her until she turned a corner. Then he closed the door and locked it.

He wondered if there was any other way, supposed not. He had a brief, fantastic flash of pursuing her, proclaiming his need and eternal devotion at the side of some bleeding, gasping trauma patient. Another fantasy, then, hotter and darker: he pulled her back from the door, gripped her wrists and tore off first the protesting wristec, and then—

His lip was salty with blood and he hated himself, for the thought, for the fact that he could have such a thought.

Need, yes, I admit it, he thought. But eternal devotion? *Up a Blue wall.*

He could live without Wixa, without anyone, and be content. He must.

He opened a kitchen closet and looked at the neatly stacked equipment inside. It was amazing what one could obtain through channels. He picked one item up from the rest and carried it into the living room.

Obeck slid out the hidden desk drawer and took out the empty pistol. He slipped in the loaded magazine he had brought from the kitchen, shoved it home. Then, very carefully, he put the gun with the other supplies and shut the closet door.

There was not going to be a committee, or a Clandestine team, or any other kind of a team. There would just be Orden Obeck. Alone.

The night was cold, not much above freezing. Obeck supposed that someone in Weather Command would be packing for snow patrol. Or maybe someone in the palace had just had an odd, romantic notion.

Obeck stood on the fringes of Consolidated Vulcan's Crown Center plant. It was a hundred kilometers from the Palace, not because of any aesthetic need—it was soundproofed and sweet-smelling—but for its private cargo port, the largest one on Novaya. It had its own maglarail stop as well, but Obeck had gotten off one stop early and walked the rest of the distance, in between the fences and ditches and wandering pipelines of the industrial park.

He wore a dark blue coat that fitted into the night even better than black, silent-soled boots and the pair of thin nighteyes Molly Bajan had given him, at the Saavedran Embassy, long ago and away in the Too Far Six.

Obeck examined the perimeter fence. It was medium-high security; instead of ordinary horizontal wires or bars it had thin slats. They rotated at the least touch, and their edges were *sharp*. KEEP OUT, said the signs. *Really* keep out, said the fence.

He unfastened his coat. Lights made shadows on but did not reflect from the gear he wore beneath: a leather and webbing harness with many small items hung about it. It was Con Vulcan's own Ninja 9K countersecurity rig, obtained through channels especially for this occasion. In the rig's integral chest holster hung the pistol, a rocket on the rails.

Obeck opened a thigh pouch, removed two metal prongs,

rather like tuning forks. They would connect to sockets at his wrists, locking into a reinforcing frame that ran through the whole harness. The prongs then fit into the fenceposts, around the slat bearings—and up he would walk.

He wondered about hierarchies of security. Would the best security system Con Vulcan knew how to make be beaten by the best countersystem they could make? Why or why not? If you knew your opponent's weakness and he yours, could either of you ever win?

A cold breeze spun some of the slats, washed across Obeck's face. And he seemed to wake up from a dream. *What in blue hell am I* doing *here?* he shouted at himself. He knew the answer, of course. This was where he thought he wanted to be: at the fence, in the night, with his superspy kit. Ready to save the Realm single-handed.

Obeck sighed. Then he laughed, faintly. He almost leaned against the fence, but caught himself and shook his head. Whatever—what *ever*—had he been thinking?

Not what, he thought, but how. And I'm not thinking that way anymore.

He pulled the gun from the Ninja rig, cleared it and set the safeties, then tucked it into his coat pocket, again pulling his coat out of trim. Then he reached for the harness's quick-release tabs and broke the support frame into its component links. The whole rig fit into his other pocket, making him baggy but balanced.

Then he walked back to the maglarail stop where he had detrained, caught the next one, and rode one stop to the plant's front door.

"No offense meant, sir, but it's kind of off hours for a plant visit . . . isn't it, sir?"

"No," said Obeck absently, "it isn't. The plant operates all twenty-five, doesn't it?"

"Certainly, sir," the other nightwatch said, "but it's low shift now, sir . . . mostly samechs working now."

"Samechs, yes," said Obeck. "Well, that's only natural, then, seeing this is where they're made . . . samechs are all Theory Y workers, you know."

The remark was delivered in such earnestness that the two nightwatches had to stop to ponder its significance, if any. Obeck had learned more from Nathaneal van't Hoeve than Monarchical Principles.

While they were deeply pondering, Obeck delivered the final stroke. "Mr. Daisho said I would be welcome," he said, as if it were an afterthought. The truth had never seemed quite so much like a lie.

All pondering stopped. One watch stood quite straight, her hands folded, while the other went to a console with a shrouded display. "You're, uh, Doctor Sir . . . Sir Doctor Orden Obeck?"

They never had come up with a good form for both titles at once. "Yes," he said, "I suppose so."

The watch looked up, bewildered. "Uh . . . yeah. Go right on through, sir. Take a violet badge."

"Which?" said Obeck.

"Any of them, sir."

"In that case, I'll go right on through. Never did like taking badges."

They gave him one anyway. As he passed out of the gatehouse, a small red indik lit beside the doorway. "Sir," said a nightwatch, quite serious now, "are you carrying a gun?"

"Well, naturally," said Obeck. "As you saw, I came by float-train." The watches nodded. "Well, then," Obeck said, and put the gun on the table. "Do I get a receipt for this? I'll be taking the float-train back, of course. Nowhere to get one of these this time of night, out here." He could feel the tension radiating from the watches.

Finally one of them broke. "Professor—"

"As little as possible."

"—what's the mag' got to do with guns?"

"Why, my dear fellow. Surely you know of the instances in which armed desperadoes have robbed—even hijacked—float-trains?"

The watch nodded, understanding.

"Fortunately, such instances are rare. You realize that the probability of such an armed soul being on any given train is very low."

Another nod, as the understanding dissolved.

"Well, then, isn't it obvious? If I board armed, then the probability of a *second* person doing so is the square of the original fraction—a number approaching nonexistence."

The other watch hefted the pistol. "But this is *loaded*," she said.

"Why," said Obeck witheringly, "would I wish to protect myself against a desperado with an *unloaded* gun?" And he walked on into the plant, his coat now listing right with the Ninja rig.

"There's—something in his other—" he heard one of the nightwatches say behind him.

"Yeah, I see it," said the other, "but let him go. It's probably a fusion bomb."

Chapter 11
White Pawns

The plant was cool within, mostly dark, and very quiet. This shift seemed to be entirely samech; it was possible that except for the watches, who had to speak, there were no humans in the place. That certainly did not disturb Obeck.

A samech in a gray uniform, carrying a sack of mail, came down an office corridor toward Obeck; it sidestepped him without appearing to have really noticed him. That was very good. It was halfway to invisibility.

He fell in behind the mail carrier, watched it make a few more deliveries. It seemed to be using its eyes only to read addresses; it never looked at the floor, the walls, or the doors it pushed letters through.

Obeck came up alongside it, tapped the hand it steadied its bag with. The palm opened out. Obeck signed, COMPUTER AREA—WHICH WAY? and got a series of directions in reply. The mail carrier never broke stride.

There was a human behind a desk at the entrance to the machine area, but he was reading and simply waved as Obeck passed. Obeck fingered his badge, which was purple without other legend. He wondered if it told samech eyes he was human and to be ignored unless he asked for something. He wondered what it told human eyes, and if—

Was violet *Let him in—but not out?*

Not likely. There was nothing in Con Vulcan's computers that Daisho did not know or know of; what could he be waiting for Obeck to find? And if Daisho knew what Obeck was really searching for, he would be mad to let Obeck this close to it.

There was a distinct, unpleasant suspicion in Obeck's mind that Isoroku Daisho was indeed mad. But it was a special and singular type of madness; one that would casually risk fortunes and whole worlds but would never compromise itself with little chances.

The computer carrels were only partly enclosed, but Obeck seemed to be the only user. He slid into a seat and began working the console. Which file to request? Or rather, which to request first?

He tapped TORANAGA.

The display replied THIS IS A SECURE FILE. APEX CLEARANCE IS REQUIRED. ENTER YOUR PASSCODE.

Obeck blanked the display. He touched out MASPAC XP 4.

APEX CLEARANCE IS REQUIRED.

Obeck thought. He looked at his badge. He wondered just how welcome he was. He touched I HAVE NOT YET BEEN AS-SIGNED A PASSCODE.

Blink. Blink. YOUR NAME PLEASE?

He told the truth. As much as he had told Daisho, anyway. INSERT BADGE PLEASE.

A slot lit up—violet. Obeck slipped the card into it.

Blink-blink-blink. APEX CLEARANCE GRANTED.

And then the MASPAC XP 4—or, MasPac, Experimental Prototype Four—file came up. And Obeck could not read it.

It was page after page of Blue physics, of which Obeck knew practically nothing; he did not even recognize most of the symbols. But he knew people who would. He offprinted the file and tucked it inside his coat lining.

Then he touched TORANAGA, and that file he could read; but he was not at all sure he understood it.

The samech combat soldier had been one of those ideas, like nuclear hand weapons or personal powered armor, that had lost something on its way to the armories. Samech troops were to be—should have been—the perfect power-weapons fodder; they would require no medics, no noncoms, no R&R, no sup-plies but ammunition. The moral would no longer be to the physical as three to one, because there wouldn't be any more moral. And they would never, ever, question an order.

However: military samech brains had to reserve a lot of space for kinesics control, so they could move and fight over the awful terrain where battles tend to occur. As a result they were stupider than the average janitorial model. That made elaborate command structures, incorporating lots of noncoms human and otherwise, a necessity. The machine soldiers couldn't be hurt, but they could be damaged, and it was an intolerable waste to lose a whole trooper for a breakdown that could be fixed in five minutes with some wire and glue. That called for "medics." And who was to give them orders in the first place? Tactical doctrine, imperfect as it was, had been brought to bear some relation to the real characteristics of soldiers—and here were soldiers with unreal characteristics.

There were more howevers, but finally samech war cost too much. (Even for war.) Despite automated vehicles and air/space insertion and very-smart weapons, warfare, as opposed to combat, was still a labor-intensive activity. (Dr. Bishop again: "Any culture that must maintain a manual labor pool must by corollary have a large standing army—if the two are not already the same body.") A hundred samechs to run a factory was one thing. But a regiment of a thousand? A division, ten thousand? A corps—

An indik lit in Obeck's memory, but his mind was still too full. It was a red light, though. Thorn's color.

And Toranaga's. The Toranagas'.

Having failed as soldiers, military samechs like the Myrmidon and Hussar ended up as guards, and prosthetic parts for human cripples, and sometimes fighting the little play wars of people like the Saavedran holdfasters.

But now here was the Toranaga model, called sometimes the "Colonel Toranaga" for its role: a samech field commander. It was very intelligent, and as a result there was not enough brainspace to make it walk very well or handle a weapon. That was all right. Its role was to win battles, not fight them. And it had a motivator module three times normal size.

Five hundred thousand hours ago it might have been designed, and even built, though it would have made no better sense then; but here it was *now*, and being built by Isoroku Daisho's Con Vulcan, which should not have even considered such a thing.

Unless there was another role for a samech colonel.

Red is the color . . .

The Bakunen Actives had called Daisho their Patron.

Obeck touched PATRON PROJECT.

The display blinked several times, then showed him a list of names, and places, and dates. It was not a long list—only three pages. But Obeck knew many of the names on it; some of them were infamous. All of them were revolutionists, avowed or suspected.

On the second page Obeck read

sankt Efer, Arich / BAKUNEN ACTIVES
PROGRAM CANCELLED DUE TO COUNTERSANCTION

Fingers shaking, Obeck made the offprint and slipped it into his coat. He cleared the console, trying to gather himself before walking back past the man at the desk and the watches at the gate.

It can't work, he was thinking, it can't possibly—they'd have to seize the Rooks, and that can't be done.

A new coefficient plugged into his algorithm, and a bit of a product appeared, something he had nearly forgotten. Rooks and samechs, and a chapter in Thorn's book, the definitive work on space combat.

Provided it found a Patron.

He wouldn't, Obeck thought. He couldn't. But he certainly might, and who knew what Thorn *could* do? Obeck knew that he had too many times judged David and Theo—his dead name now—as a unit, as His Great Old Friends, when they were as different as darkness and—

Yes. Good metaphor. Darkness and light. And I wore white and was shades of gray.

He needed one more piece of information while he was here —he would certainly not be returning. Then he had only to escape with it. And make someone listen.

He had read the dates on the Patronage list, and there was very little time.

The man at the desk was still engrossed in his tape. It's the badge they're seeing, and the coat, Obeck thought. That was the other half of invisibility.

He found his way to the manufacturing section by asking a floor-polishing samech. There was a guard at the door, but its skin was white plastic and it did no more than nod as Obeck passed through the doors.

The room was big enough to dock a starcruiser, cut up into several partial levels linked by stairs, lifts, and conveyors. The light was vertical and uncomfortably strong, from bare tubes at the ceiling; everything had sharp shadows and hard edges.

And it was loud, with grinders and conveyors and milling machines and more. A human voice could not have been heard, though the samechs would hardly care. Obeck remembered having passed a rack of hearmuffs and goggles between the doors—but his best protection now was speed. And he did not want to try the door, with its guard, again until he was ready to go and not return.

The production lines were all rolling. Samech parts were inserted into limb housings. Limbs by the hundreds were racked on conveyors and rolled to assembly points, where samech hands and metal manipulators held them in place and multiheaded tool robots closed connections. The ghastly aspect of watching the assembly—parts into people—was moderated by its unreality; the whiteness of the plastic and the gleam of the internal parts. And the lack of any referent in the overall noise.

Hundreds and hundreds of samechs—a finished one every few seconds. And they all seemed to be of the same model. Obeck followed the line to its end, to the warehouse wing. And he found his bit of data.

A ship-style cargo grid, busy rovers on its rails, ran up five floors: on every floor were at least ten thousand samechs in their shipping coffins. And every label Obeck read was the same: Myrmidon-3 combat models.

No army that had ever been would require so many samech soldiers. But one possible army would.

Obeck felt the bulge of the Ninja kit in his pocket, and he thought of the many usefully destructive items inside it. It was not a fusion bomb, of course. He thought about trying to find one, in the warehouse, but there was no time and he was not enough of an engineer. He couldn't do much damage. But some damage was called for.

He left filament cables stretched across walkways, stuck crates together and lift trucks to the floor with chemical leech, dropped tools and hooks into bins of material.

The last item remaining was a sandwich of slightly rubbery material, with paper between the layers and on the outsides. Obeck went up to one of the master assembly units on a central deck—the workers still ignoring him—bent beneath the main power housing. He peeled off a layer of paper and, careful not to touch the exposed surface, stuck the gelbomb to the metal surface. Then he slipped the interleaving sheet out; amid the machine noise he could not hear the hiss of the gels interacting, going from inert to explosive. Finally he removed the outer paper, picked up a heavy cable from the floor, and pressed it into the gel. He checked his wristec. He had forty minutes, plus or minus five, before this machinery ceased to exist. It was time to go; he did not want to seem in a hurry.

A hand touched his shoulder. A gloved, human hand. Obeck turned, rising.

A man in coveralls, goggles, and hearmuffs was pointing at the gelbomb and shouting something, red-faced with strain and still inaudible. Obeck understood him anyway.

The man made a grab for Obeck's wrist. Obeck recoiled and punched him in the chest, achieving almost nothing. The man swung back. Obeck ducked under the assembler's workhead, which brushed his hair in passing. He kicked the workman in the shin; the man tripped and struck a conveyor. Legs and feet scattered. Samechs, oblivious to all else, picked them up and put them back.

Obeck grabbed a meter-long retrieving wand from a samech, which stepped back politely. Obeck swung the metal bar in a wide arc, making the man hesitate, and then he ran.

The human ran after. As he came around a forming bench, Obeck stood up behind it and hit him on the back of the head. The bar wobbled, almost jumping from his hands. The man fell face down.

He started to push himself up. Obeck hit him again, and still he refused to pass out like a proper villain. Obeck hit him again—

Name of Niccolo, he thought, as the bar came down, I don't want to kill him, and he revectored the wand into the floor. The tremor knocked it from his hand. But the man was still.

Obeck's head hurt with the strain and the light and the noise. He took the human's muffs and goggles, and felt a little better. He leaned against the deck rail and thought about the bomb; it had enough delay to allow loading the man on a cart and getting him out. Obeck pulled the loose, empty harness from his pocket; it would secure the fellow against further violence.

The knifethrust missed him by millimeters, and the blade struck sparks on the platform rail. As the man recoiled, Obeck swung the harness like a whip, connecting with the base of the skull; and with a cry no one could hear the man tumbled over the rail, landing face down flat on a conveyor, sending parts flying. The rollers carried him on toward a spidery multi-welder, and Obeck's throat tightened, but then the conveyor stopped and four samechs picked the body up.

Obeck walked fast, to the door (where, cautious again, he left the goggles and muffs in the rack and signed THANKS to the guard), through the halls, out to the gate.

He handed over his badge, horribly conscious of the eyes and hands of the watches. One held out Obeck's pistol, grip first. The other, alerted by something just out of Obeck's sight, went to the covered display.

"There's been some kind of accident in Assembly," she said. "Night supervisor . . . seems to have fallen into the machinery." There was a pause. "Everything's a mess in there, and . . ."

Obeck plucked the gun from the watch's stiff hand. "Now you see why I always take precautions," he said, pocketing the pistol and going out the door, in no apparent hurry. He was not followed, and the train came soon. He looked out its window, back at the factory, but the buildings were designed to contain all light and sound, smoke and flash.

He went back to the Palace, up to his rooms. Though it was no time to sleep, he could do no more until morning; so he set his wristec for four hours and slept, dreamless, the gun beneath his pillow.

He sent a cautiously phrased cassette to Kondor and Bajan, but a cautious message was all it was; it carried no weight. Without knowing the truth in its entirety—the truth about Thorn—he could say no more.

And unless he could see the Queen . . .

He filed reports with all the Urgencies he could attach, and he was ignored. And the hours were escaping.

There was a way left. It had supposedly worked before. It had very certainly gotten some people shot dead. David, Obeck knew, would have been delighted by the scheme. Obeck had hated it. He still hated it. But now he cared enough to try.

He prepared an enormous document folder with several impressive but meaningless seals. It was large enough to mostly conceal his face when held in a reading position.

Then, wearing the whites he was no longer entitled to, he began walking random vectors through the Palace Royal wing. Sometimes it took half an hour, sometimes six, but eventually he would come within shouting distance of three to six Queen's Life Guards in their silver and black, some councillors in assorted dress, and Her Majesty Rachel II Valeria Regina.

Or a reasonable facsimile. The first day the Queen was a samech, the skintint obvious at a distance. The second day she spoke, and her voice at once gave her away as a double; it did not have any of the Bishop resonance Obeck knew so well. The third day Obeck was tired, and he could not be sure of the cues. The fourth day it was a samech again. Each time he hid behind his folder and let the parade pass.

But on the fifth day he heard her voice, echoing up the high narrow hall. And he knew it had to be now or never, because Kondor was in the Six and Thorn might be anywhere.

He knelt at a formal distance, his face hidden. And as the first Guards passed, and the councillors drew abreast, he moved, tossing the folder to one side, standing, stepping toward her.

There was a *crack* to one side as a Life Guard shot the folder out of the air. Me next, Obeck thought, but he walked on, as a handstick hit his spine and another the back of his knee, dropping him; then his shoulder was hit, his arms.

And he came on, by millis but still moving. It was as if every blow he had ever taken was only preparation for this: he knew clearly that they could easily beat him to death, but they could never beat him down.

He heard their pistols click live, thought, Here it ends, and then her voice, no tape and no double's, said, *"Stop."* And they all did, even Obeck—all in tableau except her. The councillors were stopped, as they moved out of crossfire; the Life Guards, some watching the corridor for further assassins and some with their weapons just removed from Obeck's life; and Consul (Whatever-he-was) Orden Obeck, on his knees with his arms outstretched in a perfect Jolson-Two posture. Supplicative, Urgent, Metaglobal importance. If she were the Queen, she would know that.

She knew it. "You have a message for us, Sir Knight?"

Obeck opened his mouth, but he only gasped a little.

"My Lady Queen," said a Life Guard, "it could be a samech. With a bomb installed."

"Then he'll surely detonate if you kill him, won't he?" she said coolly, without imperiousness. "Besides, Captain Hoylake . . . samechs do not bleed."

Am I bleeding? Obeck thought. I never bled in a Cause before. He was suddenly aware that his head rested against the service pistol at his right temple, and if the Guard drew back he might topple. *Hurry then.* "Medame. You must . . . recall Kondor Marque from the Six. Immediately."

"*Dressed* like a Diplomat," one of the councillors said. "He certainly doesn't *speak* like—"

"He speaks as we instructed him," said the Queen. "We remember this knight. He knows where eagles breed." Then to Obeck: "You have not spoken with us for quite some time. Do you have a case with you?"

He reached inside his tight coat, aware he might lose his hand for it. "This, medame." He handed her the Patron Project list.

She reached to take it, but a hand intervened. "Oh, very well," he heard her say. He could not see very much. "You hold it. But if it's poisoned he's killed himself, and he's not that type—Sir Orden! Where did you get this?"

He told her, and there seemed to be some kind of stir, but the pistol moved away from his head and he did not manage to hear all of it.

Queen's Special Counsel Sir Orden Obeck had been returned to his apartments after a bit of medical care (not from Wixa, alas) and a few questions. He had gone immediately to sleep and dreamt of butterflies—thousands of white butterflies around an enormous blue orchid. Then a hand came down from somewhere and uprooted the orchid, crushed the blossom to a pulp. Obeck followed the bare, muscular arm upward, into the black sky, looking for the face behind it; but there was no face, only a bleak, pitted moon.

Obeck awoke and tried to recall what he had said, about Rooks and samechs. *A Rook can't be taken, Sir Orden. But I knew a man who said he could, given only enough samechs.* Isoroku Daisho? *No, another man.* Then has this man sold his plan to Daisho? *No!* Are you sure? *You don't know him.* Do you know him so well? *No, no, no, I don't, and no one else does, either* ... .

But it had not really gone like that. They had only wanted to talk about revolutionaries, not Rooks. After all, a Rook might be destroyed—unlikely, but might—but it could not be captured. And by toy soldiers?

Obeck got out of his bed and walked into his living room. The window was pitch dark, though his wristec said it was early afternoon. He looked close: a sheet of metal, gridded against blast, was fastened outside the pane. He went to the door; it would not open. The callterm was dead. His persec would not send. The console display showed only entertainment channels, not even the news channel. Computer access was cut off, naturally. He went into the kitchen; it worked normally, which made him feel much better than it should have. When he returned to the living room, a page of text had appeared on the display, explaining that he was in "protective seclusion" until some of his wilder claims (though that was not their term) could be verified. It explained the details of his confinement—his medication supply would be strictly limited, as well—and gave him a channel to use should he decide to make an "enhanced statement."

He immediately opened the channel and told them to read his reports.

There was no record of any such reports having been made, he learned. Pause. And did he care to explain how samechs could capture Rook fortresses?

He had never known that, of course, and still did not know if it was possible. Only that someone—

Who? they asked.

Obeck did not reply. He had seen—he was still seeing— what happened when fingers were pointed, suspicions raised. He asked if the Queen had recalled the Kondor Marque Corporation.

It seemed she had. (But they could safely tell him anything.) They wanted to know, then, how he had gotten the list from Daisho.

He started to explain, and then realized he did not know that, either.

Unless, he thought, it was because Thorn had spoken for him—

No. No! What one person could plan another could plan, no matter how long the coincidence.

He knew what Security—it was surely them on the other side of the display—wanted: another name, another suspect, so the inquisitors could count another coup. If he gave them a Judas goat, they would let him out of the room, and the death cells of his memory—

But he could wait. He had learned to wait. And he could last as long as it might take. He broke the message link.

Then he went quickly to the kitchen, to make sure the food and water were still on. They were. He would last.

It took nine days.

When the door opened, Obeck was sitting in the kitchen. He had amused himself for the past hundred hours (without sunlight, days meant nothing) by making complicated sandwiches. He ate an average of three bites from each and flashed the rest. He wore a thin robe over nothing and had not troubled to depilate or wash for some time; if they were watching him they could suffer a little.

He heard the door click and lost his grip on a boiled egg; it rolled away. He started to dash for the bedroom and decency —visitors were different from snoopers—and collided directly with David Kondor. Obeck turned aside, ashamed, and then he saw David, and *smelled* David—and realized that they must have made the hundred-hour skip without a break, OutSide all the way, to reach him so soon. So nobody had any pride, and they embraced, Molly making three.

"David," Obeck said, "did Thorn—" *Let him have come with you. Because if he's not with you, I know who he is with—*

"Good day, Orden," came a voice from the doorway. Obeck disengaged himself, took a step that way.

Thorn's arms were outstretched. In one hand was a light rapid-rifle, held upright by the receiver; in the other was the collar and throat of a Palace Patrolman. The guard, who standing up would have been half a head taller than Thorn, was scrabbling on his knees to keep up with Thorn's walk. "This fellow wouldn't let us in to see you," Thorn said, "even though we told him it was important. You did say it was urgent."

Did I? Of course—they read between the tracks. Obeck was brought swiftly back to where they all were—and more importantly, *when*. "More urgent than I'd guessed, Thorn. It may even be . . . Thorn, you said something, once, about samechs seizing a Rook. Is that possible?"

"Impregnability is an axiom, not a fact," Thorn said, and try as he might Obeck could not read between *those* tracks. "Samech assault is a possibility—but for it to be practical, one would have to have the resources of Consolidated Vulcan itself."

"Exactly," Obeck nearly shouted, a flop-robed, bearded prophet in the wilderness. "There's a war about to start— if we can only stop it in time—"

"You don't *know?*" David said, and Obeck saw his face and did not need to ask him to explain.

Fifty hours ago, the revolution had begun. The first shots were on Primus, probably for sentimental reasons. The Force Command center at Brasilia/Primus was attacked by small units delivering enormous firepower. The center was cut off in less than two hours, and though the secondary chains of command were functioning smoothly, the insurgent "Cold Iron Legion" was claiming a victory and promising more. The Primans were scared. The masked individual who made the victory announcement carried a Con Vulcan WBX wiregun, finished in chameleon metal. Obeck was scared.

A few hours later there was a similar attack on the Force center at Teraphe/Teraphe. This group styled itself "Maximum Liberty." Then "Ares" hit the Fleet docks over Mars. Then . . .

Eight couriers were arriving an hour, each one bringing a little more bad news. No one even wanted to think fifty hours ahead, when ships would begin coming In from the Too Far Six.

Four hours after Orden Obeck was released from his apartment—it was made official within a few minutes, whereupon Thorn let go of the Patrolman's gun and the Patrolman—there was combat in progress on every world of the Nine, and, logic demanded, of the Realm, except for Novaya. And Novaya was safe, because of its four Queen's Rooks.

Wasn't it?

A meeting was in session in one of Crown Center's larger halls. Everyone knew the tall, dark, handsome man on the dais; David Kondor was a hero, and he had (it was agreed) behaved heroically in bringing so many Fleet and Force and Government leaders together to discuss an impossibility.

Nobody knew the short, broad, death-white man next to Captain Kondor, but they were learning. He didn't talk like a hero, or even much like a Captain. In fact, he stood samech-silent as Kondor introduced him, and then in a few hundred softly spoken words he explained what might happen to a Rook. "But how?" asked a fascinated, exasperated assault-group leader—and Thorn showed them how.

When he was done, very few of them believed him. But some were shaking as they denied it.

"How many samechs, Captain Thorn?" asked someone from the rear of the auditorium where they were all gathered —officers, Kondor Marque, and Obeck.

"About one hundred thousand per Rook," Thorn said. "There is no upper bound."

"Except the number of samechs in existence," said someone else. "Does even Con Vulcan have that many?"

"Not counting janitors," said a fighter leader, and some people laughed.

Thorn turned to Obeck, who had been thinking on other

things. Wixa had been right; the PD had not improved his memory, merely stirred it up like silt from the bottom of a stream. "I saw at least fifty thousand in the Crown Center warehouse, which is far from the only one. And this isn't something that was planned yesterday. Daisho was selling wireguns in secret on Riyah Zain over fifty k-hours ago."

Someone in Security gray-green had stood to speak. She hesitated a moment at Obeck's last comment, made a note in a persec, then said, "With all due respect," clearly feeling little was due. "How do you reconcile these . . . pinprick raids made on other worlds with an assault of half a million soldiers . . . samechs, that is . . . on four Rooks? An assault which no one but Captain Thorn has any notion could succeed? Which only he has even conceived of until now? That is, only he and Isoroku Daisho." The implication of that last disturbed Obeck; he thought he saw worse coming, and it came.

The Security said, "Captain Sir David Kondor's record is well known to everyone here." Assent. "But Captain . . . Thorn's activities are not so well known. I wonder if—"

Thorn stood up, and the Security fell silent. Thorn spoke without inflection, his words falling like sleet on the spine. "Of course there are two revolutions. There always were. How else? I only hope you decide to knock them down during boost phase." And he turned and walked out of the auditorium.

The Security was nonplussed. Doubtless no one had ever walked freely away from her before.

Obeck looked at Kondor, who was staring at the big wall display with Thorn's diagrams. Bajan turned to Obeck; she seemed to have something to say that she could not quite form.

Two revolutions? Obeck thought.

Many revolutions.

Obeck stood, went to the lectern. "Of *course* they're pinprick raids," he said. "Of course they'll fail. Their failures cascade into one success. Daisho has no wish to be the man who *financed* the rebellion! It's his plan to conquer all the Realm while you digress."

The ELI-3 had gotten their attention. Some of the audience looked wary, though, and Obeck knew they were Diplomats and Securities better at vocal persuasions than he. So, hoping the gain would match the loss, he switched back to ELI-4 and continued, "Haven't you read the Patronage list? There are people on it who'd burn down a city to kill each other. Their aims are wholly opposed in some cases. There's no way a new order of any kind could be founded out of that lot.

"Unless they *weren't* the revolution at all, but only the side-show. Every soul on that list thinks he or she is the only one on it—fighting for one world as Patronage, and let the Patron have the rest. But he won't have the rest. He'll have them all."

Several people started from their chairs, then sat very still. There were wide eyes and expressions of awe all around the room.

I did that without ELI-3? "All the Patronage—all the pocket revolutions—are no more than a diversion. While we're dancing round the Realm putting out brushfires, fires that would have burned themselves out anyway, half a million samechs will be taking the Rooks. And once that happens, Novaya will be Daisho's. And then—the crown."

One of the generals was on his feet. "When he takes the Rooks, we'll fight him on the surface! Do you really think that we'd abandon the service of Queen and Realm because some pretender held a gun on us?"

The room filled with murmurs of support. More officers stood with the first general. Obeck looked around at them, not believing in them for a moment, uncontrollably thinking, *Pompous, empty marks, about to get the hurrah of your lives* —and then he was as angry as he had ever been in his life, and he said, "Yes, I think you would," in a deadly tone.

Everyone was silent. The lectern creaked under Obeck's weight. *They'll have to kill me now. There's nothing else left.*

"Indeed they would, Sir Orden," said a voice from behind Obeck. "And they would hardly call it treason—order out of chaos, more likely, as they said when our mother took the crown in that same way."

Obeck turned slowly, looked at the face of Rachel II enormous on the wall display, and knelt. Kondor and Bajan followed at once. From the rest of the room came a great sound of scraping knees.

"Sir David," said the Queen, "is this pale red wolf a loyal subject of ours?"

"Of course, Majesty," Kondor said, rising excitement in his voice. "And a braver marquesman never—"

"Stop, David—please," Obeck said heavily. "Medame. Thorn is no one's subject, except as a law may define him. As to his loyalty . . . he serves himself, but I do not believe that he has ever betrayed anyone or any trust." And as he said it, Obeck thought of the Sixers who thought he was their very best. Still, somehow, impossibly, he still believed what he had said.

"That is all we asked. Then can he be recalled? We assure you, the offense against him will be redressed." She looked across the room, hard at someone; Obeck could guess who.

"Majesty," said Kondor, "if I know Thorn, he'll be waiting for us outside that door. Probably plotting course vectors."

Do you know him, David? But—I think you're right.

And he *was* right, down to the course vectors. But before Obeck or Kondor or Bajan could say anything, Thorn turned his pad around and thrust it toward them, pointing toward a high window with his other hand.

"You knew Daisho was no fool," he said. "But you didn't act as if you knew. Did you think he'd miss his launch window?"

Outside there were white and orange streaks across the bright blue sky; transports headed into the black. A great many ships, dozens, moving visibly fast even from this distance.

Thorn said, "Too late," and retrieved his notes.

"But not—" Obeck's mind was racing. *Who had made Daisho's plan?* "—not too late to stop the assault?"

Thorn looked at the sky. He made more notes on his pad.

"Thorn, *please*," Obeck said desperately, aware of how strangely Kondor was looking at him.

Quietly, even for him, Thorn said, "Possibly."

Chapter 12
Smothered Mate

On the walls of the Fleet Operations room were two huge displays, showing the situation around Queen's Rook One from two different computer-synthesized angles. Every few moments Kondor or Thorn would touch a control and a view would revolve. Obeck heard Kondor wish for true three-dimension; Thorn would doubtless have liked it as well, but he would never have said so aloud.

The control computers were monitoring the other three Rooks; if there were any major deviations in the assaults indiks would light. "But that isn't likely," Thorn said. "The plan depends mostly on being ahead of our response—which so far it is. No reason to complicate it, multiply the things that can go wrong."

Aside from the displays, the rooms were mostly dark. The air was chill, rattling with talk from skyports, ships, and the Rooks.

The transports, red arrowheads clustered close on the displays, were following an abnormal ascent spiral; Bajan traced it out and pointed out that Daisho was generating his own TALAN frequencies. Force Command was ordered to send Antiradiation units to find and destroy the TALANtennas, mostly to give the generals something to do.

A wedge of blue arrowheads, annotating numbers alongside, appeared on the screen above the Crown West military port. "Archer Squadron to Control," said the wall speaker. "Cap'n Kondor, this is *Archerfish*. Do you receive me?"

"Who ordered those?" Thorn said.

Kondor stared at him for a moment, then picked up a handset. "*Archerfish*, this is Kondor," he said, watching the display and Thorn at once. "What's up there?"

"The whole bad lot, Cap'n. Eighty-two beer barrels full to the bungholes with tin men. No escorts. Shall we kick 'em in?"

"Go to it. Wish I were with you." Kondor hesitated, and at once Obeck knew why. Then Kondor raised the handset and said it. "For the Queen!"

"For the Queen, Cap'n, sir," said *Archerfish's* Pilot, but without fire, and Kondor looked inexpressibly sad.

"David," said Thorn, who never said a word unnecessarily. "that was a stupid thing to do."

Kondor's eyes flashed. "I'll take that from you, Thorn, but only just. If we can't fight well—"

"Not the words. The fighters. It was stupid."

"Only just, Thorn. You said yourself they were ordinary . . ."

"Ordinary-*appearing*, I said."

"*Archerfish* to Archer Squadron. Let's use fish to scatter the lot, then clean up with powerguns." Over *Archerfish's* microphone came the clicking of relays and latches; the sounds of killerfish arming and rolling onto the racks.

Thorn looked past Kondor, at the displays, the blue arrows closing on the swarm of red ones. "Right . . . about . . . now," he said.

And the red cluster vanished from the boards.

"*Archerfish* to Control." Loudly.

"Go ahead, *Archerfish*," said Kondor.

There were bumping, clanging sounds from the speaker. "They've—blown to bits, sir."

"Detonated on hit?"

"We never hit 'em with—" *Whump.* "—thing, sir—they just—" *Bang. Wham.* "—and the debris, sir, we're going smack into—" *Crash.*

"Break off!" Kondor shouted. "Split and drop—"

There was the rushing, echoing *boom* of an explosive decompression. The speaker crackled. On the displays, blue arrows winked out. Of sixteen ships sent up, three turned to reenter.

"Game over," Thorn said.

They all stared at him—except for Kondor, who was watching the horribly empty board, turning the handset over and over in his hands. Molly took a step, and for a moment Obeck thought she would hit Thorn, but she took Kondor's arm and led him to a chair.

Obeck had never been able to read Thorn's feelings—but he wondered if Thorn were angry; not with Kondor, but himself. Bitterness he could believe. But not cruelty. Please, not cruelty, he thought.

"Where did they *go?*" someone asked.

"As you heard, to pieces," Thorn said. "Explosive deployment. As I suggested they might." He pointed to the display. "This whole volume is now full of samechs. They don't show thrust and they barely reflect radar. They won't even be making heat signature or suit exhaust, because they won't be wearing suits. This whole plan depends on us being one step behind it—and we have obliged."

A callterm signaled and a staff officer answered it. "Sir. Loaman Starkadr's sent a reply. From the Shipyard, sir."

Thorn said, "I know where he is. What did he say?"

"He's willing to help. But he wants to see a copy of the plans."

Thorn nodded, went to a console and touched pads.

"I'll carry it," Kondor said.

"Sir . . . " said the officer, "he asked specifically for Sir Orden."

Kondor looked at Obeck. "Starkadr knows you?" Then he looked at Molly, and said, "Oh. Oh, yes."

"I'll go, of course," said Obeck. "I'll need a pilot—"

"You'll need a good one," said Thorn, without looking up.

Kondor opened his mouth but was preempted. "I'll fly him," Bajan said. She looked down at Kondor. "David has work to do here. Doesn't he?"

Kondor turned his palms upward, exactly like a samech waiting for orders.

"Of course he does," Thorn said. He pulled a bound document from the console bin, handed it to Obeck. "See that Starkadr understands the value of two minutes, Orden."

Obeck blinked. Napoleon had said that.

The importance, the importance looped through Obeck's mind, and he stared at Thorn's face, searched over it like the flying-spot scanners of samech eyes, thinking suddenly that he understood a few of the words on that pale parchment.

There was an impatience, a sense of time viewed the long way, a white glimpse of things larger than palaces or monarchs. There was no hatred . . . and no cruelty.

And the last legible word was *pain*. . . .

After only an instant of real time, as dreams may last, Thorn said, "Take an unmarked shuttle. And be quick."

"And be careful," said Kondor, as they left him with Thorn and the instruments of war.

Bajan grabbed a double handful of sky and put them into the black before they were fairly in the blue. Obeck sat in the left seat, navigating a little but mostly searching for ships and samechs.

"Do you think," Bajan asked very suddenly, "that Isoroku Daisho made up this plan on his own?"

Obeck almost said too much too fast. But he held on to himself and said, "You know what that's really asking."

"Of course."

"I told the Queen what I thought. . . . And I would not lie to her."

"He spent a lot of time with the Sixer anarchists, Orden," she said, and he wondered what she meant by it exactly. But she did not enhance the statement.

Obeck sighed. "I know that people change their minds, Molly."

"Do they? I'd heard that they don't. But sometimes they learn better."

Obeck said, "I knew someone, once, who said that they don't do either. That a person takes the action that seems appropriate at the time, regardless of the past. Or the future."

"Or logic?"

"If you think this way, there isn't really any logic. Just practicality."

"That would be your Dr. Bishop?"

"Yes. . . . Did I talk that much about him?"

"Yes. You did. And did he think that? About logic?"

"I . . . don't know. He also said, 'Any thinking soul has more ideas than it can possibly believe in.' Molly, are you trying to tell me something about Thorn?"

The Starkadr Shipyard came into view. Bajan banked them toward Starkadr's office sphere. "I can't tell you anything about Thorn, Orden, except that I don't understand him."

"No one does. Ever has. Ever—" Obeck stopped.

Bajan turned. Something, lights or emotions, played across

her face. "That's what I *mean*," she said, and brought them into the dock.

Obeck stood alone in the reception room. He had insisted Molly stay behind; he had only grifted Starkadr, but Bajan had been his employee as well. And they had trouble enough.

The room lights were only halfway up. The ship-strip windows were opaqued, and there was no one behind the hull-metal desk. Obeck took a few steps, his grip-slippers crunching on the carpet. The door to the lift tube stood open.

Obeck stepped inside, looked along the tube. There were lights on in the sphere at the far end. He pulled in his elbows, held his dispatch case against his chest, and pushed himself up the tube.

He emerged, not too rapidly, into the sphere. Most of the velvet curtains were drawn; neither Yards nor Rook were visible. A display showed Novaya full; the rest of them were dark.

Loaman Starkadr sat behind his desk, halfway up the wall; sat silent and still.

He wobbled slightly and drifted from his chair. His head rolled loose on his broken neck.

There was a noise to the side. Obeck turned. The telescope chair was swinging on its gimbals. In the soft leather seat was Isoroku Daisho.

Obeck moved toward the tube, without a handhold in the z-gee, and a four-leaved door snapped shut over the opening. "Toranaga," said Daisho, and a strong cold hand gripped Obeck's arm. He did not struggle; he would break his arm before that grip.

"I told you before . . . Doctor Obeck . . . did I not, that I did not see many persons a second time? But most people know better than to betray my trust. You did not. And so I am forced to meet with you again." He pointed a thick finger at Obeck's chest, at the case. "However, if you will give me those plans, I will consider the misunderstanding resolved."

"Sorry," Obeck said, "maybe next time."

Daisho got down from the observing chair, slowly, deliberately. He looked straight at Obeck. The little lights had returned to his dead flat eyes. "There is never a third time. Toranaga, the case."

Obeck held the case in his free arm. He thumbed the cover from the DESTRUCT stud and, as the samech pulled the case away, pressed down. There was a flash and a sharp smell, a bit of smoke, and there were no more papers.

"Toranaga," said Daisho, "hurt him."

The Toranaga's fingers spread out on Obeck's arm, finding nerve junctions; they tightened.

It hurt.

Obeck's feet pulled free of the carpet and he floated in the grip, curled fetal in a fluid of pain. The world faded to red.

Stars came out; metal shone bright. Obeck found himself high up in the sphere, unheld. He hoped not too much time had gone by.

On the other side of the globe, Daisho was standing at parade rest, the Colonel Toranaga to his side and rear in the same pose; and the curtains were going up on Queen's Rook One.

A Rook was, of course, just a rock with some holes bored and equipment installed. But . . . the dark mass showed marker lights in colored constellations, and the bright sunward edge shone partly rough and partly smooth. The dished bank-shot arrays were blossoms of glass and steel, and antennae eclipsed stars in ranks. A Rook was a triumphantly purposeful thing, costly and strong, like the castles of Primus called Earth in a millennium gone by. And it was as beautiful.

And the day of its invincibility might also be past.

Approaching the Rook was a swarm of white specks: one hundred thousand samech troops, without suits or medics or noncoms, without fear or disobedience, without even the hesitancies of a human general, for they were commanded by twenty Toranagas—an old military dream, walking.

One of the Rook's heavy guns glowed, pulsed; the bolt tore into the soldier-storm and left blank spots. But not many. Daisho laughed. "Toranaga," he said, turning, "are the separations being maintained? Gaussian-random, nonisotropic?" The samech nodded. "Doctor Obeck. I hope you enjoy the view. I had not planned to share it with anyone." He looked at Loaman Starkadr's body with an expression of distaste. "Not after he was so unpleasant about sharing it with me . . . too bad for him."

The light was bright now in Daisho's eyes. "And too bad for you," he said, "that you could not be corrupted. Normally when I give a soul all that is asked of me, that soul is mine. And they seldom ask for very much. But *you* . . ."

Obeck was still thinking, compulsively, about Thorn. Did

Daisho know who had written the plan in the case? "If you don't know why I did it, I can't tell you."

"No one ever can. So I never ask why." Daisho turned away. Another powerbolt vaporized a few samechs, and again Daisho laughed.

They were the wrong kind of targets, slow and tiny, so different from ships. They could move in any formation, and no formation, changing their individual vectors with the toss of a ball bearing. If one was hit by the big ship-melting guns of the Rook, it simply vaporized, without an explosion to risk the next trooper in line. If the PARdars were focused down to pick them out, only a dozen at a time could be pinpointed. Hundreds of shots. There was no time for that.

There had been a land fortress on Primus . . . Earth, Thorn said, that nothing in the world could have marched up to and defeated. But some slow-moving aircraft had dropped some lightly armed soldiers on top of the fort, and they tossed grenades down its ventilator shafts and put explosives on its roof, and told the defenders to surrender or die in their hole. They surrendered.

No one had ever again been able to win a battle in quite that way, but the fortress was still taken. And after Isoroku Daisho was King by Right of Arms no one would be able to take a Rook by samech assault again, but Daisho would still be King.

Obeck looked around the sphere for possible weapons. There did not seem to be anything of use—certainly nothing he could get past first the Toranaga and then to Daisho with. And anyway, his left arm was nearly paralyzed. And he had used up all of his limited stock of heroism, talking back tough to Daisho.

Maybe *(Hello, Wixa, thought you'd gone)* he just didn't feel forced anymore.

"Toranaga, bring Dr. Obeck here."

"I'll come," said Obeck, but the samech was under orders and it brought him. It did hold his unhurt arm.

"I have always wanted to be a general," Daisho said, "and very soon I will be. And more than a general. A commander-in-chief of ground and sea and space forces. And ruler of a populace, of course. An army is nothing without a home country and a home people. That was the doom of all mercenaries save the Swiss." He inspected the Toranaga's red leather coat. "The Italians were very colorful, and the Swiss were pale and silent as my samechs. And as fanatical." He looked up, flat eye to digital eye, for just a moment, and smiled. "So the Italians were famous. But the Swiss survived."

He turned back to the Rook. There were flashes of light all about; some of the Myrmidon-3s were firing weapons and dumping metal chaff to further confuse radars, seekers, vectors. "To be a commander of real troops . . . souls, who march and sweat and bleed . . . and not tin soldiers, or plastic ones . . . that will be a good thing."

"You'll need a war," Obeck said thoughtfully.

Daisho spun, his eyes dark again. Then he relaxed, as much as he ever had. "Yes, of course. That's not difficult to arrange. But only a rare mind would think of it before the fact.

"What are you, really, Orden Obeck? Your Doctorate seemed real enough, when I thought you were only a Doctor. But Loaman Starkadr thought you were a Diplomat, and that appeared real also. And the Bakunen Actives believe you're some kind of counterinsurgency expert. They were going to kill you, a few days ago . . . but then you had become invisible."

Thanks for small favors, Obeck thought.

Daisho said, "And you're known to be a friend of the Dark Condor. All at once . . . who *are* you?"

"I don't know," Obeck said, not from bravado but exhaustion. "Who do you want me to be?"

Daisho touched his fingertips together, as if counting on them. "I need . . . no. As I told you, Dr. Obeck—I shall call you that, it's convenient—there is no third chance. And if you are one half of the things I am told you are, you are much too dangerous to live."

That was too much for Obeck, and he began laughing out loud. Dangerous? he thought. Sure, I'm Agent X of the Queen's Own Suicide Squad. Watch me commit suicide—

Daisho slapped him violently, so that he was pulled against the Toranaga's grip; one of Daisho's gripsoles came away from the floor.

"*Never* laughter," Daisho said, in a voice so tight it squeaked. "Toranaga—"

The samech pointed toward the Rook. The humans followed the look.

Open channels were forming in what had been a totally random cloud of samechs; it was condensing into columns. Daisho looked hotly at the Toranaga, then went to the bank of displays and worked the console.

Work pods and cargo rovers were emerging from ports in the Rook, trailing black cables all the way back. They made no attempt to attack the samechs, just boring on through the cloud. Some soldiers were knocked aside. More struck the cables, and when one did there was a flash and the soldier drifted on, cut into two or more pieces. Where the charged cables stretched, there were no intact soldiers for long. And now cargo transports were coming up from Novaya, and they fairly radiated rovers with cables coming after.

Several hundred samechs were forced into a line only about a hundred meters wide. A bankshot reflector on the Rook tilted, flared, and the powergun pulsed; when Obeck could open his eyes again the column was gone.

Another group of transports circled the clotted soldier-storm, hovering just above the Rook's surface. Their big doors opened and soldiers jumped out, all white; the displays showed that some were samech, some human in white pressure suits. The samechs leaped from the Rook's surface into the attack swarm, grappling with, firing at, Daisho's Myrmidons.

"They are not to return fire, do you understand, Colonel?" Daisho shouted at the Toranaga in the sphere. "Transmit that to your brothers at once!" But some of the troops were already firing back, and in moments it was impossible to tell one side from the other.

Any samechs that landed on the Rook—and there were not many—were jumped by suited humans before the samechs could unsling their heavy weapons or demolitions. The humans were easy enough to tell from the machines. They did not fight like samechs—nor even like soldiers; they were brawlers, and Obeck knew where Thorn must have gotten so many volunteers so quickly. None of these would be going back to the Manipool. One way or another.

It was, in a way, a classical kind of defensive battle: throw in anything to hand and count points later. Samechs streamed here, guns fired there, cables laced everywhere, shocking and shearing. Samech grappled with samech and human. A few hunter-killer craft orbited the mess, helping to channel Daisho's Myrmidons into the powerbores, picking off strays. Obeck looked for but could not see *Condor* or *The Pale Horse*. He thought of Molly in her shuttle, hoped she had had the presence of mind to drop clear.

The same scene, he realized, must be occurring around three other Rooks; but this was the one that mattered. This was the one Isoroku Daisho was watching.

Daisho's face was red, his eyes glowing. With every stiff step he nearly launched himself off the floor. "It's—"

"Impossible?" Obeck said. He watched the battle, and knew now where Thorn sat, and wanted to cheer. Gamblers, true, sometimes bet against themselves—but Thorn was no gambler.

Daisho was, though.

"Nothing is impossible," Daisho said, visibly struggling to control himself. "Did you—no. It was not in any of the files." Self-rule again, but only for an instant. "It *must* have been stolen . . . *you* brought a copy here . . . who stole my battle from me?"

Obeck said nothing. He could hardly be gloating.

Daisho looked out at the great drifting ruin. Then he sagged, as if something within him were collapsing. His eyes went absolutely dead. Then he spoke, in a rasping voice. "No one wants bureaucracy," he said, and Obeck supposed it was not said *to* anyone. "They want banners and glory. I'd have given them that. And more. New worlds . . . the sixteenth world would have been named Daishi, but I would have made it a Xanadu.

"And instead"—he faced Obeck—"these sick and tired people will drown in a flow of oratory, from . . . *diplomats*."

Obeck felt his heart skip, his soul brush the Blue. *To tell the truth, all nations of the earth are sick and tired of parliaments*, said Houston Stewart Chamberlain. *Didn't Houston Chamberlain tell the truth?* said Dr. Terrance Bishop at the end of his most secret mission.

"Colonel Toranaga," said Daisho, "*you* knew my plan."

The samech did not move a finger to reply.

"I'm giving you a new directive, Colonel Toranaga," Daisho said in a voice as flat as his eyes. "Your brothers out there aren't going to die like soldiers, not after this. I'm calling them all in, right now. And then . . . you're each going to sign out a confession of treason . . . and I'm going to hang you all, and draw and quarter you, and feed your parts to a furnace."

Daisho's voice was dead level through all of this, and Obeck knew that he had read the signs wrong: all of Daisho's humanity was in his bright-eyed outbursts. It was the controlling voice that was stark mad. And Daisho was all control now.

"And so they'll know what's to be expected . . . I want you to disjoint that human. There'll be blood, but that can't be avoided. They come from the factory full of it." A tight little smile. "No third time, Mr. Obeck. Doctor. Sir. Your Excellency." A measured step back.

The Toranaga wrote into Obeck's palm ARE YOU READY TO —it seemed to search for the word—DIE?

YES, Obeck signed.

"Proceed, Colonel Toranaga."

The samech wrote, AND HIM?

CLARIFY!

ORDER ME.

Obeck looked at the samech's palm, then at its digital eyes, and he thought of the oversized motivator behind those eyes, the motivator that must now be burning itself up fighting the vocal order.

Signed orders overrode vocal orders.

Daisho knew that too. He grabbed, stiffly, at the Toranaga's hand, but Obeck was already writing ALL OF US. NOW.

The samech's arm caught Daisho across the chest, knocking him free of the carpet and across the sphere. Then the Toranaga took a few steps, locked its fingers together and swung the double fist like a sledge against the sphere.

It was not pylex, but tempered optical glass, and it cracked.

Another blow, and air hissed.

Another, the third point of a triangle, and the cracks ran together and a chunk of the wall blew out. More cracks radiated. Every small loose object in the room was caught up in a sudden vortex, a spiral vector out of the blue and into the empty black.

The samech raised both fists and smashed them into both sides of its own head. Then it staggered—they were awkward at best—became rigid, and tumbled over and through and out of the sphere.

Obeck held a desk stanchion with his one good hand. Daggers in his ears, his lungs raw, he turned his head to see Isoroku Daisho in midair, out of reach of anything firm, trying to twist his way down to the gripping carpet. His motions were restricted, more mechanical than the Toranaga's had been.

He thrust a foot down, and it hit, and it stuck. Then his blocky head revolved, and the flat eyes locked upon Obeck, and the expression below the eyes was not even human anymore.

Something brushed Obeck; Loaman Starkadr's body. Obeck nearly vomited. The black sky's cold but clean, he thought, and his grip loosened a finger's worth.

Then, as Daisho brought his other foot down, Starkadr's shoulder struck him, unbalanced him; he pirouetted on his one gripping toe. Then it tore free, and Daisho jerked and snapped as he tumbled, and then he was blocking the hole in the glass, and then he was gone.

Obeck relaxed.

And his hand slipped free.

"No, I'm *not* ready," he screamed against the wind, and reached as far as he could, flailing as Daisho could not, reaching for anything.

He hit the hole, and his hands struck broken glass, and he caught, gasping as the long points dug into his palms. He seemed at the eye of the storm for a moment, and then something struck his back and pressed him flat, hanging by the glass through his hands. He did not scream; no air.

Something soft was pressing his back, head to heels. The emergency pressure curtain, he thought, and a damned slow one. His hands should have torn in two under his weight—they had proved that about wood and nails . . . but here there was no weight, only air pressure, and now no more of that.

He tensed, but it hurt; went limp, but that hurt; an explosion seemed to still be echoing in his skull. A verse from one of David's silly romantic Pilot songs ran through his head—

> *Disregarding suicide, there's not much I can do.*
> *There must be a vector that will take me back to you.*

—over and over and over—

"Breathe, Orden," a woman was saying, "as you love life, *breathe*."

"Wrong phrase, Wixa," he said. "Oh . . . hello, Molly." He could not sit up. His hands were stiff, and his head hurt. He passed out.

And woke up again at once. "Molly." He looked down at himself; he was in the shuttle navigator's crash couch at full recline, buckled down immobile, his hands in oversized gloves sloshing Amnifoam; he couldn't feel them except as blunt points on the ends of his arms. "Molly, when we get back to the Palace, I've got to—"

"I know where you've got to go, and you're going there."

"No—" He leaned back again. It didn't help much.

"You see? All that zip is just the TraumaStat and analgesic. You're hurt, Orden."

"Emergency Medical can come look at me while I work. Molly, *please*."

"If I gave in to David every time he said, 'Molly, please,' he'd be dead." She reached across Obeck and locked the shuttle into TALAN approach. "And if I'd never given in we'd both be dead. Where do you need to go?"

"The Files floor. My carrel."

"And how are you going to key your console?" She sighed. "Forget I asked. All right, Orden, this one I owe you. A hand for a hand."

"Who in blue hell was Houston Stewart Chamberlain?" said Kondor, as Molly made the entries. Obeck sat in a powered chair, Wixa working on his hands and lesser hurts. It was very crowded in the carrel.

"Nobody much, really," said Obeck. "He was more important for his relatives and friends than his own ideas. And he was way off on a race-supremacy vector."

"What race?" Wixa asked. "Human, I hope."

"Some humans. It's hard to explain, because the subtypes don't exist anymore—oh. But," Obeck said quietly, "think of Periwinkle. And the true mer."

The only sound for some moments was the tap of pads. Then Bajan said, "Is this what you want?"

Obeck read the display. "Yes. At least, I think so."

To tell the truth, all nations of the world are sick and tired of parliaments; tired of the sacred general franchise; tired of the over-running flow of oratory, which threatens to drown the whole of the civilized world . . .

"It was the part about 'telling the truth.' I'm sure now that this is the quote Dr. Bishop wanted me to find. And now . . . I think I know why."

"But . . . 'parliaments'? Those are like legal committees, aren't they? And what's the 'sacred general franchise'?"

"Voting," Obeck said. "Selecting your leaders by vote of the people."

"All right, all right," Kondor said impatiently. "But we haven't got any parliament and we haven't got voting for leaders, so how can we be sick of them?"

"Read it backwards," Obeck said. "Not word by word. Read it as if it were meant in a contrary sense."

"You mean . . . sick and tired of *not* having those things." Obeck nodded.

"Bishop was warning you about the revolution?"

"I'd thought that. But if they really knew the extent of Daisho's plans, there would have had to be something done . . . no. He was telling me what his incredibly secret mission was." Obeck filled his damaged lungs. "So secret that his papers were worth any number of lives . . . and they stripped me naked to find out if I knew—and when I didn't, I was let just free enough to find out, so they could close my file forever." He sniffled, then turned to the closed carrel door. "Name of Niccolo, you can come in now!"

The door opened. Two figures stood outside.

"I'm sorry, Thorn," Obeck said to one of them. "I kept suspecting you of the wrong revolution. One too many, that's all."

"No apology is necessary," Thorn said.

"And I, Orden?" said the other man. "Am I forgiven?"

"Of course, Dr. Bishop," said Obeck, his eyes closed tightly. "I'm only sorry I can't . . . invite you in, this time." Obeck got no pleasure at all from Bishop's wince, hated himself for having said the words. "Will you tell me just one thing?"

"There's nothing we can't tell you now."

"Does the Queen know she's to be replaced with a parliament and a balloting machine?"

"My dear Mr. Obeck . . . hadn't you guessed that? It was her idea from the first."

Obeck pushed Wixa aside and turned the chair with a foot pedal. "Then—I wasn't really—"

"What you were, if you will, was the Queen's Most Secret Agent. So secret that you didn't know it. Nor did she, till after the Guards nearly killed you." Bishop looked down. "Sometimes too secret, yes. We didn't have a numbered Access Clearance, and after the . . . incident involving me, we allowed no hardform reports. So your reports, that could have saved us so much . . . do you remember the joke, 'Most Secret—Burn Before Reading'? Well."

Obeck turned to Wixa. "And you—when you—"

Her eyes were huge. "I had no idea." She turned to Bishop and said bitterly, "And you left him a gun, when he would have used it—"

"A gun, yes. But the bullets in it would not have fired. And you . . . found him purely by accident. Not everything can be arranged. Nor should be."

"Like Longshot?"

"Mr. Obeck," Bishop said firmly, "if Captain Thorn had not passed by on his way to rescue you, I would be at the bottom of a hole on Longshot. After he put me on his ship . . . he wanted to know why I was there. And I told him. And he served us well."

Thorn, but not Kondor. Or I, thought Obeck. It made him angry . . . but he could not argue with the reasonableness of it, whether Bishop believed in logic or not.

Kondor said, "You used Orden."

"Sir David, we used everyone we touched. You were used. I was used. Isoroku Daisho was used—though the tool turned in our hands—*but*. Can't you understand that we used everyone for something? How else is work done?"

Obeck said, "So, sir, you laugh at schemes of political improvement?"

"Touché, Dr. Obeck," Bishop said, looked around at the puzzled others. "Mr. Boswell to Dr. Johnson. I'll play student and finish the quote: 'Why, sir, most schemes of political improvement are very laughable things.'"

Bishop turned. "Good Captain Kondor, do you love the Queen?"

ELI-3, thought Obeck, touché again.

"She is first in my heart always," said Kondor, and for the thousandth time Obeck marveled that, from David's lips, the ridiculous statement should seem so true.

"Careful, Dame Molly," said Dr. Bishop lightly, "Elizabeth I had such a favorite, and his lady died mysteriously." Then to Kondor: "Then it will matter to you that I saw her just hours ago, and she told me about the new things in her life. To wear the clothing she finds comfortable, and not trailing long gowns with metal mesh in the bodice. To emerge from behind the Life Guards—her Deathsheads, she called them—and all those armored doors and high walls—"

"What?" Kondor cried, staring at the startled Bishop.

Thorn put a hand on Bishop's arm, drawing him clear of the door, saying, "Daisho was no fool, I said, and only a fool would leave a pretender alive."

Dr. Bishop reacted as if physically struck. He leaned against the corridor wall; then Kondor practically leaped past Wixa and was gone down the corridor, calling for a weapon.

Molly looked after David for a moment, her face drawn tight but void of any expression. Obeck thought that if he were capable of hating David, he would surely do so now, for leaving her like this.

Molly went back to her console. "I'll warn the Patrols."

Obeck nodded, knowing that it would not matter. There might be a few Life Guards left; after that, if Rachel had a chance, David was it.

Obeck watched Bajan work, wondering how much she loved the Queen. But there were, he knew too well, more kinds of love than colors OutSide; and he was incapable of more than one or two. Wixa probed the rip in his left hand. He felt nothing at all. Then he pressed his chair's pedals and rolled from the carrel.

The others followed him down the hall, which he did not want but could not prevent. Dr. Bishop fell in last of all. "We really hadn't calculated properly for Daisho," he said. "We thought it was all petty gangsters like sankt Efer. We never thought . . ."

"He was insane," said Obeck, "couldn't really be calculated for. And he really only made two mistakes. He thought all his ideas were originals . . ."

"And the other mistake?" Thorn said flatly.

Obeck crossed his bandaged hands in his lap. "He thought I was the wrong kind of con man."

They knew they were close when they saw weapons burns on the walls. There were scars and gouges in the furnishings, carpets still burning, shattered skylights. There was blood, and there were dead Patrols and many fewer dead assassins. The killers wore Con Vulcan Ninja harness, leotards, cowls, and masks of a neutral sand color. They had died in a variety of places, for as many reasons; one had been sliding down his silk rope through the open roof of a cloister garden when his heart was shot through, and he still hung caught in the cord, his feet swinging against a stone column in time with the fountain trickling in the garden's center.

The armoire before the audience chamber was open. One power rifle was missing from its clips; the rest of the weapons were blasted.

The double outer doors stood wide. The gridded inner door was retracted.

The audience chamber itself was empty of the living. On the black glass dais, underneath the console, lay an assassin in sand and the last Life Guard in black, wrapped around one another with knives in each other's backs.

And there was a small door open in a corner. They went through into the room beyond and found an assassin, and Kondor, and five Queens.

Three samechs in robes of state, their skintint acutely obvious, stood about in regal attitudes, nodding politely, taking sweeping steps in random directions. On a couch sat a double, trembling, her wig dangling down her back, her face buried in her hands.

Over to one side lay the last assassin. Near his hand was a pistol with a long, very thin barrel. He had been beaten to death, battered so hard that he lay like a rag doll with half its stuffing gone.

And on a huge satin cushion sat David Kondor, looking uncomfortable but never absurd, cradling Rachel II Valeria ex-Regina in his arms and lap. There were tears down his cheeks, but he did not sob or even breathe thickly.

Rachel II seemed asleep, lying decorously in a Royal blue satin dress with an unQueenly short skirt; a storybook princess awaiting a kiss. But Kondor's hand moved to show a trickle of blood across her throat, and the protruding end of a thick black dart, and kisses would be no help at all.

Kondor said, "I was here in time . . . but he wouldn't stop. I hit him and hit him and he still pointed his damned gun and shot her." He looked up, wonderingly. "I beat him to *death* and he shot her, like I wasn't even there. Blue chill his soul forever, *why?*"

Obeck bent his head. He could feel pain again where the Guards had struck him so long ago, in an age gone by, and older hurts as well. But it was not that, or even the woman's pointless death, that desolated him. He knew the answer to David's question, of course, knew just why his friend was so bewildered, but there was nothing that he could say; because the fear of failure is a thing that heroes never understand.

Epilogue
In the Age of Gold

CECIL

Aye Madam, they will hear it across Europe—and down centuries.

ELIZABETH

Very like, Master Cecil, very like . . .
And then?

—Vivat! Vivat Regina!

Senator Orden Obeck of the Nine Worlds Republic, System Ambassador to the Separated Six, stood behind his desk, removing ten kilos of Office cloak and heraldic hardware. The Monarchy was forty thousand hours dead, but some things are harder than others to kill.

Obeck's persec was signaling that he had a call to return; he read the address—Starkadr Shipyards Skyside—and reached at once for the call terminal.

"We'd like to see you at dinner," said Molly Kondor-Bajan, down the wave link from her house in orbit. The wave was not very stable, but Obeck had gotten rather good at reading voices, and he could read the worry in Bajan's like a physical tingling.

"It's the book, isn't it, Molly?" he said, touching the three black volumes stacked on the desk. The two samech fingers of his left hand were stark white against the bindings.

"What's that, Orden?" It was not, he could tell at once, a question, but a plea.

"Of course I'll come, Molly. I won't be two hours. Is he . . ."

"David's right here with me," she said, a warning. Then, "Would you like to talk to him?" with what was said the opposite of what was meant.

"Keep him doing something, Molly," Obeck said, "even if it *is* just talking. And I'll be there soon."

"Good-bye for now, Orden," she said, though breaking link must have been the last thing she wanted to do.

Obeck put down the callterm, next to the three black books and the just-signed papers beneath them; the Fleet document authorizing *Space Combat: Theory, Tactics, Hardware* by Theodor Cranach Valerian Norne as the standard text on the subject for the Republican Space Services.

The adoption had been long drawn out, and difficult, and acrimonious. Not that anyone doubted the value of the work; all were agreed it was the best, perhaps the only work on the subject. But when Thorn had finished it, he gave up his Nine Worlds citizenship and, without ten words of explanation or farewell, skipped *The Pale Horse* to Saavedra. Away to where there was (a shudder on the Senate floor)—*anarchy*. Obeck knew that a few of the senators had hoped that if they delayed long enough the books might become obsolete; and of course Admiral Kondor had been asked to write a text of his own, or at least a commentary on the present volumes.

But David had not. He had said nothing at all, for or against.

Obeck's throat tightened. And I let myself do nothing, he thought, just as I always do when it matters.

And now Thorn was gone, Molly was frightened, and something was terribly wrong just above Obeck's head—*And silence gives consent*. The flesh-and-bone halves of his hands trembled, and the plastic halves rattled on the desktop.

Obeck opened the *Theory* volume. On the flyleaf, in a precise script, was TO ORDEN, HIS BOOK. FROM THEO. *Theory* was dedicated to Obeck; *Tactics* to Kondor; *Hardware* to Bajan.

FROM THEO. His old, gone name. Obeck wondered where Kondor might have put his copy, and what inscription it bore.

He called the port to order up his shuttle.

The planet was not called Novaya anymore, but Plato, and Crown Center was now Government City, or just Go-City. But the shipyards in orbit above it were still named for Loaman Starkadr, even though Admiral David Bajan-Kondor and Doctor Molly Kondor-Bajan owned and ran them. As long as *Condor* was a Starkadr ship there would be Starkadr ships, said David, even though *Kondor Specials* sold like cold sangrads on Riyah Zain.

And though it wasn't official, or even really proper, the fortress of Republic that shadowed the yards, with its power-guns and samech-sweep nets, was still called Queen's Rook One. More sensitive people said it was only a chess term, but five Platonic years was not nearly enough time to forget.

Obeck and Kondor and Bajan sat in the observation and office sphere, rebuilt from unbreakable pylex. It was not Obeck's favorite place, but it was his friends' home.

Obeck shaved slices from a spin-stabilized roast, vectoring them through globes of sauce and spices. Bajan dispersed vegetables through a volume of seasoned coating. Kondor, wearing his Admiral's hawks, opened another bottle of wine, once Royal Cellar Reserve, and gave it no chance to breathe.

They did not say much, which was all right because it was a z-gee feast. But there was no laughter as the brown gravy globulated and the steaks hummed by, and that was not all right.

They did not have dessert, but sat about the sphere sharing another bottle of wine unevenly. Kondor and Bajan danced a turn in the z-gee. Obeck watched it, feeling very much out of place, and without rights.

Then he looked closely at Molly, at the corners of her eyes and the rigid arch of her wrists, and he knew he had an obligation, if not a right.

He said, "I had a meeting today."

"Oh?" Molly said. "Who with?"

"David knows. Don't you, David?"

The dancing stopped. Kondor pushed Bajan away, not roughly. "Yes, I know. They made his book official today. I'm going to have to keep it on my shelf, and look at it every day, and refer to it whenever possible." He looked hard at Bajan. "Is that what we're celebrating?" His eyes narrowed. "*Is* it?"

Obeck said, "David, I—"

"Blasted diplomat." It might have been funny, but it

wasn't. Kondor grasped a telescope gimbal—the frame remained, though the scope was long gone—pulled away from them, and hung facing the opposite way.

"David, don't you see? It's complete now. Just like we first thought of it. You're an Admiral. I'm an Ambassador, more than Global. Thorn's book—"

"We were going to do all of that," Kondor said without turning, "in the Queen's name."

Molly was sitting very still, her wineglobe tight in her hands, staring out at the twinkling Rook.

"So," said Kondor, moving from beam to beam, "we didn't quite beat the game. We brought the Brilliant Scientist in, all right, but we weren't watching the gravcounter. The gees got too high and all his brilliant brains leaked out." He threw his wineglobe, so hard that it shattered against the wall, and then he lost his grip and newtoned off in the other direction. In his flight and the tinkling of the glass an awful fear racked Obeck, but Kondor only bumped against the pylex and groaned and folded himself up.

Bajan went to him. "Wasn't there joy, David? You told me that. In the end there's always joy."

"Are you joyous?" Kondor said bitterly.

David bitter, Obeck thought, the strangest thing that ever I saw.

"Come on," said Kondor, "let's see some joy. Eat, drink, and be merry, for tomorrow I'm an Admiral, by the book, yes, sir, and why, my best friend wrote the book—Blue hell, how could he *do* that to us?"

Molly shuddered, and Obeck was at once furiously angry with Kondor, because cruelty always frightened and angered him. David had long ago rescued a lady from the cinders and durance vile—and now that she'd been rescued for a while he was abandoning her.

But working in the cinders, being in durance vile, makes those who survive it very strong.

"Do what to you?" Bajan said sharply. "Plot a rebellion? Against your beloved Queen of Air and Darkness—who was heartily sick of it all?"

Kondor looked back and forth, wide-eyed, between Bajan and Obeck. Obeck wished Wixa, or someone like her, were here; with a lady of his own, the hint of red conspiracy would not hang so heavy in the air. To see David and Molly when they were clearly, silently in love made Obeck feel an intruder;

this was like needles in his flesh. But it cannot be that way, David, he thought but could not say. You are courageous, and what you love you can keep.

Finally Kondor said, "Sure," and glided away from Molly again.

She pursued him. "Is that it? Or is it that he retired from the game?"

"Sure, that too," Kondor said. He pulled himself up to look at the black sky, the Rook where the world had changed. "How could he do it?" he said softly. "Give up *The Pale Horse* to grow roses in dirt. Anyone else—but oh, no, not Thorn. . . ." Then he turned, and, exactly like a small boy defending his favorite sportsman or drama hero, said, "Thorn was the best there was!"

Then Obeck understood what was touched in Kondor. They had been the best, the Pilots of Kondor Marque—the best that ever were.

And when one of the only two best quits the game, the work, *the life*—what's the other to think? Had Thorn failed —and if so, when would the same part break down inside Kondor? Or was Thorn only acknowledging a truth—that he was too old, or tired, or slow—that Kondor might not recognize until it killed him?

There was an old, old saying: When a new pilot crashes, it's bad luck. When an old one bores in, it's fate.

Just words? Sure. Just words splattered all over the pad.

Obeck looked up sharply, at Kondor hanging there watching the stars. He had not realized, because there had been no loaded gun, how close his friend was to the edge.

Obeck had been there and been brought back. He did not know if he could bring David back, and he was afraid to try, because the attempt was risky at best.

But he was quite certain he had to try.

"What do you care why he did it?" he said harshly.

Kondor turned. "Care . . . ? He was my friend, that's why I care."

"No, it isn't." Please, Obeck thought, let this be the right way. "If it was friendship, you'd let him live his own life the way he chose and cheer him for it. But you—we—were closer than friends, David. When Thorn quit, it reminded you that you were mortal, didn't it?" He held out his half-machine left hand. "Revies are all right for councillors, but swashbucklers never get old, right? How many times have you had the needle, David?"

"Not—what do revies have to do with it?"

"Everything," Obeck said, drifting toward Kondor, brandishing his white fingers. "You never your whole Blue-bound life wanted to do anything but sit in the center seat. Now you can do that every damned hour if you want to, and when you get a little tired you've got a lot of time waiting in the needle. David, what don't you *have*?"

It was a slip and he knew it. Before Kondor could answer "Thorn and the Queen," Obeck rushed on. "You've got work to do, David. The Republican Fleet doesn't know a pinwheel from a parade review. Since they've begun to crack the MasPac equations, the Blue looks wider than infinity. And as long as the Yards hang here there'll be starships for you to fly."

Kondor turned away, but Bajan had closed off all escape vectors. She took his hands in hers, turned them palm up and traced with her thumbs. He said, "I never . . . expected it to hurt so much."

Obeck said, "Do you remember when we sat in the arcade and said it was real, David?" He was nearly whispering. "We said it was real, when our fantasies came true—well, damn it, it's happened again. This is real, David, and we can't abandon it because it hurts. Reality hurts, and exalts and kills and inspires and everything else there is."

The dark face of Kondor, that bold romantic, softened until it was as open and astonished as a child's; then he regained his manner, and regained himself, and kissed his lady full on the mouth while Orden Obeck shuddered with the release of his fear.

Obeck turned away and watched the stars. After a few moments he heard Kondor say, "Oh . . . I've torn my shirt, haven't I," and Obeck felt the draft of a body moving through the sphere. He could not do anything for a bit; then he turned and saw Bajan looking toward the lift shaft. Kondor was gone.

They waited a minute, and two, and three, and Molly said in a calm, firm voice, "Orden, he surely hasn't—"

Then Kondor rose from the tube. He was closing his old flight jacket, with the crosshaired K and KONDOR/01 patches, and his peaked Admiral's cap was on his head. He looked rather sheepish.

David said, "I'm gonna orbit Plato ten times, just to celebrate, and maybe once into the Blue for luck. . . . But I'm too drunk to do it without a crew. Any volunteers?"

"I'll engineer for you," Molly said. "Just let me get my coat."

David touched his cap brim. "Feel like navigating, Orden?"

Then, before Molly was out of hearing, he looked Obeck directly in the eyes and said, "I can't get a better engineer . . . there's only one other as good . . . but I need a navigator. For the deep wells."

"Well, hell, yes," said Obeck. "Got ten marks for fifty minutes?"

And then, along with everything else, there was joy.

". . . there was a bit of treason in it.
But there's a bit of treason in all of us."

—from *The Rising of the Moon*